Book
of Love

Book of Love

◆ ◆ ◆

William Kotzwinkle

Houghton Mifflin / Seymour Lawrence
Boston

Library of Congress Cataloging-in-Publication Data

Kotzwinkle, William.
Book of love / William Kotzwinkle.
p.   cm.
ISBN 0-395-56335-6
I. Title.
PS3561.O85J3   1990   90-35822
813'.54—dc20   CIP

Printed in the United States of America

AGM 10 9 8 7 6 5 4 3 2 1

Houghton Mifflin Company paperback, 1990

This book was previously published
under the title *Jack in the Box*.

I

Persons attempting to find a plot will be shot.

—Mark Twain

Chapter 1

The Masked Man Is Attacked
by the Palm Street Gang.
The Life Goes Out of His Thundering Hoofbeats.

◇ ◇ ◇

The Masked Rider of the plains reined up in back of the tailor shop, his mighty horse raising the dust in the road.

"Whoa, big fellow, whoa there."

A jet of steam came out of the tailor shop window and disappeared in the air above the tailor's little goldfish pond. The Masked Man took his horse over for water. Goldfish swam beneath the green lily pads, rippling the water with their tails. The tailor waved through the steam and the Masked Man waved back, taking care not to trample on the flowers. Sometimes flowers leaned out under your thundering hoofbeats and you got the blame.

The goldfish swam around slowly. He had to get back on the trail of the bank robbers.

Hi-yo Silver, a-waaaaaaaaaaay!

He galloped back into the alley, the dust rising again at his feet.

Maybe the bank robbers are hiding in that old garage.

He rode slowly toward it, hand on his six-shooter with the

silver bullets. It was actually only a one-shooter, loaded with a rubber dart, but it could stick good to a window or somebody's head.

He opened the garage door. There were stacks of newspapers around and some tires, and a pile of greasy rags. Maybe he'd use this place as his own hideout. Nobody would find him here, not in a million years.

He crawled in back of an orange crate; it was filled with rusty nuts and bolts, good for throwing at anybody who tried to attack him.

Ropes and coils of wire and old fan belts hung down from the crossbeams, and a big piece of rotting canvas was draped over it—he'd use it for an Indian tent.

Footsteps spun him around quickly, gun drawn. The side door banged open and a man stood there, a pail of ashes in his hand.

"C'mon get the fuck outta there . . ."

Not wishing to have ashes dumped on him, the Masked Man rode quickly out of the garage; he'd been hit before with big ash-clinkers and it was no joke; they could leave the mark of Zorro on your head, forever.

He rode hard up the alley, climbing the high hill, upon his magic pony that never tired. Giddy-up, giddy-up, boy, up!

He rode into the very heart of the badlands at the top of Palm Street, where there were guys who'd make you piss in a pot and drink it. He feared this; neither silver bullets nor his Tom Mix Glowing Arrowhead With Compass And Magnifying Glass would be of any use against the Palm Street Gang.

Palm Street had no palms. He often wondered where they were.

He rode down to the avenue, taking his horse into heavy traffic. Horns sounded and he dodged upon Silver, over the trolley car tracks.

"Hey, why don't you cross at the corner!"

Who could catch the great white horse and his masked rid-

8

er? Down here, boy, down to the end of Palm Street to the dump, where they'll never dare go because of the rats.

He galloped into the trashcans and bed springs, over old dolls and broken bottles and smoking mattresses with the stuffing turned black and stinking. He didn't give a shit, he was the Lone Ranger.

Then, out of nowhere, a terrible pain stung him in the ass. He whirled, heard the sound of a bee-bee gun being cranked in the distance, and then the soft bpffffffff as it fired again and raised the dusty ashes at his feet.

Crank-crack-bpffffff

"Owch! Ow!"

Up there, Kemosabi, on the bank, hiding in the weeds.

Yes, Tonto, but all I've got is this rubber dart-gun. Range, two feet.

Bpffffff

Then ride, Kemosabi, ride hard!

Through the smoke of the burning dump, the Masked Man rode for all he was worth, his ass burning in two places. He had to get himself a bee-bee gun somehow.

And a mighty hi-yo Silver, a-waaaaaaaay!

He followed the winding alleyway out of the dump, toward Bobby Yacavola's house. The front door flew open and Yacavola came running out, with his old lady after him.

"You no-good little bastid!" She had the broom on Yacavola, swinging it hard. Yacavola ducked and jumped over the porch rail, landing in the alley beside the Lone Ranger.

"And don't come back!"

"*That whoreson bitch,*" hissed Yacavola as they rode off down the alley.

The Masked Man said nothing. He was not accustomed to cursing out his mother, and was always amazed at goings-on in the Yacavola house, which smelt like the dump alongside it.

Yacavola scratched violently in his curly blond hair. Deep as the Masked Man's feelings were for his faithful companion, he rode slightly apart from him, as he didn't want his horse to get lice. Yacavola didn't seem to mind lice, seemed to like scratching and destroying them. He picked one out now, held it up to the light and smiled as he pinched it to death between his long yellow fingernails. They were like a lady's nails, and were dangerous in a fight. There was always dirt underneath them and if they scratched you, you got blood poison.

Yacavola trotted quietly beside him now, but there wasn't much life in their thundering hoofbeats. Old Lady Yacavola had scared their ponies. It was the problem with magic ponies, they were very shy and scared easily. But when they wanted to, when they were happy, they could take you anywhere in South Side in no time flat. The Masked Man loved that kind of ride. Everything came alive and your dreams jumped out all around you.

He put the spurs to his pony, made him rear up, and Yacavola did the same. The ponies shot forward, happy again. They galloped up the alley. The dust clouds rose behind them, like a whole outlaw band, and you could almost see the palm trees.

"Gettum up, Scout. On Silver, on big fellow!" The Masked Man's pony danced and pranced. The fence posts smiled with knotty eyes and splintery mouths, and the old garages stared with their big glassy eyes. There was nothing like it, when you rode with a pal, out on the range. Yacavola waved his invisible lasso in the air, shouting "KI-YIPEEEEEEEEEEEEEE!" and the Masked Man felt far-off memories of strange places he'd been to in his sleep.

They rode along the dusty trail, with the smell of cinnamon buns in the wind, then reined up in back of the bakery, where their horses could drink from a puddle.

The smell of the buns blew out through the big fan in the wall of the bakery. The outlaws crept toward the bakery door. Inside were the men in their aprons and white hats, working the ovens. The racks were piled with cinnamon buns. "*Keep low,*" whispered Yacavola.

The Masked Man knew the procedure. You hide along the edge of the rack and when the baker turns his back . . .

You grab!

"Hey! Hey, you little cocksuckers . . ."

They can't catch us, we know the alley too well, over this wall and through this yard.

The baker stood at the wall, waving his wooden spoon.

"I'll report you to the cops!"

"Report this," said Yacavola, giving him the long curving yellow nail of his middle finger, and they ducked between two houses and ran down a narrow stone gutter that drained toward the avenue. They stayed in the shadows of it, eating the sweet buns. "I'm going to join the Foreign Legion when I grow up," said the Masked Man.

"I'm going to be a crook," said Yacavola.

They rode out of the drain, licking the warm sugar off their lips. The street sloped down and they rode fast, hoofbeats pounding. Summer was coming soon, you could feel it in the air. "Couple of girls ahead," said Yacavola.

The Masked Man had nothing to do with girls, though he sometimes followed them secretly behind trees and bushes.

It was Dorothy Dillon, swinging on the gate with her girlfriend Patsy Sotnowski. Yacavola began flirting.

"Couple of creeps you are."

Patsy smiled, showing her braces. Her braids stuck out like little black tails and her socks were white. The Masked Man loved her little socks. She swung the gate, leaning over it toward him.

"Got any gum?"

He had none, and was unable to speak straight. But Yacavola was pouring on the charm.

"What's that thing crawlin' up your neck?" He reached out his long yellow fingernails.

11

Patsy drew back, giggling. The Masked Man was beginning to feel strangely dizzy. It was time to ride on. He needed the sound of mighty hoofbeats.

"Hi-yo Silver, a-waaaaay!"

He looked back, saw Yacavola riding right behind him, riding hard and well. The girls had brought him up straight in the saddle. He could ride like Lash LaRue when he wanted to and he rode that way now, whipping the air and scratching himself as he galloped. They rode past Hank's Hair Parlor, and onto the last rocky sidewalk before the end of town. The sidewalk was like a roller-coaster because the coal mines had heaved beneath it, and the houses were all abandoned and falling apart. They rode through them, throwing stones, and then the big open field was ahead of them, with a campfire smoking down by the railroad tracks.

"It's the bums," said Yacavola. "Let's ride down and see what they're cookin'."

The two riders rode into the grass and down the embankment, their hoofbeats soft as Indian ponies when they're sneaking up on a wagon train. They rode quietly through the grass, and circled the campfire, where the two bums were sitting. One of them had a nose like a pimply squash.

"What the fuck do you want?" The pimply-nosed bum looked up from the fire.

"What's in the can?" Yacavola pointed to the bubbling mixture over the flames.

"Screw, you little Jap." The other bum was squatting on his haunches, his large hat-brim turned down over his eyes. The Masked Man touched his plastic dart-gun. He was well within range.

"How about sharin' your beans?" asked Yacavola.

"You can share my dick," said the squash-nosed bum.

The bubbling can sent its aroma into the air, of tomato sauce and peppers.

"Gimme just a spoonful," said Yacavola.

"A kick in the ass if you come one step closer to this fire."

These weren't the wonderful bums you saw on the screen of the Ravino Movie Theater, who shared everything with other guys on the road. These were a pair of pricks. The Lone Ranger whipped out his gun and fired, hitting the squash-nosed bum in the middle of the forehead. The dart wobbled and hung there, like an arrow between the bum's eyes.

"I'll kill you, you fucking little Polack bastard!"

"Ride! Ride, Kemosabi!"

They rode up the railroad tracks, their ponies galloping hard, into the sunset.

Chapter 2

. . . In Which the Masked Man Thinks
About Titties.

◇ ◇ ◇

The wading pool glistened in the sunlight, with water spraying from a nozzle at the shallow end and making a rainbow in
the air. He raced into it, the rainbow breaking around him as
he splashed toward deeper water.

"Yay, yay!" Yacavola jumped in from the side, his huge
Salvation Army bathing suit flapping back and forth around
his skinny legs. The playground director made him wear a
bathing cap too, because of his lice. This the Masked Man
couldn't understand. Wouldn't it be better to drown them?

"Yay, hooray!"

They splashed and dove forward together, flattening out in
the pool. Yacavola couldn't swim, and clawed frantically at
the water until he sank. He stood up, his bathing suit falling
down, his bony ass coming out of it. He yanked it up and
tightened the long drawstrings; it bunched up around his
waist like a curtain.

"The Great Submariner!" Yacavola dove, hitting the water with a loud smack and then paddled desperately, finally sinking. He rose up, choking and coughing, the floppy legs of his bathing suit so big on him his balls were hanging out the side. He yanked the strings tight again, but his balls still hung out. Dorothy Dillon and Patsy Sotnowski pointed at him, giggling.

"Tarzan of the Apes! Ah-aaaahhhhhhh-aaaahhhhhh-aaaaahhhhhhhhhh!" He beat on his chest and drove handfuls of water at them, backing them to the edge of the pool.

"You stop that, Bobby, right now!"

"Ah-aaahhhhh-aaaahhhhh!" His bathing cap had a flower pattern on it, and the cap kept working upwards, making him look like Denny Dimwit. He took another leap and went under, his bathing suit floating out around him like a huge balloon. Fart bubbles came out of the billowing legs and the Masked Man moved away, into the falling spray from the nozzle, the spray beating all around in a million little dancing points of light. He dropped into the rippling mirror and swam away, head down, underwater. He could see Yacavola's bathing suit flopping and falling down again. He surfaced alongside him and Yacavola said, "Let's pull Patsy's suit off."

"I'm going to tell the lifeguard on you," said Patsy.

"G'wan, tell him," said Yacavola. "He's a fruit."

Yesterday the lifeguard had put Yacavola out for pissing in the pool, had dragged him away by the strap of his bathing cap. Now the Masked Man noticed another suspicious trickle coming out of one leg of Yacavola's huge suit, and he jumped up, onto the edge of the pool.

Yacavola stood in the water for a moment, smiling, then climbed up beside him. "Let's go look in the girl's bathhouse." They circled the edge of the pool, feet slapping on the hot black pave. The playground director was judging the Ping-Pong tournament, his head going back and forth and

15

they snuck on by him until they were out of sight, behind the bath-house.

"Lemme stand on your back," said Yacavola, and the Masked Man crouched low. He could hear the girls talking and whispering, as his faithful companion climbed up and hung there until there was a shriek from inside, and then the lifeguard's whistle blew.

Yacavola dropped to the ground alongside him, his bathing suit falling down around his ankles.

The Masked Man helped him to his feet and they rode off, but Yacavola's bathing suit kept falling down and it tripped him up, slowing his thundering hoofbeats as the lifeguard's whistle got louder.

"Come on!" shouted the Masked Man, but Yacavola was tangled up in the drawstring, and the lifeguard cut him off at the pass.

The Masked Man beat it around the corner of the bath-house alone, and when he'd circled all the way to the other side of the playground, he saw Yacavola being dragged along by the strap of his bathing cap, toward the gate. The lifeguard swung the gate open and snapped him out. Yacavola spun away, holding up his bathing suit. The Masked Man joined him on the sidewalk.

"What did you see?"

"*These.*" Yacavola pointed a long-nailed finger at the Masked Man's chest.

They walked along in their bare feet, bathing suits trailing water. "I'll get that lifeguard," said Yacavola. "I'll drown the whoreson bastard."

The Masked Man was thinking about titties. All of the girls who swam at the wading pool screamed if you tried to pull their tops off, but their little titties weren't any different from his own. He wondered why they made such a big fuss.

Yacavola turned back toward the playground, where the lifeguard was still watching them. "I'll get my old man to

16

come over and kick his ass." Yacavola yanked his drawstring tight.

The Masked Man nodded. The only ass he'd ever seen Yacavola's old man kick, was Yacavola's. He'd kicked him out of the house, over the porch railing, into the rabbit pens.

Chapter 3

. . . In Which the Brave Commando Yank
Is Heard to Remark,
"Whoreson fucks. They're no good,
to Jap a guy that way."

◇ ◇ ◇

Captain Marvel and his pal, the brave Commando Yank
Yacavola, stood perfectly balanced on the high wall of Herbert Hoover School. The fall winds were blowing and it was
thousands of feet to the schoolyard below, where Dorothy
Dillon and lots of other girls were watching.

Commando Yank stuck one foot out in the air and twirled
it around, defying gravity.

"You get down from that wall this instant!"

Startled, the daring Yank lost his balance and wavered,
hands clutching at the air. Captain Marvel moved quickly
and saved him from falling, but the jig was up. Below them,
hands on her hips, face twisted with rage, was the vicious
Miss Kneedle, worse than a Nazi general.

*"Did you hear me? I said get down from that wall at
once!"*

It was going to be a tough one. Marvel's hands trembled as
he lowered himself down the wall.

"Miss Duffy too," said Commando Yank softly, his long nails scratching on the stones.

They landed, Miss Duffy charging toward them, like a Jap, her buck teeth flashing, her big tits wobbling. Behind her Miss Kneedle came goose-stepping, like the evil Nazi general, Baron Glutz.

"How dare you climb that wall!"

Marvel put his hands in his pockets.

"Take those hands out of your pockets!"

Marvel took his hands out of his pockets. Miss Duffy grabbed him by the collar and marched him toward the school. Commando Yank Yacavola was in the grip of Miss Kneedle. Nervously, Yank killed a few of his lice and flicked them away.

"You stop that!" Miss Kneedle whacked him across the head.

Captain Marvel stiffened. If Yank used his nails on her, it'd be reform school for sure.

"Wash your hair with kerosene," said Miss Kneedle. "Tonight."

Commando Yank laughed, half-closing one eye in a secret look that said, *go fuck yourself.*

Captain Marvel took an apple out of his back pocket, emergency rations for when you were captured by the Axis. Miss Duffy held the door and they marched through, into the hallway.

"Straight to my office."

Nazi Headquarters. Hideous tortures awaited them.

"Get in there, the pair of you."

The American flag hung by the window but it was only camouflage.

". . . might have broken your neck . . ."

". . . and wash behind your ears, with *soap*."

Captain Marvel took a bite of his apple.

"Take that apple out of your mouth!"

19

"How dare you eat in front of us!"

He tossed it up and down in his hand.

"In the wastebasket," said Miss Kneedle coldly, pointing to the only place for such an apple.

"Hold out your hands."

Captain Marvel steeled himself for the blow. He was bullet-proof, but a metal-edged ruler was something else—ARGGHHHHHHHHHHHHHHHHHHH

Miss Kneedle pointed the ruler at Commando Yank. The brave Commando held out his hands.

"And cut those filthy fingernails!" Miss Kneedle wound up, and slashed the ruler down. Commando Yank twitched, and his lice jumped. Captain Marvel saw one land on Miss Duffy's collar and begin its climb upward, toward her hair.

◇ ◇ ◇

"I'll get them suckers someday," said Commando Yank, as they walked home at the end of the day. "I ain't never forgettin'."

"Through here," said Captain Marvel, leading them between some garages, into Fido Decontino's yard. Old Man Decontino was in back, hammering out a fender.

"Whattyaz up to . . ."

"Where's Fido, Mr Decontino?"

"Idano." A cigar stuck out from between Mr. Decontino's teeth, and when he hammered at the fender the tip glowed and sent up smoke signals.

They looked around at the different cars and jacks and welding tools. Tall grass was sticking up through old bumpers that were piled around. You could dig in behind them if the Japs were charging you. Mr Decontino wasn't fighting Japs though, because he'd lost two fingers in a fan belt.

Captain Marvel started to fly, out of the yard, back into the alley. His arms were spread out, making wings, and Commando Yank flew with him, making airplane noises with his mouth, as Captain Marvel sang, "*Off we go, into the wild blue yonder . . .*"

They flew over a couple of fences and some ashcans, fighting Jap Zeros. Captain Marvel knew what a Zero looked like; he had silhouettes of every plane in the war, in case of attack.

". . . *we live in fame or go down in flame, 'cause nothing can stop the Army Air Corps!*"

The Army Air Corps flew around a big bend in the alley, right into a real battlefield, Fido and Big Joe Decontino shooting at each other with bee-bee guns.

"Hey Fido, hey Big Joe!"

They ran in alongside of Fido, and crouched with him behind a wall. Across the alley, between some garages, Big Joe was cranking his rifle.

"Watch me get him this time," said Fido. He raised up and aimed. Big Joe swung out at the same time, and fired. Fido fell backward with a scream, holding his eye.

"I'm shot! I'm shot in the eye!"

Big Joe ran down to them. "Lemme see."

Fido took his hand away. There was a big red spot on his eyelid.

"You're ok," said Big Joe.

"I was fuckin' near blinded." Fido touched at the red spot.

"You shouldna stuck your head out," said Big Joe.

"What'll I tell Ma? She'll take away our guns."

"Tell her you fell into some glass."

"Yeah, ok. I fell down the steps into some glass. Somebody left glass layin' around and I fell into it."

Big Joe Decontino looked at Captain Marvel and Commando Yank. "Start movin'."

"Hey, Joe, don't point that gun—"

"Move," said Joe. "I'll give you three."

Joe and Fido raised their rifles. Captain Marvel looked at Yank.

21

"Ride, ride!"

They rode hard. It was rough being a little guy without your own bee-bee gun.

"Ouch! Ow!" Captain Marvel jumped in the air. A direct hit in the ass. He'd ask for a bee-bee gun for Christmas, promise that he'd never point it at anybody.

Then he'd wait in a tree for Joe Decontino, and plug him.

They reined hard around the corner, out of range. "Whoreson fucks." Commando Yank rubbed the seat of his pants. "They're no good, to Jap a guy that way."

Captain Marvel nodded. It was a rotten trick to pull on your pals, and it'd still be hurting tomorrow. Anyway Fido got shot in the eye.

They walked on, nursing their wounds, into a big pile of leaves at the gutter. They shouted and whirled, kicking and stamping in the leaves.

"Hey, what in Christ do you think you're doing! I just raked those leaves."

"On Silver, on big fellow!"

With the long rake swinging in the air behind them, they rode away, spurring their gallant steeds.

"Let's swipe some baloney," said Commando Yank.

"Alright," said Captain Marvel, who'd been without food for hours. They slipped quietly toward the back of the butcher shop, and crept through the door, into the room where the bacon hung. They could grab some of that and cook it on a fire, just like a bum. Marvel pointed and Yank nodded.

The office door swung open and the butcher stepped out, grabbing them by the neck.

"Where you goin', boys?" He shook them in his huge bloody hands. A cleaver was stuck in his belt and he smelt like hot dogs.

"I was comin' in to buy somethin' for my mudder," said Commando Yank.

"You always shop in the back, do you?"

The room pitched upside-down, the walls flew past, and they went sprawling into the alleyway.

"I'll get the old man after you!" shouted Commando Yank.

"Bring him around," said the butcher, slamming the door shut.

Captain Marvel picked himself up, brushing off his invisible cape. It had been a rough day all around—whipped, shot, and tossed out on their ass—but that's the way things went sometimes when you were serving the cause of freedom and justice in the land.

Chapter 4

The White Rider Prays to God for a Bee-bee Gun.
Old Man Yacavola Comes Out with a Brick.

◇ ◇ ◇

Raised in a valley hidden from the eyes of men, where the tremendous pressure of gravity made them stronger than any ordinary horse or man could be, the WHITE RIDER! *and* SUPERHORSE! *have dedicated their powers to the cause of law and order.*

He rode into the parish yard of St. Michael's, and reined Superhorse up at the steps. Father O'Hora was sitting on the front porch. "How're you today, my boy?"

"Good, Father," said the White Rider, climbing the stairs.

"And how's your mother?"

"She's tryin' to find some money." *If only I could find some money*, she'd said. He'd been keeping his own eyes open, looking along the sidewalks and gutters, but all he'd found so far was a cigar butt that'd made him terribly sick.

"Well, now, what's this here, behind your ear?" Father touched the White Rider's ear, and brought out a nickel. "And right here inside your hair. I think I see a . . . "

"Nit?"

"No, wait a moment—it's a dime." Father handed the coins to him. "You've got money all over you."

"How do you do it, Father?"

"It's God's work." Father took out a cigarette and tapped it on the porch railing.

The White Rider put the coins in his pocket and sat on the railing, thinking about God in His long white beard and gold chair and wondering if God had a bee-bee gun. One He could spare. Then, as if in answer to his prayers, Fido Decontino came around the corner, carrying his.

Does God want me to have Fido's gun? wondered the White Rider.

"Hey, Fido, hey . . ."

Fido turned into the parish yard and walked toward the steps, like a soldier, the air rifle on his shoulder. He marched up the steps, and Father saluted him. "Fido, how's business?"

Fido leaned his rifle against the railing. "Hey, Father, got any more magic tricks?"

Father flicked his cigarette ash over the railing. "Well, now, Fido, I just might, but first tell me how you got that sheriff's badge you're wearing."

Fido looked down, and Father reached out. "My mistake, it's a nickel." The coin flashed in his fingers and he handed it over. "Keep your money in your pocket, Fido."

"Thanks, Father." Fido put the coin away and leaned against the railing beside the White Rider. The White Rider eyed his rifle. He could just grab it and run but maybe God didn't want it to happen like that.

"Fido," said Father, "hand me that rifle of yours."

That's it! thought the White Rider. He knew God wouldn't let him down.

I promise to be careful and good with it.

He waited for Father to give him the rifle. The first thing he'd do after he shot Fido would be to hide in the grass when

25

Miss Duffy and Miss Kneedle came by. They'd jump alright, holding their behinds and looking around for what stung them, but the White Rider would be gone, on Superhorse.

"You just crank it, Father," said Fido.

"Yes, I see . . ." Father cranked the handle once, slowly, and turned in his chair, looking across the parish lawn. He raised the rifle to his shoulder, sighted along the barrel, and fired.

A fluttering little figure fell from a tree at the far end of the yard.

"Hey, Father, you're a great shot!"

Father brought the rifle quickly down. "I didn't mean to . . ." He looked at Fido and the White Rider, his face suddenly pale.

The White Rider knew, he'd seen the rifle take right over, aiming itself perfectly.

"You'd better go now, boys," said Father, handing the rifle back to Fido.

"A bull's-eye," said Fido.

"Yes, well, we won't tell anyone about it." Father was going toward the dark glass parish door.

"See you later, Father."

Father didn't wave good-bye. They rode down the steps and up the street, looking over the parish fence. "He must have fallen outside the yard," said Fido.

They went into the alley and found the bird, on the grass just beyond the fence.

"He's still alive," said the White Rider, looking into the bird's tiny blinking eyes. The bird's breast rose and fell with quick little breaths. The White Rider picked it up carefully, and the scratchy feet moved for a moment against his palm. "We'll nurse him back to health."

"Yeah," said Fido, "I read somethin' about it somewhere." They started walking toward the alley.

"What'd you read?"

"I dunno, I forgot." Fido laid the rifle across his shoulders.

They headed down toward the body shop. The garage doors were up and they could see the welding torch shooting a long tongue of white fire at a fender. Fido's old man was under the helmet, working the torch. They entered the shop and stood alongside him, the White Rider gently holding the wounded bird in his hand. He could feel the bird's heart beating against his palm.

Mr Decontino turned off the torch and pushed back his helmet. "Whaddyaz up to?"

"Look, Pop," said Fido, "a wounded bird."

Mr Decontino looked into the White Rider's hand, then looked up at Fido. "I told yez not to shoot birds."

"I didn't shoot him, Pop. Father O'Hora did."

"Don't hand me that shit." Fido's old man whipped him across the ass with a radiator hose. Fido yelped, jumping out of the way.

"Honest, Pop, I ain't lyin'."

"You're always lyin'. Get outta here." Old Man Decontino picked up a rubber hammer. They backed out the big open doorway.

"Father shot him," yelled Fido. "Right from the parish house."

They ducked out of sight, behind the shop, and hopped the fence. The White Rider looked at the bird, at its little black eyes staring into space, and its smooth shiny feathers. He and Fido were its only pals now, and they'd save it, like in the story Fido couldn't remember.

"I think we should feed it." The White Rider led them toward his house. They went up the front steps, to the apartment, and he opened the door. The apartment was empty. He went to the bread box and took out a slice. The bread was fresh and soft. He laid the bird on the bread. "Go ahead, eat that. You'll feel better."

A little drop of blood fell from the tip of the bird's beak, onto the bread, staining it red.

"He don't look too good," said Fido.

"We better take him down to Father."

They went out onto the street and down toward the parish house. "He's got some ladies on the porch with him."

"That's ok, he'll wanna see what happened."

They opened the parish gate and walked across the sidewalk to the porch. "Hi, Father." They climbed the steps. The White Rider held out the slice of white bread.

"Here's the bird you shot, Father."

Everybody looked down at it. Another drop of blood fell from the bird's beak onto the bread, making the red blotch bigger.

"He's still alive," said Fido. "See where you got him? Right in the chest." He pointed to the spot where the feathers were ruffled.

"You'd better go and play, boys," said Father. "It was an unfortunate accident."

"It was a bull's-eye," said the White Rider to the ladies, wanting Father to get the credit. The ladies smiled nervously and looked at each other, and the White Rider could see how impressed they were.

"What'll we do with him, Father?" asked Fido. "I read a story once about this guy took care of a bird."

"Say a prayer for him," said Father, and the White Rider did, immediately, adding a little reminder to God about what *kind* of bee-bee gun he wanted, a repeater, not a single-shot.

"Run along, boys, I'm busy now. You can come back this evening."

The White Rider nodded. Father was probably going to pull nickels and dimes out of the ladies' hair.

Fido led the way back to the gate. "Whyn't we go down to Yacavola's? I seen his old man fixin' up one of their rabbits once, that the cat clawed."

They walked to Truck Street and down it, to the little yard in back of Yacavola's where the rabbit pens were. Mrs Yacavola was out, with a pan full of feed.

28

"A wounded bird," said the White Rider, holding out the bread to her.

"How'd that happen?" she asked, looking down at Fido's rifle.

"Father O'Hora shot him."

"Don't tell stories."

"We thought maybe Mr Yacavola could fix him up," said the White Rider.

Mrs Yacavola turned toward the house.

"Stawshu!"

She had a voice like a wrecking ball, and the White Rider cringed. Old Man Yacavola got up from his seat by the window and came out. He wasn't fighting Japs because one of his nuts hung down to his kneecap. He walked across the porch, leaning to the side a little, easing his nut.

"Whaddya wan'?"

"They got a bird," said Mrs Yacavola, and the White Rider held it out to him.

Old Man Yacavola looked at it, and touched it with his finger. "Set 'im down."

It's alright now, said the White Rider as he laid the bird on the ground. *You'll be flying soon.*

Old Man Yacavola reached behind one of the pens, came out with a brick and brought it down with all his might on the bird.

"Bury 'im."

He turned and walked back into the house.

They carried the squashed bird back up the street and dug a little hole in back of the parish house, just outside the fence. The White Rider made a little cross out of two sticks and put it on the grave.

"I remember the story," said Fido. "The bird comes back to the guy, every spring, like."

Chapter 5

. . . In Which Hitler Commits Suicide,
and the Masked Man Loses His Horse.

◇ ◇ ◇

"Superman stands astride the hills, his legs apart, his hands braced on his hips, a blue colossus with red cape streaming. He's brave, he's strong—but how will he be able to hold off the entire Japanese army single-handedly? To find out, listen tomorrow to the next thrilling episode in—

"The Adventures of SUPERMAN! . . .

"Brought to you every Monday through Friday, same time, same station . . ." The radio crackled again and another voice broke in.

"WE INTERRUPT THIS PROGRAM TO BRING YOU A SPECIAL BULLETIN. THE BRITISH NEWS SERVICE HAS ANNOUNCED THAT ADOLF HITLER JUST COMMITTED SUICIDE IN HIS BUNKER IN BERLIN. THIS, PREDICTED ONE SPOKESMAN, WILL MEAN THE VIRTUAL END OF THE SECOND WORLD WAR IN EUROPE. AND NOW, BACK TO OUR BROADCAST . . ."

Hooray, hooray! He could cash in his war bond and buy himself a bee-bee gun!

30

He ran across the kitchen and out the door and down the steps, hoofbeats thundering.

Ride, cowboy, ride! Hitler committed suicide!

The smell of wet grass filled the air. Drops of water fell from the gate as he swung on out of the yard, his pony prancing and dancing. The garage roofs glistened with raindrops. The sun was scattered in puddles all along the alleyway. He jumped the puddles, saw trees floating upside-down in them, and then he was thundering on through the mud and stones. The old broken fence leaned way out, water dripping from its gray face. The magic pony galloped in the cool fragrant air, and he rode tall, along the winding trail. The pony whinnied and tossed his head happily, stamping and rearing way up in the air.

"Easy, boy, easy . . ."

He spun in the muddy alley, hoofs biting deep, and then leapt a low crumbling wall, scattering loose stones behind him.

This cayuse is wild today.

He pulled hard on the reins, but couldn't keep the high-spirited horse in check.

"Yipppeeeeeeeee! Ki-yii-yipeeeeeeee!"

He waved his invisible ten-gallon hat and slapped it against the mighty haunches of the prancing pony.

"Hi-yiiiii! Hii-up there!"

He galloped out of the alley onto Fetterbush street, slapping and bucking in the saddle.

"Yippy-yip-yipeeeee!"

"Stop that dreadful noise!"

He spun in the saddle, saw a woman standing in her yard, pointing a finger at him. "You're too big to be carrying on that way."

The magic pony stumbled. He stuck his hands in his pockets and shuffled away. The woman called after him, over her fence. "A big boy like you, you ought to be ashamed."

31

"Hitler committed suicide," he said, and ducked between the garages, trying to get his feet going, get them making the sound of mighty hoofbeats again, but he couldn't. The magic pony was hobbled; his legs were stiff and heavy.

"Giddyup, big fellow, giddyup there . . ."

His voice echoed emptily between the garages. He looked up into the clouds and felt the pony go through them, toward the lonesome draw.

He tried to gallop, but his legs were stiff as wood, stiff as a wooden soldier's legs. He called into the wind, called "KI-YIIIIIII!" as loud as he could, but the hoofbeats he loved were so far off he could hardly hear them.

"Hitler committed suicide," he said, trying to feel better, but it didn't help because something had happened to his pony. The lady had scared him away, had maybe even killed him.

She killed my pony, he said, walking along. The window-eyes of the garages were empty; the old picket fence had lost its mouth and nose and had nothing to say. He felt more grown-up, the way he never wanted to be.

He started to run, shouting into the backyards, "Hitler committed suidide, Hitler committed suidide!"

Somebody said, "*What?*" and he said, "I heard it on the radio," and ran on, feeling very important, and older, spreading the news, the real news about Hitler.

Ahead on the corner he saw Yacavola, and Yacavola started to ride toward him, but the Masked Man didn't really ride himself, he just ran ordinary, he was a cowpoke without a pony, it had happened all of a sudden, with a lady, like he'd heard it on the radio or something—you're a big boy now— and Hitler committed suicide. The two were all mixed up inside him, and his pony was gone.

Yacavola shouted, 'Ya-hoooooooooooooooooo!" and waved his invisible ten-gallon hat, but the Masked Man didn't wave back, because people might see.

He ran along, trying not to show that he was a cowboy. He felt like he'd just popped out of a box, like a jack-in-the-box. He'd been living inside the box where nobody could see and now he'd popped out.

Chapter 6

The Lone Rider and Mrs Loopo's Great Big Ass

◇ ◇ ◇

Smoke and faces were behind the window, and he could hear people singing.

Mrs Loopo opened the door, with a glass in her hand. "Come on in, everybody's here."

"We brought Jacky," said Mommy. "I hope he won't be in the way."

The Masked Man did not like being called Jacky. He had lots of other names—secret, mysterious names.

"He can keep my nightmares company," said Mrs Loopo, pointing to Jerry and Joy Loopo, in cowboy hats, riding up alongside her.

"The B-Bar-B ranch," said Jerry.

"I'm the Durango Kid," said Joy.

"A girl can't be the Durango Kid. She has to be Dale Evans."

"I don't want to be Dale Evans."

They rode off through the crowd, whooping.

"Have a pretzel, Jacky," said Mrs Loopo, handing him the

34

dish. The Lone Cowpoke took one, and looked at her through the curling hole in it. Mrs Loopo was chubby and pretty, with a great big ass one of the men was tickling while looking the other way and talking to somebody else.

"People are in the bathtub, Ma!" Jerry reined up alongside her again.

"You mind your own business."

"Without any water."

"It's near your bedtime, young man."

The Lone Rider snuck off through the crowd, following his father, over to where the men were singing. They had their heads together like hound dogs, their voices harmonizing a tune.

He listened a long time, and felt like he was dreaming, way back in the old days his father'd told him about, before he was born, when his father was a little boy and went to the German bar with a bucket to get beer for the family. Daddy'd told him all those stories, and they seemed to float like ghosts in the air, over the heads of the singers.

Mr Loopo saw him and said, "Have a beer, pal," but gave him a soda and told him to have a good time. He liked Mr Loopo a lot; he had a little mustache and slicked-down hair and sometimes he took out his false teeth and clacked them at you.

Jerry Loopo rode up. "Hey, Pop, why do people get in the bathtub without any water?"

"They're relaxing, Jerry. They're tired."

The Masked Man walked through the living room; the Loopo house was falling apart, with tape on the windows and big stains on the wallpaper. There were people in every room, talking and dancing. He ate pretzels and saw Dolly Loopo go by, helping her mother serve sandwiches. She was older than he was, and pretty like her mother. She saw him and smiled and said hello. A piece of pretzel fell out of his mouth.

"Are you having a good time?"

He loved her. She had a bowl haircut, because Mrs Loopo

35

cut it herself to save money, with a bowl. She had freckles too, over her nose and he wished he knew how to dance so he could ask her to and turn slowly with her in the smoke.

"I'll see you later," she said, and went off with the tray. He watched her go and sucked on another pretzel, dissolving the salt slowly on his tongue. Jerry Loopo rode up, waving a pair of lady's underpants, pink with yellow flowers. "Capture the flag! Capture the flag!"

Everyone cheered except Mrs Loopo who slapped him behind the head. "Where did you find these?"

"Nowhere."

"Did you take these from the bathroom?"

"Somebody threw them in the hall."

"Young man . . ." She went to hit him again but he rode off waving the panties and everybody laughed and the Masked Man thought he should go upstairs and check out the bathroom too.

He went through the kitchen and up the back steps. They were dark and creaky, and the sound of voices and singing and tinkling glasses floated up the stairs behind him, growing softer as he turned the first landing, toward the stillness of the second floor. The walls smelled old, as if nothing had ever changed on this back staircase. He peeked around the corner of the top landing. Mr Loopo was standing in a doorway down the hall, with his hand up a lady's dress. Her skin was white as snow, and she was leaning against the edge of the door, her knee bending more and more.

The Masked Man backed down the staircase and sat on one of the steps in the dark, his heart pounding. He'd have parties like this all the time when he grew up.

He crept up again slowly; the bedroom door was closed. He tiptoed down the hallway, through the old-timey smells of wallpaper and dampness that filled the whole house. He stopped at the closed door and listened, but couldn't hear a sound.

He moved on to the end of the hallway and down the front

stairs, underneath an old hanging lamp with flowers painted on it, the flowers chipped and fading.

Below, someone had started to play the ukelele, and people were clapping and singing a song about doing the hula-ha.

He followed the singing into the living room, and saw his-mother dancing in a grass skirt. She was laughing and shaking her hips, making the long blades of dry grass rustle back and forth.

"Your mother's very pretty," said Dolly Loopo, suddenly beside him. He nodded, but he was still too amazed to speak. His mother had her hands in her long blond hair and was lifting it slowly over her head as she turned, the grass skirt swaying across her knees. She was a different person, someone he'd never known. He stared at her, trying to figure out who she was.

"My father," said Dolly, "brought that skirt home from the war."

All the men were clapping time, and he felt like he was suddenly very far from his mother, and would never be able to return, except the singing stopped and she started talking and joking and was familiar again, the mother he knew.

"Time for bed, kids." Mrs Loopo shooed them off, and Dolly said, "I have to find Jerry and Joy."

He followed her to the kitchen, and into the laundry room. Joy was on the sink and Jerry was in the washer. "Tank Commander," he said, and slowly lowered the lid and sank down.

"Time for bed," said Dolly.

Jerry's voice echoed from inside the washer. "Run them down. Man the machine gun."

Joy said, "He was going to put me in there and turn it on."

"He wouldn't do that," said Dolly.

Jerry opened the lid. "Yes, I would."

Dolly grabbed him by the arms and pulled him out. He

37

kicked but she dragged him along to the back steps. The Masked Man followed, with Joy, and they went upstairs to their bedroom.

"Freezin', ain't it?" said Jerry. "We had to cut back on coal, because we're broke."

He jumped on the headboard of his bed, balancing there for a moment, and then dove forward in a somersault. The mattress sank down and the bed springs creaked.

"You're going to break that bed some night, young man," said Dolly.

"I'm Green Arrow and Speedy."

"Get undressed."

He jumped up and down. "Someday I'm going to break my neck."

Joy danced out of her clothes, whining about how cold it was.

"I like it cold," said Jerry, yanking on his pajamas. "I wisht we lived in an igloo."

"Can we make one?"

"Yeah, sure . . ." They disappeared under the covers, and raised them up in a dome, their voices coming softly from inside. Dolly stepped into the closet. It was big and deep with a light in it, and she closed the door behind her.

Jerry climbed out of the covers. *"She's changin',"* he said in a whisper. *"We can watch her, come on."*

"Ever see this one?" The Masked Man put his hands together and demonstrated the thumb-that-comes-apart.

"Hey . . ."

"It's easy."

Joy looked out from the blankets. "I put my big toe in the onion dip. Mommy had to throw it away."

"Be quiet, I'm learnin' a trick."

"You be quiet."

Dolly stepped out of the closet in a long flannel nightgown with little blue dots on it, like Wendy Darling in *Peter Pan.* "Jerry, get back under there."

38

"Wait, I'm tearin' my thumb off." Jerry twisted his fingers together but Dolly went to smack him and he crawled back under the blankets with Joy.

Dolly turned down the covers of her own bed. "It's lots big," she said. "You can sleep in it with me till your parents go."

He took off his shoes and socks and crawled in. She smoothed out the pillow and then switched off the light.

He'd never been in a colder room. It was like being outside. The street light shone on the frosty window and he could see his breath in the air.

"Are you freezing?" asked Dolly.

"No, it's ok."

"Feel that," she said, and put her ice-cold foot against his. "Isn't that awful?"

A shadow slipped from the other bed, going softly to the door. Light from the hallway entered, along with a woman's voice from the record player, a voice that had silenced all the other voices at the party.

"This old whore come down the road . . ."

The woman's rough voice was covered by laughter from the party and then a man's voice came on the record, saying, *"Lemme touch it."*

"Why should I let you touch it?"

"Because I want to touch the goddamn thing."

"Maybe I'll let you sniff it."

"Alright, lemme sniff it."

The Masked Man felt how far away the downstairs was, far away in another world he couldn't understand. Something darkly mysterious was down there, making the grown-ups very quiet, all you could hear was the tinkling of their ice cubes.

"Smells ok, lemme touch it."

"How much will you give me?"

"Give you twenty-fi' cents."

"Well, give it to me."

39

The woman let out a heavy sigh. He felt himself melting into the mystery, melting and floating down the stairs.

"Take it out, goddamn you!"

"I jist got it in a little ways."

"I says, take it out!"

"Alright, I'm takin' it out."

"Goddamn you, you took it out and put it back in again."

It was the truth about everybody, crackling on a record, crackling and rasping, but he couldn't understand it, it was out beyond him somewhere, in the darkness.

"Did you shoot in me, you buzzard?"

"Jist a few drops."

"Well, you are a no-good buzzard."

"Jist a few drops . . . a few drops . . . a few drops . . . drops . . ."

The record kept sticking, and then it stopped, and the grown-ups were clapping and laughing. The bedroom door closed, and Jerry crept into the middle of the room. "We've heard it lots of times," he said. "We know all about what it means."

"Get into bed," said Dolly.

Jerry's shadow slipped back under the tent of covers, and he and Joy started whispering again. The Masked Man lay in silence. Dolly turned over. "I hate that record," she said softly. The Masked Man stared at the frosted window. The frozen swirls were like palm trees in a jungle garden, and the falling snow beyond them seemed to make the palm trees move, to sway and gently toss around, as if fairies were in the silvery leaves. He watched for a long time, till his eyelids grew heavy, but the garden still remained, shimmering and glistening as he went toward it in his sleep, walking with slow uncertain footsteps.

Chapter 7

... In Which the Masked Man Hears of the Boy Scouts and the Bare-naked Girl.

◇ ◇ ◇

They were moving. His guns were in the truck. He climbed into the front beside the driver. Yacavola stood on the sidewalk, scratching. "I'll come visit ya."

The driver started up the truck, and Yacavola ran alongside it, scratching and waving.

"Your pal's got bugs," said the driver. He was a fat man, with a cigarette behind his ear. "I get itchy lookin' at him." He turned the wheel and the truck rolled onto the avenue, Yacavola growing smaller and smaller behind it as the Masked Man waved out the window.

The truck bounced along, over the trolley car tracks. The Masked Man watched all the old trails falling away behind him. He was moving on. Up ahead was the big bridge, into the center of town.

They went onto the bridge above the scummy river. If you fell in it you got typhoid and died. He looked at it way below and then they were over the bridge and into central city. They passed the bums on the benches around the courthouse square. He'd be a bum when he grew up, and drink out of a wrinkled paper bag.

"I'm going to be a bum."

The driver burped and lit his cigarette. They drove on through town, following the trolley car tracks. The tracks curved out of central city, past the car lots and the electric company. Ahead was the jail, with ivy growing on the walls and bars on all the windows. He got the feeling he was going to die in the electric chair.

He touched his scalp, feeling all around it carefully, where they clamped the juice on you.

"Bugs," said the driver, scratching inside his shirt. "A couple jumped on me too. Somebody oughta give that pal of yours a bath."

"He's going to be a crook."

"You're gonna be a bum and he's gonna be a crook . . ." The driver puffed on his cigarette, and then threw it out the window. They went over a bounce and the Masked Man heard everything rattle around in back. Mommy and Daddy were somewhere up ahead, driving in their car to the new house. Daddy'd said there were woods and ballfield, and they were moving there for him, so he'd have a decent place to play, something a little better than the alleyway. The Masked Man said nothing of this to the driver, that all the stuff they'd had to carry and pile in the back of the truck was because of him.

"Smell that?" The driver pointed out the window, toward a burning mountain in the distance. "That's the culm dump. If you was to walk up there, you'd be dead in no time from the coal gas."

What a wonderful neighborhood!

"They been tryin' for years to put it out, but it just keeps burnin'."

This was the place for a Masked Man alright, with a mountain on fire right in the neighborhood. Things were working out better than he expected.

42

They turned a corner and climbed a hill, turned again and pulled in to the curb, alongside an old gray house. Daddy's car was in the drive. He jumped down and ran into the backyard. It was filled with bushes.

He snuck through them quickly, and came out by the cellar door. It creaked open when he pushed it, and he went inside, into the dark old basement. This would be his headquarters, down in the shadows.

The cellar stairs were dark and creepy, and he went up them fast, coming out into the kitchen. Mommy was there, unpacking dishes.

"Did you see the poisonous mountain?" He pointed out the kitchen window. "You die in a minute if you go near it."

"We'll never smell it up here on the hill," she said, but he could tell she was a little worried, the way she turned toward the window to look at it.

"Could I get a gas mask and go there?" He ran up the stairs and down the hall, to the back room. There was the mountain, clear as could be, smoke curling off it.

He opened the window and climbed out on a sloping little roof over the back porch.

I'll come across here secretly at night and drop down into the backyard.

I'll have to get a real cape, and silver pants.

He climbed back in and opened another door, onto more stairs, dusty and wobbly, going up. He climbed them and a dream jumped out of his head, about an attic filled with every toy in the world.

He climbed quickly, but when he reached the top the attic was bare, with only cobwebs hanging around. He pried up a loose board. It was the perfect place to hide his cape when he got one, so that his true identity might never be revealed.

Raindrops were beating right over his head. He looked out the little attic window. Below, a yellow rainsuit was coming along the sidewalk, with a limp, one leg twisted to the side and dragging. The rainsuit stopped in front of the house and watched the unloading.

He went quickly down the staircase, through the house and into the cellar, then out the cellar door into the bushes, which were already turning out to be very handy. He snuck along through them, to the front of the house and spied on the rainsuit.

It turned toward him, and he ducked away, back through the bushes and into the cellar again.

He crouched in the shadows, near the coalbin. He was a lone rider, banished from the society of others, forced to live a life of flight and hiding because of the mask he wore and the misunderstandings it caused.

"Hey, anybody in there?" The voice was at the cellar door. "I'm comin' in, ok?" The limping footsteps came through the cellarway.

The Masked Man could remain crouched no longer. He'd been cornered in his own coalbin, five minutes after checking into the new hideout.

He stepped out of the shadows, ready to draw. The yellow rainsuit came forward.

'You're the new kid, ain't you?"

"Who are you?"

"Paul Kane," said the rainsuit. "Everybody calls me Crutch. You know, Crutch Kane." He imitated a person walking with a crutch under one arm and a cane in the other.

"What happened to your leg?"

"I got hit by a beer truck." Crutch pointed to one of the wooden posts supporting the ceiling. "See this?"

The Masked Man joined him by the post. A name was carved in it, the name *Douglas Davis*.

"He used to live here." Crutch lowered his voice. "He's dead."

The Masked Man quickly glanced into the shadows of the spooky cellar. "How did he die?"

"He was explorin' one of the old mine shafts and it caved in on him."

The Masked Man looked at the letters carved deep in the wood. A strange feeling came over him, and he knew he'd carve his own name there—*Jack Twiller*—and after he died in the electric chair a legend would begin, that anybody's name who appeared on this post was fated for a terrible end.

"It's stopped raining," said Crutch. "Wanna go out? I'll show you around." He put back the hood of his rainsuit. He wore thick eyeglasses.

They went through the cellarway, into the backyard, and across it to a paved court that ran along behind the houses. "That's my house up ahead," said Crutch.

"We could flash messages with a mirror."

"And flashlights at night."

"I'll be getting a cape and silver pants."

"See that house there? Sometimes the lady goes by the upstairs window without anything on."

Kids! Own your own telescope. Close-up view of sports, nature study, etc. Amazingly sharp details. Loads of fun and thrills galore. Rocket Wholesale Company. Pay postman only $1.98 on arrival.

The ballfield was ahead of them. "I play ball," said the Masked Man. "My father's been trainin' me."

"Yeah, I don't play much," said Crutch.

"I'm gonna be a shortstop." They stepped onto the ballfield and the Masked Man picked up a stone and wired it.

"My old man was trainin' me too," said Crutch, "but he gave up because I kept fallin' over the first base with my bum leg."

"We can have a catch."

"I mostly play cards," said Crutch. "And look in windows."

Compare with telescopes selling for much, much more.

45

Try it—enjoy it—at OUR RISK *for 10 whole days. Your money back quick if not thrilled.*

They cut across the ballfield and climbed the bank, into the woods. "I know all the trails," said Crutch. "You could take me out in these woods blindfolded, I'd find my way back in no time."

They walked along a winding path. "The state troopers had to hunt all day for me once, but I wasn't really lost."

The Masked Man breathed deeply. He'd never smelled anything so wonderful as the rain-soaked woods. This was the place for real hiding. He'd stalk with his shoes off and shoot flaming arrows at people. "Ever get any Indians in these woods?"

"No, but they found a bare-naked girl tied to a tree. Spider Pronka did it."

"Who's Spider Pronka?"

"His old man's in jail."

"I passed the jail today."

"Well, that's where Spider's old man is. He knocked off a gas station."

"Who found the bare-naked girl?"

"The Boy Scouts. I'll be joining them when I'm old enough."

The Masked Man walked slowly, thinking of the bare-naked girl. It made him feel crazy inside, and he figured he'd have to join the Boy Scouts too, to help with the untying.

"If Spider feels like it, he'll de-pants you and you'll have to walk home in a cardboard box."

The path led to a small open patch in the woods, covered with hard grey silt. "There's an old mine shaft just over this hill. Sometimes you can find dynamite caps."

They scrambled down the hill. Rusty mine-car tracks curved through the grass, disappearing inside a dark opening in the hillside. The Masked Man crept to the opening and stuck his head into the damp dark shaft. Crutch moved in

46

alongside him. "If we find any dynamite caps we can blow somebody's front steps off."

They crept deeper into the shaft, Crutch taking the lead. The Masked Man crawled along, listening to the drip-drip of water somewhere ahead in the darkness. It was the worst place he'd ever been in. This new neighborhood was going to be alright, so long as he didn't get de-pantsed.

"I'll show you a shortcut to school tomorrow," said Crutch.

A chill of fear ran through the lone rider of the sagebrush. A new school was worse than being crushed to death in a mine shaft.

Chapter 8

Barney Baxter in the Air with Miss Olson

◇ ◇ ◇

Everybody in the class was looking at him. They'd been looking at him all morning. He kept his head down and stared at
his desk. His stomach was churning, like when Barney Baxter
In The Air falls out of his plane and drops hundreds of feet
and lands in a barrage balloon.

Miss Olson was talking but he couldn't hear her, he was
falling hundreds of feet through the air. The room started to
spin; his stomach churned wildly, and he raised his hand.

"Yes, Jack?"

"I'm going to faint."

The class snickered. He rose from his seat and the room
spun faster, with Miss Olson in the middle. She took a step
toward him, and he grabbed onto her to keep from faint-
ing.

The class roared with laughter, and it sounded like air-
planes, Barney Baxter's airplane, out of control. He pressed
himself into the folds of Miss Olson's skirt; she was a pretty,

plump lady, soft as a barrage balloon and he wrapped his arms around her.

What am I doing? he asked himself in amazement, but it was too late. He'd done the horrible thing and the class was banging on their desks and whooping, and somebody said, "What a fruit!"

"You be quiet, all of you!" snapped Miss Olson. "It's hard being in a new school. We must think how we'd feel if it were us."

Miss Olson, Barney Baxter will never forget you for this. He'll defend your barrage balloon his whole life long.

She patted his back and brushed the hair out of his eyes. "Are you feeling better now?"

"I'm going to be sick," he said, and raced to the door. He got his hand on the knob and puked all over it.

"That's alright, Jack. Go on down to the lavatory. I'll call the janitor."

He stepped into the big gloomy hall. This was worse than anything that had ever happened to Barney Baxter, Tailspin Tommy, or Secret Agent X-9, put together. His nose was burning, his eyes were watering, and everybody thought he was a fruit.

The door opened again, and Crutch stepped out behind him. "Miss Olson said I should go with you." They walked together through the hall and down the stairs to the basement. "I got to tell Mr McKlusky." Crutch knocked on the janitor's door.

A burly gray-haired man opened it and scowled at them.

"Somebody puked in Miss Olson's room."

The janitor turned and picked up his mop and pail. He waved them aside with a short swing of the mop, then climbed the stairs and disappeared into the big gloomy hall above.

"OK," said Crutch, "let's go." He led the way through the basement corridor, and into the lavatory.

49

Barney Baxter lowered his face over the sink and splashed water on his face. He'd like to shoot a flaming arrow into this school.

Look—flaming arrows! Run, run for your life!

This way, Miss Olson. I, scoffed by all and called a fruit, am in reality Flaming Arrow, the Arapahoe.

"If McKlusky catches you writing on the walls down here, he sticks your head in a toilet." Crutch swung one of the stalls open and pointed inside. "See? Clean as a whistle."

"He wouldn't stick my head in a toilet."

"That's what Spider said when McKlusky caught him pissing out the window."

"What happened?"

"McKlusky stuck his head in the toilet and flushed it. Spider said he fuckin' near drowned."

His flaming arrows, though specially coated with a secret lignite process, are harmlessly extinguished in the thundering waters of Mr McKlusky's toilet.

"You ok now?"

"Yeah."

"Don't ever come into the lav alone if you see Floyd here."

"Who's Floyd?"

"He's in our class. He'll try and play with your dick."

"Why does he do that?"

"He likes to. He'll be Head of Patrol Boys someday."

◊ ◊ ◊

The lines formed at the front and back gates of the schoolyard. The Patrol Boys kept everyone quiet and marched around importantly, their big metal badges gleaming in the late afternoon sun. He stared at the badges, his nose plugged up and burning from vomit, and his head still spinning. Principal Chicken Legge came to her office window and gave the

50

signal for the lines to proceed. He walked along in silence with the others to the corner.

The Patrol Boys stopped traffic and waved everyone across. As soon as he reached the other side he felt better, his dizziness suddenly gone. He saw a guy from his class start to ride, feet galloping, hands holding imaginary reins.

Why isn't he ashamed of himself? wondered Flaming Arrow.

Maybe we could ride together.

"Who's that guy?"

"Rider Wendorf," said Crutch, as the lone figure galloped off up the block. "He runs that way 'cause of his hand. He had polio and it bent his wrist, so he makes believe he's ridin' a horse."

Flaming Arrow watched Rider Wendorf disappear over the top of the hill.

"That's where Floyd lives." Crutch pointed to a big yellow house on the corner. "He's got a Daisy air pistol. He'll give you a quarter if you let him shoot you in the ass with it."

Flaming Arrow made some quick calculations, figuring how many times he'd have to get shot before he'd earn enough for his own bee-bee gun. "Does he give you a running start?"

"He makes you bend over, right in front of him."

It would be hard-earned cash, but it'd have to do until he could get some other odd jobs around the neighborhood.

They walked over the hill and he saw Rider Wendorf still galloping, across the ballfield. Some guys were already on the field, throwing a ball around. "I'm goin' home and get my glove."

"There's Spider," said Crutch. "He musta skipped school today." Crutch pointed to a skinny black-haired guy walking along the edge of the field with a funny sideways kind of movement, like he was coming along on a thread and looking over his shoulder to see if anybody was following him. He stopped by the backstop, talking with the players. He didn't have a glove or ball with him, but the players were gathering around him.

"He's sellin' hotbooks," said Crutch. "Ever see one? Popeye and Olive Oyl, like, without any clothes on."

He hadn't seen that one. It sounded like *Tiny Folk and the Giant*. The tiny folk didn't wear any clothes either. You could see their little asses in every picture, and the gold-digging dwarfs were always giving them a hard time. "I've got a boxful of comics."

"Not like Spider's."

He'd have to work a trade, maybe give Spider two for one, *Barney Baxter In The Air* and *The Human Torch* for *Popeye and Olive Oyl Without Any Clothes On*.

Chapter 9

. . . In Which Flaming Arrow Asks Himself,
  "Does Schunkenfeld really eat peanut butter
  and toilet paper sandwiches?"

◊ ◊ ◊

It was his birthday. He sat by the window, waiting for his guests. He didn't want a party, but his mother said it would be an opportunity to make new friends.

"And, Jacky . . ."

"Yes?"

"I don't think you should tell your new friends that your name is Flaming Arrow."

"Why not?"

"Because Jacky Twiller's a perfectly good name."

"I don't want any new friends."

"Yes, you do."

Twiller walked over to the table where his birthday cards were standing, and shook them all again, in case he'd missed some money.

Yacavola's card really stood out. It was a Valentine's Day card somebody'd sent Yacavola. Yacavola's name was crossed out and *Jack Twiller* was written in underneath it. He wished good old Yaco were coming to the party; Mother had

53

said it was too far for Yaco to come but he figured it was Yaco's lice. Everybody would catch them and he wouldn't make any new friends.

He tried to loosen his tie but the elastic neck band was already stretched all the way out. You had to wear a suit and tie on your birthday, you couldn't wear anything else. His hair was plastered down too. At least he was wearing his Zombie Skull Ring, *weird, mysterious, and frightening.*

He went back to the window. The girls were coming up the street—Harriet Blibbert and Louise Jaballo and Anita Crumpf. They were all from Miss Olson's class and had seen him throw up on the doorknob.

"Your guests are coming, Jacky."

He let them in. They were giggling as if they knew something he didn't know. He flashed the *ghastly skeleton's head with realistic crossbones and ruby-colored eyes,* but they didn't seem to notice it. They were looking around at furniture and things.

He led them into the living room and they put their presents on the couch where Daddy always napped like Dagwood Bumstead, underneath the painting of a lake. Daddy had pasted a trout in the painting, leaping from the water. Not everybody knew about that, you had to look closely. He knew something the girls didn't know, a fish was jumping right over their presents.

Mother asked if they'd help her set the table and they went off giggling and asking her questions and looking at things.

The doorbell rang. He went to it, twisting his Zombie Ring.

"Happy birthday," said Crutch, handing him a present.

"There are girls in the kitchen."

Crutch looked toward the kitchen door, then looked back. "Did Wanda come yet?"

"No."

Crutch took off his glasses and wiped them with his shirt.

54

"I think she likes me. She hit me with a rock yesterday. Right in the back."

The girls came out carrying party hats. Twiller backed away, but Anita Crumpf came straight at him. "Here," she said, and slapped a dunce cap on his head. "That's the cap for *you.*"

Crutch said, "What about me?"

"You're a dunce too." Anita whacked one down on his head. Twiller started to like her a lot. She was little and bossy and was telling everyone how to set the table. ". . . put those horns on one side and the two little candies on the other . . ." She bent way over the table, and Crutch sang, *"I see London, I see France . . ."*

The doorbell rang. Twiller went and opened it. Schunkenfeld stood on the welcome mat, smiling. He was a moron, and the poorest boy in Theodore Roosevelt School. Twiller'd been told that Schunky was so poor he sometimes brought sandwiches made of peanut butter and toilet tissue. *Don't laugh when he eats them,* Anita Crumpf had said.

Schunky followed him in and stared around the living room, the same smile on his face, as if everything he saw made him happy—chairs, ceiling, radio, floor lamp. "Someb'dy stuckt a fish in that pitcher."

"Here," said Anita Crumpf, and handed him a little paper derby. Schunky put it on, carefully adjusting the rubber band under his chin. The little derby hat sat on the very middle of his head and made him look more like a moron than ever.

The doorbell rang again. It was Lily Induris, and Twiller let her in, stammering a tongue-tied hello. She had fuzzy brown hair almost like cotton candy and very cute legs with Band-Aids on the knees.

"Here's your present," she said, and he put it with the others. The growing pile of presents made him feel a little embarrassed, but secretly he felt he deserved them.

"Rider's coming," said Crutch, looking out the window.

55

They watched Rider riding up the block, reins in one hand, present in the other. He galloped across the lawn, and rode up the steps.

"Howdy . . ." He trotted slowly through the doorway, and then just sort of stayed in the saddle as he looked around.

"Hey," said Crutch, "here's Wanda."

"Then *you'd* better watch out," said Anita.

"Why?"

"Be-*cause*," said Anita.

Twiller opened the door for Wanda. She could make a real fist. It would be awful to have a girl beat you up. He was very polite to her. "Have a paper hat."

"Hi, Wanda," said Crutch.

"Ugh." Wanda made a face, and then they saw Spider coming up the driveway, looking back over his shoulder.

"Spider, hey, Spider . . ." Twiller opened the door, really glad that Spider was his new friend because now Spider would never de-pants him.

"How ya doin', fuckhead." Spider walked in, without a present, because his old man was only making a nickel a day sewing mail bags in jail.

"Is everybody here?" asked Mother.

"Yep."

"Well, then, I guess we should put all the lights out . . ." She pulled the blinds and turned out the lights, and Spider said to him softly, *"Your mother's a good-lookin' dish . . ."*

Twiller filled with pride. His mother *was* beautiful; he thought she looked just like Blondie in the comic strip. She came in, carrying the cake. The candles were burning brightly, each candle carried by a little animal stuck in the icing—there were camels, elephants, horses, all in a ring, and everyone sang *"Happy birthday to you . . ."*

He made a wish for a bee-bee gun, leaned over and blew, and caught Spider blowing too and spoiling the wish.

56

The lights came on. Tiny curls of smoke were rising over the cake. Mother took the candles away and handed him a knife. He cut the cake down the middle and then she took over, making slices for everyone. Spider blew his paper snake, which unrolled with a *braaaaack* and struck Twiller in the eye. There were sodas for everyone and the little candies were all wrapped in silver foil. He took a bite of cake and found silver foil stuffed in the icing. Spider was smiling.

He spit out the silver foil and adjusted his dunce cap. Rider Wendorf was sitting across from him, making clip-clop sounds with his tongue and holding the reins as if the table were a stagecoach.

The cake was disappearing, roses and all, but now came the ice cream. The girls were whispering and giggling and Twiller looked at Lily Induris, who had some cake crumbs in her fuzzy hair. She smiled at him and said, "Happy birthday," and it made him feel funny inside. He blew his paper snake toward his plate, into his ice cream.

When the ice cream was finished they all went into the living room. He heard Anita Crumpf asking his mother for an empty milk bottle.

"Now everyone get in a circle," said Anita, coming in with the bottle.

They all did, the girls giggling again and Crutch wiping his glasses off with the end of his tie.

"OK," said Anita, setting the bottle in the middle of the circle. "Here we go." She gave it a spin and the bottle went around and around. Rider made fast galloping sounds. The bottle stopped between Louise Jaballo and Schunkenfeld.

"I'm not kissing *him*," said Louise.

Schunky smiled and looked around happily and the bottle was set spinning again. It stopped between Wanda Locomovitz and Crutch. "Well," said Wanda, "I'm not kissing *him*."

"Come on," said Crutch, "you've got to."

"Well, take your glasses off first."

Crutch took off his glasses and leaned into the middle of the circle, his eyes weak and watery. Wanda kissed him real-fast-on-the-cheek and pulled back, wiping her lips. *"Ugh . . ."*

She spun the bottle, and Rider got a kiss, in the saddle. They spun again and again, with the whole party kissing except Twiller, who got passed up by the bottle every time. It stopped a lot at Schunkenfeld, but none of the girls would kiss him and he sat grinning in his derby hat.

"Hey," said Spider, "how about some post office?" He put his arm around Wanda and gave her a squeeze. She gave him an elbow in the ribs.

Twiller opened the large closet off the living room, where his books and games were stored. They counted one-potato-two-potato and Anita Crumpf got to go in first. She called Rider and he rode into the closet and was in there with her for a long time, making faint clip-clopping sounds.

"Come on," yelled Spider. "I got a special-delivery letter to mail . . ." He pounded on the door and they opened it.

Twiller watched his new friends going in and out of the post office and prayed for one to ask him. He'd never kissed a girl before; everybody seemed to like doing it, and he didn't want to miss out on the fun, but nobody was asking him. Was it because he'd thrown up on the doorknob? Did they still think he was a fruit? He could play ball better than anybody in the neighborhood, they should see him play ball with the big guys, then they'd know.

Spider stepped out and pointed to him. "She wants *you*."

He went toward the closet, feeling very fluttery inside, like he was falling through the air again. He opened the door and Lily was waiting for him, and when he closed it he could smell sweet soap. Her hand fumbled toward him and her fine-spun hair brushed his cheek. Behind him were his books—*Huck Finn, Tom Sawyer, A Treasury of Dog Stories, Buddy in*

58

Deep Valley, A Boy Scout's Destiny. Then Lily's lips were touching his, and a magic land was opening softly all around them, with soft velvety paths, her lips not trying to get away like he thought might happen, but pressing against his and tasting like cake. Kissing, he realized, was the most wonderful thing you could do, almost as good as finding a dynamite cap.

Chapter 10

Twiller Tries to Impress a Friend.

◊ ◊ ◊

**YOUR NAME WILL
GLOW IN THE DARK**
A thrilling new ring! Your first name or nick-name written on it in PHOSPHORESCENT LETTER-ING! *Fits all sizes—protected by sturdy plastic dome. Will glow any-where in the dark! Order today! Only 25 cents!*

He finished his cereal and went upstairs to his room, to his Mystery Bank—*Engineers, Mechanics, Magicians—all agree that this Mystery Bank will mystify and baffle everybody.*

He pulled at the Special Invisible Drawer, but couldn't make it work. He banged on the bottom and twisted the top, but the money only rattled around inside.

He threw it against the wall, and then kicked it with his foot. The Mystery Bank remained sealed, the Special Invisible Drawer refusing to Glide Mysteriously Open.

He shook it, jumped on it, and flung it against the wall again, tears of frustration welling up in his eyes.

"Jacky!" Daddy shouted from his couch downstairs. *"What're you doing up there!"*

"Opening my Mystery Bank."

"Well, don't make so much noise, I'm trying to nap."

It was Daddy's Saturday morning nap, the one right after he got out of bed.

He took the pliers from his junior mechanic's box and yanked the Special Invisible Drawer out by the teeth. The metal tore, the Secret Hinge snapped, and his money spilled out. He went back downstairs.

> *Print your name carefully on the coupon.*
> *It will be glowingly reproduced in*
> PHOSPHORESCENT SCRIPT.

He printed his name on the coupon and taped a quarter to it. Then he went to the cupboard, opened up a new box of cereal, and filled in a second coupon, carefully printing another name.

◇ ◇ ◇

The brass slot in the door lifted, and the package dropped through. He ran downstairs before anybody else could get to

61

it, and carried it on outside and down the street, unopened. Nobody must know the secret—but he could feel the glow already, in his pocket.

He cut through the alley and slipped into one of the old garages, straight to the darkest corner. He opened the package.

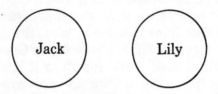

The names glowed side by side, soft as moonlight.

He took his ring out of the box and slid it on his finger. Now Lily's ring glowed by itself in the box, surrounded by white cotton, like the moon in a cloud.

He closed the box and stepped back into the alley. He could give her any of his other rings, but a Jet Plane Ring didn't seem right; the tiny plane launched off ok, but then it just fell on the floor.

A Glowing Name Ring was perfect.

He hurried down the alley and took the corner on the run, the houses and trees going by in a blur beyond his outstretched finger. The ring caught the sunlight, the little dome glistening, and his name curving inside it.

He ran along the ballfield, and across the avenue to Kleinbauer Street. It sloped sharply downward and his feet were flying now. Lily's house was at the bottom of the hill, and he knew she was home, he knew every move she made. Early this morning she'd had a ballet lesson at the Kherlacombe School of the Dance, and come home on the trolley car at ten-thirty, carrying her little dance bag. Spider said he'd seen her practicing ballet and while she was twirling on her toes her underpants fell down but that was a Spider story and not to be believed, although he liked to think about it.

He stopped at the hedges just beyond her house and took her ring out of the box. He was nervous, but it was now or never; if he waited around to think about it he'd still be thinking in the middle of the night, the little moon glowing in his hand.

He walked up the sidewalk to her front door and rang the bell.

Impress Your Friends!
Luminous Hand-painted Script.
Phosphorescence easily recharged
under the ordinary light bulb.

Lily's mother opened the door. She was a tall pretty lady and she looked at him blankly, maybe thinking he was selling salve.

"Is Lily home?"

A question flickered in her eyes for a moment, and he suddenly felt the whole life of this house he'd never been to before, with strange people and furniture and smells, a world he now wanted to escape from. But Lily was coming toward him, and the ring was in his hand.

"Here," he said, "it glows in the dark."

Lily took it, read her name and handed it to her mother, who read it too and then looked at him. "Where did you get it?" she asked, as his cheeks started to burn.

"I found it."

"You found it?"

"Yeah, I found it. On the street. I saw Lily's name on it, I figured it was hers, figured she lost it."

"I see you're wearing one," said Lily's mother, a smile spreading across her face. "Did you find it too?"

He turned quickly and started back across their lawn. It was a million miles wide, and Lily said "Thank you," and her mother said, "Wouldn't you like to come in?" but he was running, around the hedge and along the sidewalk.

He ran up the street, past the cellar where Spider lived, past Wanda Locomovitz's house and then past the driveway where the two coal trucks parked.

He ran over the top of the hill to the avenue, raced across it, raced the trolley. The motorman clanged his bell, but he was already gone, over the curb and into the field, jumping the puddles, the little box still bumping in his pocket. Someone waved from behind the backstop but he just kept running, leaping the last puddle and climbing the bank into the woods.

Chapter 11

Good-bye, Kemosabi

◊ ◊ ◊

A bald-headed man came forward, with a flower in his buttonhole, and said very softly, "Right through there."

Twiller walked into the softly lit room. "You can go over to him," said the man, putting a hand on his back.

He walked over to the casket and stood beside it. Yacavola was stretched out, his eyes closed, arms folded on his chest. A rosary was wound through his clasped fingers. His fingernails were cut way down and weren't yellow anymore.

Somebody came in sobbing, it was Miss Duffy, with a handkerchief to her nose. Miss Kneedle was beside her, holding a handkerchief too.

He looked back at Yacavola, and leaned closer to see if Yaco's lice were still on the job. There didn't seem to be any. Had they washed his hair with kerosene? It didn't smell like it, but you couldn't tell with all the flowers.

Miss Kneedle came up behind him and whispered, "You can say a prayer for him, Jack." She pointed to a kneeler in front of the casket.

He knelt down, peering closer into the casket. Yacavola didn't really look like himself, with his hair washed and combed and his fingernails cut. He looked kind of like an angel. Would God keep him out of heaven because he'd called his mother a whoreson bitch and a bastard? God probably wouldn't even recognize him now, with his nails cut and his lice gone, all dressed up in a suit and tie. You had to have a suit and tie when they buried you, he knew that, but it didn't fit Yaco too well. It was probably from the Salvation Army, like his bathing suit. He'd never seen him in those shoes either, polished and all. They looked strange, sticking up in the air with the toes pointed out a little to each side.

Good old Yaco.

He started to cry, and Miss Kneedle took him away. Mrs Yacavola came in and she was crying too. Old Man Yacavola was alongside her, leaning a little to take the pressure off his nut. Yaco had shown them all the old man's truss one day, as big as a shopping bag.

"We're very sorry," said Miss Kneedle, and Mrs Yacavola started crying more, and Old Man Yacavola said, "Now, now . . ." and straightened up, pressing two fingers in along his pants leg.

Father O'Hora came over and took Mrs Yacavola's hand, and said, "He's with the angels now."

So there it was, Yaco had gotten in, God hadn't spotted him. Or else He was overlooking all the times Mrs Yacavola had gone after Yaco with her broom, and the time Old Man Yacavola had kicked him into the rabbit pens.

"How do you like your new school?" asked Miss Kneedle.

"OK," he said, looking at her bony knees. If she gave you one of those in the back you'd go down like a shot.

He edged away from her, saw the butcher come in, and tried to get out of sight; the last time he and Yaco had swiped some hot dogs the butcher said he was going to put their ass in his sausage grinder. He didn't look mad now, though. He looked big as ever and was running one finger inside his collar to loosen it, but he wasn't pissed off about the hot dogs, he looked real down-in-the-dumps as he shook Old Man Yacavola's hand.

"I'm sorry as hell about this, he was a good kid."

"Yeah," said Old Man Yacavola, "yeah . . ." He shifted his weight again, easing off on his swollen nut.

"Stawshu," said Mrs Yacavola, "take a chair."

"I'm alrigh'," he said, sticking one hand down under his belt.

"He usta come into the shop," said the butcher.

"I know," said Old Man Yacavola. "He brung the baloney."

"A good kid," said the butcher, shaking his head.

Miss Kneedle and Miss Duffy were whispering with Mrs Yacavola about how they'd noticed Yaco starting to get thinner and weaker, and Mrs Yacavola said yes and then he finally couldn't get out of bed at all and Father O'Hora said the blessing was it came quickly.

He listened beside a vase of flowers. It was quite the thing to die, everybody was really nice to you.

He looked at his watch, which didn't work, and pretended to remember an important engagement somewhere else. He had to go now, the smell of the flowers was making him sick.

He waved toward the casket, to his faithful companion, and walked back out through the dimly lit hall.

Chapter 12

The Next Adventure of Superman;
or, Will Someone Please Kick Lois Lane in the Ass.

◊ ◊ ◊

The little carriage wheels caught the sunlight, and turned it, around and around. Anita Crumpf and Wanda Locomovitz pushed the carriage along, fussing inside it. The spokes flashed, the axles creaked, and he came out of the bushes and started following them, but pretended he was just looking in his wallet, with the picture of Romantic Mexico on it and the secret pocket known only to himself, *to keep important papers and money safe from prying eyes.*

They turned and saw him, and started whispering to each other over the carriage handles. The flashing wheels spun webs of light along the sidewalk, and Anita and Wanda did some more fussing inside the carriage. He started closing in on them; he had to get to the movies pretty soon, for the next adventure of Superman.

". . . enough here for the movies," he said, quietly counting his money as if that was all that concerned him, but out of the corner of his eye he tried to spy into the carriage.

"Do you want to see what's inside?" asked Anita Crumpf.

"No."

"Good, because I'm not going to show you."

He zipped his wallet closed, *gorgeously embossed, with a roomy currency compartment* except he never had any currency. He was walking in the flashing webs of light beside the carriage wheels, and Wanda said, "We'll show you—just for a second."

The silvery-gray fringe on the hood of the carriage swung back and forth, and a strange feeling came over him, as if the fringe were shimmering and swaying inside his stomach. "OK," he said, "show me."

"No," said Wanda, "I've changed my mind." She reached inside the carriage and rearranged the covers.

The webs of sunlight at his feet seemed to be getting thicker and stickier, it felt like warm threads were creeping up his leg. There was something mysterious going on in the neighborhood, more mysterious even than kissing, something that had to do with girls, something very tickly and warm that was wrapping itself around him right this minute. He wanted to run, but he couldn't, he was caught alongside the carriage and had to know what was in it. "Come on," he said, "let me see."

"No, we can't."

"Why not?"

"You're not old enough."

"Yeah, sure I am. I just had a birthday."

He tried to peer through the fringe, and they pushed the carriage faster. He made a grab for the blankets under the hood, but Wanda belted him, screeching, "You're too fresh!"

Her shrill voice nearly deafened him, and he stopped where he was, in a fading hopscotch square. The carriage pulled away. Anita and Wanda had their heads together

69

again, whispering. Anita turned back to him and said, "We've decided to show you—but only if you promise not to tell anyone."

"I promise," he said, jumping along the hopscotch squares toward them.

"Cross your heart and hope to die right hand up to God."

"Yeah, sure," he said, quickly sealing the promise.

I'll send the message to Crutch in code, through a tin can.

He followed them around the corner, in under the shade of a big chestnut tree. Anita drew the blankets aside and let him look.

Two little dolls, no bigger than his wooden soldiers, lay on a satiny pillow. The girls had made little dresses for them, just like the capes he'd made for his soldiers. But the inside of a carriage was no place for a soldier; he started to back away, no longer interested, but Anita pointed to the lettering stitched onto the dress of one of the dolls. It said *Anita*.

She lifted the doll's dress slowly.

He wanted to move, but he was caught in the web again.

"Swear to God and hope to die," said Anita. "No fingers?"

He showed her his uncrossed fingers and she lifted the dress a little more. He'd heard somebody say she had dirty blond hair. It didn't seem too dirty to him. Did she have lice? He stepped back a little.

"You're going to tell," said Anita, stopping.

He quickly crossed his heart again and stepped closer. "I won't tell," he said quietly. He could see a little ways up under the doll's dress, to her flesh-colored legs and he could feel the mysterious secret of the neighborhood pulsing there, and pulsing now inside himself, making his heart go faster.

Anita lifted the dress up over the doll's belly and up still higher, until two red bulging titties appeared. He swallowed, his mouth suddenly watering.

"*Touch them,*" said Anita, her voice almost a whisper, right beside his ear.

He was itching all over with lice, and his stomach was churning.

"Go on," said Anita. "Are you afraid?"

He touched the red titties. They were soft and squashy. "Hey . . ."

They were gumdrops, cut in half and pinned to the dolls.

Anita and Wanda burst into squealing laughter, and Anita pulled the dress back down. "That's enough," she said. "We'll show you more when you're older."

They pushed the carriage down the block. He cut through the backyards, toward the movie theater, stopping first at the candy store.

"Box of gumdrops, please."

Clark Kent was taking a lot of insulting talk from City Editor Perry White, and Lois Lane was being snotty as usual. He hated her for being so rotten to Superman and wished somebody would kick her in the ass. He stood up in his seat and threw a piece of popcorn toward the screen; it flashed like a comet in the bright white beam overhead, and a shower of popcorn flashed in from all sides like a swarm of fireflies. He sat back down, satisfied that Lois had been shown she couldn't get away with that guff.

The guy alongside him got down on the floor, crawled under the seats, and disappeared.

He liked to change his own seat a lot too, until he got one that felt right.

Anita Crumpf came up the aisle, peering into each row. She looked down his row, saw the empty seat beside him, and pushed in through everybody's knees until she was right next to him.

"Surprised to see you here," she said, and sat down in the empty seat.

Why did she say that? She knew he went to the movies every Saturday afternoon, like everybody else.

He didn't bother to answer her, because at this very moment Clark Kent was removing his suit and tie and glasses, and now he was emerging from the closet as SUPERMAN!

"Yeah, yea, hooray!"

The man of steel raced for the nearest window and jumped into the sky. Anita twisted toward him in her seat. "Aren't you going to kiss me?"

She leaned closer and then they were kissing. Her mouth tasted of Teaberry gum. His popcorn fell on the floor, spilling all over. He bent down for it, and Anita got out of her seat and wedged into his, stepping on his popcorn. He scooped a handful off the floor and tried to sit up, but could only get halfway because Anita was in his seat.

"Hey, Anita . . ."

She kissed him again. Bullets were bouncing off Superman's chest, and flying lead was ricocheting all over the place, but Anita's head was in the way and he couldn't see the screen.

She put her arm around his neck and leaned her head against his, the way big kids smooched in the back row. Superman crashed through a wall, dust and bricks flying, but then Anita started kissing him again and hogging the whole seat and he couldn't see a thing.

"Kent, where've you been? Superman just cleaned up the entire gang!"

"I'm sorry, sir. I was delayed in traffic."

He tried to kiss and watch at the same time, but Anita was kissing and chewing her gum and somehow it popped in his mouth.

"Give me back my gum."

"I swallowed it."

72

"That was my last stick."

He heard Superman whistling through the air, high over Metropolis, cape snapping in the wind. It was always his favorite part, but he couldn't see it, Anita was complaining about her gum. The music swelled to a mighty finish and the cartoon came on, he could hear Popeye's theme song, with whistles and toots.

He tried to move Anita out of the way, but she was kissing him again. *"You're my boyfriend now,"* she whispered. *"Do you have a ring to give me?"*

He thought of the rings he had—his Zombie Skull Ring, his Jet Plane Ring, his Sky King Ring, his Compass Ring, his Magnetic Automobile Ring, and the one he'd just gotten in the mail—his Straight Arrow Golden Nugget Picture Ring, look into the cave entrance and see *your* picture *inside the ring*, with Straight Arrow and his palomino, Fury, in the secret golden cave.

He didn't want to give any of them to Anita Crumpf.

"I don't have one."

"Then you can't be my boyfriend," she said, slipping out of his seat and stepping back into the aisle.

Chapter 13

Did Captain Marvel Junior Jack Off?

◊ ◊ ◊

"We'll make tunnels," said Crutch, digging beside him. "We'll come up wherever we feel like. Maybe we'll come up in Wanda's backyard."

"I'd rather come up in Lily's." Twiller threw a shovelful of dirt out of the hole.

"You like her," said Crutch, filling his own shovel. "I'll tell you something . . ." He emptied it over the side. "She wears a training bra."

"What's that for?"

"To train her tits."

Twiller stuck his shovel into the ground and heaved out some more dirt. He didn't even know Lily had tits. He wondered what she was training them to do. Tricks, probably.

"We're pretty deep," said Crutch. They huddled down in the hole and slid some boards over the top. "Just room enough." Crutch lit a candle. "All we need now is Wanda. And Anita."

"Anita won't kiss you unless you give her a ring."

Crutch's thick glasses mirrored the candleflame and his huge magnified eyes blinked slowly. "I'll give her my *bicycle.*" He leaned back and stuck his leg out of the hole. "All the comforts of home." He stiffened suddenly and let out a scream, his knee twisting upwards like a corkscrew, and Twiller saw Spider's grinning face through a crack in the boards.

He shoved the boards aside, as Crutch flopped around, groaning. "Hey, Spider, hey, that's my bum leg . . ."

Spider let go and knelt beside the hole. "Whattya doin' down there, jackin' off?"

Twiller wanted to ask him what jacking off meant, figured it must have something to do with lifting a car. Spider was probably planning to steal a car, that's what his old man had gone to jail for, the time before last.

Spider moved off and they followed him down the alley toward the ballfield.

"Hey, Spider," said Crutch, "got any hotbooks on you?"

"We can trade," added Twiller.

"Yeah, whattya got?"

"*Airboy, Mary Marvel, Justice Traps the Guilty.*"

"I don't want any of that crap."

They crossed the street, into the ballfield. Twiller picked up a rock and winged it, nailing the base of the flagpole.

"Pinyatta Party!" Spider grabbed for Twiller's balls. Twiller jumped out of the way, covering with both hands. A pinyatta party had to be the worst kind of party there was, somebody squeezing your nuts till you screamed. There'd been a guy at the YMCA swimming pool with only one nut, he'd probably lost the other one at a pinyatta party.

They climbed the far bank of the field, into the woods. Summer'd really come, and Spider might tie a girl barenaked to a tree. They walked along quickly, then froze suddenly as running footsteps sounded ahead—the lunatic that lived in the woods! Spider whipped out a pistol.

75

Rider Wendorf rode out of the trees, reining up alongside them. "Whar you bound fer, podners?"

"You're lucky I didn't plug ya." Spider showed them how he'd drilled out the chambers of a cap pistol, so that .22 caliber bullets could fit inside. He fired a blast into the air, a long tongue of flame leaping from the barrel. Twiller decided Spider was the most important person he'd ever known.

"The cops come after me," said Spider, "these woods is where I go. You guys bring me food."

Twiller knew the cops would be chasing him someday too. "If they catch us, we'll fry."

"That's right," said Spider, eyeing him coldly. "Your hair burns off and your brain starts to boil."

"What the fuck are you guys talkin' about?" Crutch goggled at them. "We're just goin' for a swim, right?"

"You never can tell," said Spider, sticking his gun into Crutch's ribs.

Crutch edged away from the muzzle. "Hey, Spider, they ever put your old man in solitary? I hear it's pretty rough."

"The old man knows how to handle stir. He knows the score."

Rider galloped on ahead, toward the Man-Made Mountains. Buried trees stuck out of the slag piles, and they grabbed onto the branches, scrambling upward. Rider reached the top and disappeared over it, and they followed, down the steep wall of the ravine to the muddy pond below.

They piled their clothes on the shore, and Spider and Rider cannonballed in, sending up two big clouds of mud. Twiller set himself carefully on the edge and then dove through the swirling scum to the muddy bottom. He turned and kicked upward through the brown water, toward a pale shapeless blur that suddenly became the bright burning sun.

"Pickle on a platter!" Spider floated, his prick flopping over on his stomach, just above the surface of the water.

Rider floated beside him, right hand still holding the reins, toward the sky. Crutch waded in slowly, brown swirls of mud rising around his waist. He walked to the middle and stood there with his glasses on, looking around, water up to his chin.

"Half-moon over the Hudson." Spider dove under, sticking his ass in the air; it sank slowly out of sight. He climbed the muddy bank and sat down. "Whattya say we have a jack-off contest?"

"You're gettin' a head start." Crutch climbed out of the water, with Rider behind him and they joined the contest— the strangest one Twiller'd ever seen. He knew it must be against the law if Spider dreamed it up, and it felt that way, a sneaky silence falling over the guys as they touched their privates, that's what his old man called them, his *privates*, and Twiller always thought of a bunch of soldiers. It looked like soldiers now, a little bit, holding their rifles and polishing the barrels. He watched them for a while and then decided he might as well join the contest too.

He climbed up the bank. "Hey, wait for me."

"Suck . . . my . . . bone." Spider lay back in the grass, polishing very fast. The other guys stopped and looked at him. Suddenly he made a terrible face, his eyebrows coming together and his eyes narrowing. He looked like he'd just been shot in the back with an arrow. He twitched and a couple of white drops spilled out of his bone. "There it is," he said, as if it were some kind of dangerous experiment, "that's it."

He drew a long milky thread into the sunlight, showing it to them. Twiller could see how sticky it was, like something out of a milkweed pod.

"Jism," said Spider, and seemed to be very proud of it.

They climbed into their clothes and Rider led the way out of the ravine, galloping back into the woods. Spider took a running jump into a big gnarled birch tree and scrambled quickly up the thick branches toward the top. He edged half-way out onto a heavy limb and set himself in the middle of it.

"TARRRRRRR-ZANNNNNNNNNNNNN!"

He jumped toward the next tree, arms out, and caught one of its branches; his momentum whipped him completely around the branch in a loop and he lost his grip. He hurtled down, arms still stretched out overhead, fingers clutching toward the sky. He hit the ground on his back, across the thick roots of the birch.

". . . jesus . . . fucking . . . christ . . ." He lay on the root, gasping for breath.

"You alright, Tarzan?" They brought him up slowly.

"My . . . back . . . my fuckin' back . . ."

"Take it easy, just walk a little . . ."

"You guys . . . saw the jump I took."

"Right, a full back-spin."

"There was . . . sap or somethin' . . . on the branch."

"You were sabotaged, Spider."

"I'm comin' back . . . with an ax . . . you cocksucker." He kicked feebly at the tree.

They helped him onto the trail, and he walked along, crouched over, one hand on his back. "Let's catch a snake . . . and roast him alive. They come out lookin' like a burnt pretzel."

The trail joined up with an old mine road and they walked down it, Rider trotting back and forth into the bushes, rearing and prancing. "Hey, look at this!"

They pushed in after him, onto a huge flat rock. Lying on it were a couple of fat cotton pads, like bandages, with blood on them.

Spider was hunched over, smiling. "We know what happened here, right?"

Twiller knelt down. The sun was hot on the back of his neck. A girl had been here with somebody and taken her clothes off, he could feel it in the air. She seemed to still be

78

here, that's why the guys were so quiet, they could feel her too, lying bare-naked on the rock. She'd probably been with one of the older guys from down by the mill. Had he punched her in the nose?

Twiller stared at the white pads, white as could be in the sunlight, except for the spot of blood in the center, spread out on the white gauze.

He lifted one of the pads with a stick and flopped it over. The sun seemed to be burning right through him, and the hot wind closed him in.

He went up to his room, closed the blinds, and sat in the armchair. Pale greenish light came through the blinds and he started practicing for the next jack-off contest, but nothing seemed to be happening. It was probably the kind of thing only Spider could do.

He practiced awhile longer, but still nothing happened, so he gave up and just leafed through his comic books.

Did Captain Marvel Junior jack off?

Probably not. He was too busy putting guys like Spider in jail.

Just then . . . from the bowels of the earth—come the Tusk Men. They see the soft slender figure of Tiger Girl in the cave's entrance . . .

They always showed Tiger Girl in real good poses, in her little tiger-skin bathing suit with her ass sticking way out when she jumped off a zebra.

He started practicing again and it felt kind of different.

"Oft have the jungle drums told of such a tribe. And here come more of them."

A sort of tickly feeling was beginning.

"Where do they take me?" wondered Tiger Girl. "An underground city . . ."

79

Very, very tickly, like a feather was whirling around inside of him.

A bloodstained altar. A series of commanding grunts. Tiger Girl is roped down. The beautiful creature struggles but the crude blade is lifted over her . . .

"No! No!"

The tickling rose up, unbearably tickly. He dropped *Tiger Girl* and stopped practicing, he couldn't stand it. That's why Spider looked like he'd been shot in the back with an arrow. You had to keep practicing until the tickling made your eyebrows come together, and the sticky white stuff came out.

He'd never be able to do it, it was too terribly tickly and scary, his legs were still shaking.

He put *Tiger Girl* on the bottom of the pile and took out *Porky Pig*.

Chapter 14

... In Which Twiller Meets
the Beautiful Undressing Lady.

◊ ◊ ◊

Spider turned the first page, and Crutch leaned in from the other side. It was Maggie and Jiggs from the newspapers, only Maggie had her legs spread out over the end of a couch. *"Come on, you worm, give it to me."*

Jiggs was standing in the doorway in his top hat, looking at her. His pants were bulging way out. *"I'm coming, my dear . . ."*

Twiller shifted nervously. The only thing he had even close to it was *Fight Comics* where the *daring! glamorous!* Señorita Rio pulls a derringer out of her stocking and you could see her panties.

But Maggie's panties were down around her ankles.

"Where did you get this, Spider?"

Spider turned the page. "From the old man's drawer."

Twiller knew his father wouldn't have such things in his drawer.

"Stick it in from behind, my little man."

Spider wet his finger, but Crutch grabbed the page. "Wait

81

a minute, I'm not done readin'." His magnified eyes were popping and his mouth was hanging open, and Spider said, "What's wrong with you guys? Never seen pussy before?"

"Let me have it first, Daddy."

Jigg's pretty daughter, Norah, had come in, with hair between her legs. Twiller's heart was pounding. He had only three twisty little hairs around his pickle, and a mole, but the great mystery of the neighborhood was getting clearer now, it was in Spider's hotbook. The Sunday funnies didn't show the half of it. This was the *real* Maggie and Jiggs.

"Oh oh oh . . ." Norah was waving her legs in the air and Jiggs was bouncing up and down on her, wavy lines around his ass to show how fast he was going.

Crutch slipped down off the wall, slowly, easing his bum leg to the ground. "I'll be in the bushes, fellas, don't go without me."

"I have to go home," said Twiller.

"Fuckface has hot nuts," said Spider.

"Naw, I've got to wash the windows."

He jumped down and came up on the run. "I'll see you guys later." He ran along the street sideways, so the neighbors couldn't see his pants.

What a great hot comic that was. Hot comics showed you what was going on, not like Theodore Roosevelt School where all you learned was long division and the capitals of South America.

The house was empty. He hurried upstairs to his father's bureau, and pulled it open. There was only socks and handkerchiefs. Daddy would never have hotbooks in his drawer, he wasn't a jailbird like Spider's old man. Everything was neat and folded and the only other things were a fingernail kit and an old straight razor and a piece of cardboard that said Compliments of Duke's Barbershop.

He turned it over and saw a faint shape on the other side, in a piece of film. He held it up to the light.

It was a lady in a nightgown.

In the top of the cardboard frame was a little tab that said *Pull Here*. He pulled and the lady's nightgown disappeared. She was completely bare-naked!

His father had Spider's old man beat all the way—not just a drawing but a photograph of a bare-naked lady.

He knew his father would come through, his Dad was the best in the world.

He carried the beautiful undressing lady down the hall to his room, and undressed her again and again. He loved her with all his heart, and started pulling his pickle.

The tickling began, way down inside, rising quickly as he stared at her, it was too much, he couldn't stand it, he had to stop.

He brought her nightgown back up and turned the little card over.

Duke's—that's where he'd get his hair cut from now on, wherever it was.

He looked at the lady again. Her nightgown was thin and filmy. He took it slowly off her shoulders and watched it slip out of sight at her ankles.

He started pulling his pickle again, pulling it and dreaming of her being nice to him, getting down on the floor with him like you're supposed to and bending her knees, going *oh oh oh* as he rode the terrible tickling feeling, on and on, higher and higher, it was torture but he kept on, faster and faster until something opened inside him, a door of slippery silky candy, opening on feathery hinges, the best most perfect thing he'd ever felt, Compliments of Duke's Barbershop.

Chapter 15

... In Which Spider Lets Out a Yell,
and Shudders All Over.

◇ ◇ ◇

"Don't touch it." Crutch poked a stick in the end of the white balloon and held it up to the sunlight. "Some guy had this on his dick."

Twiller stared at the balloon; he could see now—the tip was filled. Ballons like this must be made especially for jacking off, to save on Kleenex.

Crutch flicked the stick and sent the balloon off into the bushes. It caught on a branch, the contents slowly trickling out of it.

"Where do you get them?"

"At the drugstore. You have to knock three times on the counter."

But then Mr Schlappe the druggist would know you were a jack-off. And sometimes his wife worked with him behind the counter and she'd know too.

He'd stick to Kleenex, he didn't have to be fancy.

They walked along the mine road, over the cracked mud

drying in the sun. The heat came back up off the road, faintly wavering, and he started thinking about Maggie and Jiggs again, with Jiggs going in and out of Norah on the floor.

"Girls have a hole, right?"

"Yeah . . ." said Crutch. "So what?"

"Well, what's wrong with the asshole? I could stick it up your ass."

"It's no good." Crutch pushed his glasses back on his nose. "I tried it with my cousin. You get shit all over your dick."

They pushed on through the brush to the little grove where the spring was, but the grove was splattered with mud, and the water was gone.

"Some fucker dynamited it." Crutch knelt beside the raw muddy hole.

"Spider."

"He musta found some dynamite caps." Crutch stood. "Up by the Man-Made Mountains."

They pushed back out through the muddy leaves and followed the mine road around the last big bend, to the mountains. There were fresh footprints in the big slope, going upward.

They climbed slowly and silently, then took the last few yards flat out, crawling to the top without a sound and inching their heads over the edge of the ravine.

Lying beside the swimming hole below was the strangest creature Twiller'd ever seen—four-legged, squirming on the sand.

"*He's giving it to her*," whispered Crutch.

Spider's ass was going up and down like Jiggs, and underneath him was his sister Nancy.

She was only in the fifth grade, and wasn't very big, but Spider was going as fast as he could on her. She didn't move a muscle and Twiller wondered if Spider had her tied, but then he saw her scratch her head.

Spider stopped for a second, sweat glistening on his bony

85

back. Nancy picked a piece of grass and put it in her teeth. Spider muttered something at her, and started going again.

She turned her head, looking along the canyon floor as two dragonflies zoomed by. One of her black braids fell across her forehead, and she tucked it back. Spider's ass was a blur now, like the dragonfly wings. He let out a yell, shuddering all over, and Twiller knew he'd gotten the arrow, right in the privates. The dragonflies flew straight up in the air, high over the swimming hole, and disappeared.

Spider stood, and cannonballed into the water, a halo of mud spreading around him as he hit bottom.

Nancy sat up and took a picker out of her toe. Her chest was flat. She had buttercups in her braids and Twiller loved her.

"Nazi submarine!" Spider floated through the water, holding his half-stiff dick above the scummy surface.

Nancy stood up; she wasn't tall and skinny like Spider, she was short, with a puffy little mound between her legs and no hair, just a dark slit. She was white there from wearing shorts all summer.

Crutch shifted in the grass. *"If only I had a sister."*

She waded into the water, and the dragonflies zoomed back down, hovering over the swimming hole. She dove away from them, her short legs going smoothly under, and Twiller watched her blurred shape frog-stroking beneath the surface. He loved her more then he ever knew you could love someone.

She came up in the cattails, whacking water at Spider, and they climbed up the muddy bank. She put on her T-shirt and shorts. Spider yanked out his rod and fired in the air. Twiller hugged the dirt with Crutch, the bullet whining over their heads.

Spider fired again, twisted flame shooting from the barrel of his fucked-up rod. The smell of gunpowder floated up the ravine, as he and Nancy started to walk. They left a long chain of footprints in the silt, all the way to the rain gully at the far end. They climbed up it and Spider let off another blast, and then they were gone, across the far slope.

"Come on," said Crutch, "let's go take a look."

They went straight to the place where Spider had been going up and down on Nancy. Crutch stared at the sandy grass. "I thought you had to do it on a flat rock."

Chapter 16

. . . And the Bodies of the Wicked Shall Be
Hideous and Wretched.

Sister Norma followed them into Sunday-school class, her
long black gown rustling along the floor, and her rosary beads
clicking at her waist. She was pretty and laughed sometimes,
but she could turn mean in a second, and her room was
gloomy, with pictures of saints all over the walls, and cruci-
fixes everywhere. Theodore Roosevelt School was bad, but
this was worse, with a teacher *and* Jesus watching every move
you made.

"We'll review today." Sister Norma rapped her ruler on
the desk and started asking them questions, about Who Is
God, *God Is the Father*, and he knew the answers, but the
Undressing Lady compliments of Duke's Barbershop was at
the edge of his thoughts, trying to get in. He kept his eyes
fixed on Sister Norma, and concentrated on every question
she asked, but found himself thinking of her with a strip of
cardboard sticking out of her back.

He started praying to himself, *O my God I am heartily*

sorry for having offended thee. How could he escape from these sinful thoughts, about Jiggs going up and down on Sister Norma.

"What do we mean by the Resurrection of the Body? What happens to man at his death? Lily Induris?"

Lily stood. *"The soul, separated from the body, appears before the judgment seat of God, while the body returns to dust . . ."*

"You may sit down. How long does the body remain separated from the soul? Anita?"

"The body shall remain separated from the soul till the day of the Last Judgment when God will reunite it to the soul and raise it to life."

"Shall all bodies be alike when raised to life? Jack Twiller?"

"No, the bodies of the wicked shall be hideous and wretched." He knew that's the body he'd have, with his prick coming out of his ear.

Footsteps sounded in the hallway. Sister Norma rose from her desk. "Stand please, here's Father."

They all stood quickly. *"Good morning, Father."*

"Good morning, good morning." Father Witcavage came in, smiling.

Sister Norma returned his smile. "We're reviewing the Creed, Father, beginning with what happens to man at his death."

"Good, good—and I hope you remember it well." He looked at them, and put his hands in his pockets, like a regular guy. "Because it will help *you* to die."

Die? A chill ran down Twiller's spine, and he tried to think about baseball.

"Yes, my young friends, I've been there when Death presented his calling card. And nobody wanted to look at it. But they had to." Father pointed a finger at them. "We all have to."

89

Twiller saw the candles burning by the dying man's bed. The face was his own and Father Witcavage was kneeling beside the bed, praying.

"But those who die with Christ in their hearts have no fear of Death. They die peacefully, praise for God on their lips. It's a most different sight from the one we behold in the homes of those who have lived a life of ignorance and sin . . ." Father put his foot up on the edge of a seat and Twiller felt Death's clammy hands on the back of his neck. He peeked out of the corner of his eye at Nancy Pronka and she was sitting stiff as a stick, her head down.

"I listen to their last confession, I learn of a life of wickedness and perversion, and then I hear the death rattle in their throats."

Nancy closed her eyes, the color draining out of her cheeks.

". . . so keep that sound in mind, my dear young friends, whenever you're tempted to sin. The rattle of Death will one day be in *your* throat, and only God can calm its fury as he takes you to Himself, through Christ Jesus everlasting."

Father turned to Sister Norma, a smile on his face once again. "And now I think Sister has something for you, which I'm sure you'll enjoy. God bless you, and good day to you."

"Good day, Father."

Father Witcavage left the room, his footsteps echoing in the hallway, echoing and rattling as he reached the stairs and descended them.

Sister Norma opened her desk. "You may each come up and take a *Treasure Chest*, and I expect to see you all at Holy Communion next week."

Twiller stood and took his copy of *Treasure Chest*, with a Roman soldier on the cover, holding a dying Christian boy. *Treasure Chest* was just like a regular comic, but about Christ and the saints. You couldn't trade them in the neighborhood.

He stepped into the hall. Nancy and Lily and Anita were

ahead of him but he didn't look at them; his mind was filled with the house Death had visited, and his prick felt like it was already dead.

He went out the front door into the cool fall air. He'd been jacking off all summer long, and now the leaves were turning and he was still jacking off, he'd jacked off yesterday to *Sheena, Queen of the Jungle* comics, she'd looked so nice swinging upside-down from a vine.

He took the new *Treasure Chest* out of his pocket and read while he walked, about Tarcisius the boy martyr. That's the sort of boy he'd be from now on, ready to die for his faith.

"Yield, Christian. Give up your secret!"

"Never while I live."

It sent a thrill through his whole body, to see the boy he might be, with sandals and a golden halo, and he ran the rest of the way home, up the block and around the corner, through the driveway and into the backyard. He was Tarcisius, running from the Romans who sought to detain him and destroy his faith.

He ran into the house. Mommy and Daddy were at eleven-o'clock mass. He ran upstairs to his room, grabbed his whole pile of comics and raced back down, through the kitchen to the cellar door, and down to the secret catacombs.

"Is this the fair Tarcisius?"

"Yes, madame, they beat him because he would not deny his faith."

He went to the furnace, sifted through the pile of comics, and threw in everything at all tempting—Sheena, and Nyoka the Jungle Girl being carried off by a buffalo, and Fire Hair of the Dakota Tribe, and Connie Courtenay Newspaper Woman. It left him with only stuff like Charlie Chicken and Donald Duck but it was worth it, he'd saved his soul.

He picked up the remaining comics and put them under his arm. Daisy Duck would never get him hot. She had pretty eyelashes but her legs were skinny and her shoes were too big.

91

Then if he could stay out of Daddy's drawer he'd be completely ok, and he thought he could because he always felt like a rat when he snuck in past the handkerchiefs and socks. It was a rotten thing for a son to do, look in his father's private drawer. It wasn't even good to think about because he'd just thought about it and the Undressing Lady was flashing in his mind, lowering her nightgown.

He'd better stay in the catacombs awhile longer.

He walked around the piles of stuff in the cellar. Lots of it was old, from before he was born. He stopped by the photographic enlarger Daddy'd built, a great big thing made of wood, but Daddy never used it anymore, he usually just napped on the couch in the evening, snoring toward the wall.

The enlarger was covered with dust, and so were the old magazines alongside it.

He sat down and picked up one.

Darkroom Shortcuts, How I Get My Dog to Pose, Fish Pictures Made Easy.

The magazine had a damp, musty smell, and the pages had turned yellow.

Need Money? We loan money on all kinds of cameras.

He leafed through slowly, carefully lifting the curling corners.

Just what you've been waiting for, the all-new, all-American 100% precision, fully guaranteed . . .

Tits.

Plastic Study, said the caption, but she wasn't plastic, she was real, and bare-naked from the waist up.

What a thing to happen to a Christian boy in the catacombs on his very first mission.

He looked toward the furnace.

He couldn't burn his father's photography magazines.

He looked back at *Plastic Study*. She was looking at him, and waiting.

The fair Tarcisius closed the magazine and picked up another. He'd conquer all temptation, wouldn't think of

Plastic Study again; he'd just concentrate on learning photography, getting tips on being an ace cameraman with a ticket in his hatband.

Flesh Tones in the Shower.

The fair Tarcisius took out his Kleenex.

Chapter 17

. . . In Which Twiller Wonders
What Miss Chicken Legge Would Say
If She Knew That Floyd Shot People in the Ass
with a Bee-bee Gun
and Then Didn't Pay Them.

◇ ◇ ◇

He straightened his Patrol Boy sash and walked toward the schoolyard gate. Miss Chicken Legge was at the window, looking down, seeing *that silence and order will be maintained until the adjacent streets have been crossed.*

The first graders, assigned to him, approached his gate in silence, carrying their book bags. He made certain they were lined up properly and turned toward Floyd Flynn, Captain of Patrol Boys.

Floyd looked at the other gates, to see that they were all being approached in orderly fashion. If you didn't maintain silence and order he'd stick you in the back with his umbrella. He was tall and thin, and had fancy manners. He'd shot Twiller in the ass with his bee-bee pistol and then didn't pay the quarter, just laughed.

Miss Chicken Legge gave the signal to proceed. Floyd raised his umbrella and the gates were opened.

Twiller stepped into Cudge Court, leading his first-graders

along over its rough-tarred surface, toward Kleinbauer Street. They walked quietly as mice, because you never knew when Miss Chicken Legge might trail along behind and hit you with her ruler, she'd done it more than once since half-wit Schunky had his foot run over by an ice wagon at the intersection. He'd only had one toe crushed but Miss Chicken Legge didn't like it at all, as silence and order had been broken, mainly by Schunky screaming and jumping around when it happened.

"Quiet there, no talking." Twiller surveyed the terrain ahead for possible traffic hazards. His badge caught the bright noon sun and flashed with a thrilling light. He was fully authorized to stop cars at the intersection by holding his right arm straight out, palm raised. "Look sharp now, we're coming to the corner." He prayed for a car to be coming, or even better a truck, so he could walk out into the middle of the intersection and stop it.

Some girls from the high school were on the corner, with long beautiful legs and dog collars on their socks, he loved that, the way the dog collars sparkled with little rhinestones. The girls turned his way when they saw the line coming and he went crazy inside, shouting "Let's go!" to the first-graders and running across the street, waving them after him like a band of rough riders.

"Yea, hooray!" They ran behind him, swinging their book bags, screaming and dancing in the intersection.

The big girls watched, as first-graders tumbled beside him, falling in the street, rolling in the gutter, yelling and cheering.

◊ ◊ ◊

"Disgraceful! An absolute disgrace to the Order of Patrol Boys!"

Miss Chicken Legge had a face like a chicken too, with a

long nasty beak that kept stabbing the air in front of her, and her beady little eyes made his prick shrink, he could feel it trying to hide up in his stomach as she bent over him.

"Breaking order and silence—*running*."

"All the way across the street." Floyd was sitting beside Miss Chicken Legge's desk, ratting.

"I won't stand for this," snapped Miss Chicken Legge. "Do you hear me, young man?"

She opened her desk drawer and yanked out a metal-edged ruler, but it slipped out of her knuckly fingers and landed on the floor. She snapped her beak his way, eyes accusing him of having made it fall, and he bent down to pick it up.

"Don't you dare touch that!" She bent down, creaking over to retrieve it. Her skirt spread above her bony chicken knees, and her heels came out of her shoes. She rose up, pointing with the ruler at the Patrol Boy's Oath on the wall.

"You've violated every one of its rules." She leaned her beak in toward him again. "You're to be stripped of your sash."

Floyd stood and removed it, while Miss Chicken Legge supervised. Floyd had tried to kiss him on the cheeks when he'd been made a Patrol Boy, saying that's how the French did it.

He walked in silence with the others, toward the corner. He knew they were laughing at him, at his being stripped of his sash after just one day. Even Richard Malatesta had lasted longer than that, had lasted three weeks before Miss Chicken Legge snuck by the boys' lav and smelled him smoking a stogie. She'd run in and yanked him right off the toilet.

The Patrol Boys stepped into the street, stopping a moving van with upraised hands, and he crossed, hands in his pockets, trying to look like he didn't give a shit.

Floyd was up ahead by the candy store, talking to one of

the other Patrol Boys, his voice carrying down the street. ". . . and when she bent over to pick up the ruler, she peed, right there on the floor."

Twiller stopped, astonished by what Floyd was saying, but he could see it in his mind anyway, just the way Floyd said— Miss Chicken Legge squatting down, heels coming out of her shoes, and a dark little puddle of piss forming on the floor beneath her.

"She couldn't hold it in any longer . . ." Floyd made a face and squeezed his knees together. "That's how it happened, isn't it?" He turned toward Twiller.

Twiller walked quickly away, into the candy store. "Tootsie Roll, please." He took it and went over to the comic books, pretending to be picking one out, but he was listening to Floyd's shrill voice coming through the screen door.

". . . and when she stood up she covered the wet spot with a handkerchief."

Twiller raced out of the candy store. "You're a liar!"

Floyd hit him, *crack* on the head with his umbrella. "Don't contradict me!"

Twiller saw stars for a second, and then Floyd was standing tall and stiff in front of him, screaming, "Tell the truth! Tell how she peed on the floor!"

"She didn't!"

"She did!"

He was wrestling with Floyd, twisting and turning with him on the sidewalk, and Floyd was fighting like a crazy person, scratching and screaming, "That's how ladies pee, they squat . . ."

Twiller found an opening and started to punch, but Floyd's face was suddenly so near he could see into his eyes and he didn't punch him, he dropped his arm and stopped fighting. Floyd kept pushing him, and knocked him down, but he didn't fight back, he suddenly knew how wrong it was to fight with Floyd, that you shouldn't do it even when you hated him; Floyd's face was white and his eyes were wild and

Twiller knew it was wrong to get him like that. "OK," he said, "I give . . ."

Floyd let him up slowly, and he saw how Floyd was trembling all over, his knuckles white as chalk. It wasn't like a regular fight, there was something terrible in the air, and Twiller moved away quickly and up the street.

He ducked into a yard, going quickly through it and over the back fence. A couple of first-graders popped out of the bushes. "Come on," they said, "we know where a dead fish is buried."

Chapter 18

. . . In Which Crutch Says,
"We'll be late for the fuckin' hazatska."

◊ ◊ ◊

Mr Kherlacombe wore black tights and a floppy shirt. He moved with funny little steps, like a chicken with an egg wedged up its ass. "Do you see?" He turned to them. "Please try it."

They took their positions and started, tap shoes clacking one-two-three-and-turn, Crutch's bum leg jammed out sideways. He was there for therapy, to get his bum knee working the doctor said, and Twiller followed him along the floor, wishing he hadn't let Crutch talk him into it, but Crutch had given him his *Wham-O* slingshot for joining with him and he couldn't back out now.

"Lightly, *light*-ly." Mr Kherlacombe put his head in his hands. "You sound like you're hammering a brick."

Crutch thumped and turned, tap shoe dragging.

"I suppose," said Mr Kherlacombe with a sigh, "we could bill you as the wooden-legged sailor from Venezuela."

◊ ◊ ◊

They walked down the hallway. Music and tapping came from all the studio rooms, one of them sounding like fifty machine guns, where the Star-Spangled Girls were tapping together in a long line. The door was half-open. The tail end of the line came around, the girls in little dancing costumes, tapping thunderously.

"Hubba, hubba," said Crutch.

Twiller edged closer. The girls were twirling on their toes, maybe somebody's underpants would fall down. Miss Rafalko saw him and waddled to the door. Her ass was like a huge pumpkin, you could see everything through her black tights. She slammed the door in his face, and he stood listening to the Star-Spangled Girls tap off toward the far end of the studio.

"Come on," said Crutch, "we'll be late for the fuckin' hazatska." He limped up the hallway, using the wall for support.

"How's your knee?"

"Gettin' stiffer all the time. It'll be ok once my twenty-six lessons are over."

They entered the large studio at the end of the hallway. Mr Kherlacombe was waiting in his canvas chair, legs crossed, one slippered foot swinging back and forth nervously. The other guys were already there, shadowboxing and tripping each other, and Mr Abda the piano player was sitting at the piano, head down, plastered as usual, a cigarette dangling in his lips.

"All right, gentlemen . . ." Mr Kherlacombe rose and moved to the center of the room. ". . . please take your places."

They formed in a circle, joining hands. Kherlacombe gave the downbeat toward the piano. "Begin!"

Mr Abda looked up, startled. Kherlacombe gave him a cold stare. "If you're *ready*, Mr Abda . . ."

Abda struck the keys and the hazatska music jumped out, sending them off in a spinning ring. They twisted, turned,

100

kicked to the side and leapt. Twiller floated in the momentum, Crutch beside him, bum leg flopping along. Mr Kherlacombe squatted by himself in the center of the ring, shooting out one leg, then the other, shouting "Hiiiiiii! Hiiiiii! Hiiiiiii!"

The ring spun faster. Twiller whirled past Abda bent at the keys, fingers flying, a long ash dangling from his cigarette, and then Abda was out of sight behind him and the windows of the studio were flashing by. He looked out, saw some shoppers on the street below, and then they were left behind as the circle pulled him on past the studio door.

Mr Kherlacombe was still dancing with his arm crossed at his chest and his legs flying in and out, his ass lowered over the floor as if he were going to lay his egg.

"Hiiiiii! Hiiiiiii! Hiiiiiiii!"

The sound of the lone tap dancer echoed in the hall and Twiller stopped to watch through the doorway. Classes were over but Dominick Panaro was the best dancer in the school and always practiced late, clicking coolly up a little wooden flight of steps to nowhere. He spun around at the top of the steps and clicked back down, a straw hat tipped over his eyes.

The hall suddenly filled with Star-Spangled voices and Lily came out of the ballet room with the other girls. Twiller walked to the hall stairs and started tapping his way down.

His shoe tips slapped softly in a sideways step, and he felt himself gliding gracefully on the stairs, tapping and clicking. It was like a dream, of flying or floating, weightless and free—he could do it, *better* than Dom Panaro.

The stairs slipped out from underneath him and he was pitching forward, grabbing at the air. His gym bag whipped around, the stairs rushed up at him and he bounced on his head and kept bouncing, step after step down the staircase, the stair rail twisting past him. He flopped over and continued bouncing down backwards, the horrified faces of the Star-Spangled Girls above him as he rolled off the last step and collapsed on the floor in a trembling heap.

He was up in a flash, adjusting his bag.

The girls rushed down and gathered around him. "Are you alright?"

"Yeah, sure." He straightened his shoulders. His ribs hurt worst of all and his head felt swollen around the top where he'd bounced on it. "I did it on purpose. It's a special roll, you do it right, you don't get hurt."

"Everyone onto the bus, please." Mr Kherlacombe looked like a duke or an earl in his shiny suit and lacy shirt cuffs. Twiller tugged at his own collar, loosening the elastic in his permanently knotted tie, and Crutch stood beside him, hair slicked down. Everybody was dressed up, all the guys in suits. The girls wore party dresses, and Miss Rafalko still looked like a pumpkin, but she was all made up with a fancy comb in her hair and Twiller started to be in love with her.

The bus driver sat at the wheel, counting heads as they got on. Twiller tried to sit next to Lily, but Dominick Panaro moved in beside her, wearing a string tie, dangly with little gold tips on the ends of it. His clothes were always like that, one step ahead of the other guys.

"Keep moving, keep moving . . ."

"We'll get a seat at the back." Crutch limped along behind Twiller, and they sat down in the last seat, beside Mr Abda. Mr Abda's hat was over his eyes and his hands were in his pockets.

The driver closed the door and swung the bus onto the avenue, as the Star-Spangled Girls began to sing.

The bus passed the bums on the courthouse square, and

then they were crossing the bridge toward the highway and climbing out of the valley. Mr Kherlacombe leaned from his seat and gave everyone in the bus a cheerful wave, his white cuffs flashing. Twiller looked out the window as the houses went by, and then the roadside diners and the supermarket, the bus rolling on into the state forest.

Mr Abda pushed his hat back, looked around, and climbed over their legs, into the little lavatory next to their seat.

Crutch winked and made the motions of tipping a bottle to his lips. They sat waiting, and when Mr Abda came out he was smiling and a faint smell of booze came with him.

"You been to New York City before, Mr Abda?"

The piano player slouched back down, hands in his pockets. "It's my town, boys."

Miss Rafalko rose from her seat and waddled up the aisle toward them. She reached for the lavatory door just as the bus hit a bounce and threw her sideways toward Mr Abda. She fell on his lap with a little giggle. "Oh, Mr Abda, I'm sorry . . ."

"It's alright, Viola," said Mr Abda from under his hat. "We'll make room for you.'

"I really must go." She pulled herself to her feet. Her dress was hiked way up in back; Twiller saw her stockings and the heavy white softness of her thighs, and he loved her more and more.

Traffic in the great city was snarled up and the bus moved through it slowly. Twiller gazed out the window at the thousands of New Yorkers moving along the street, every kind of face in the world going by. People were talking to themselves, and a man was playing a flute through his nose, and beautiful women with tiny little dresses and wild hair were hanging around in doorways. An old lady with a sign on her back was

103

shouting at a trash basket. He tried to read the sign but it was written all crazily about Christ and Moses and her landlord.

The bus pulled over to the curbstone beside the ballet, and Mr Kherlacombe and Miss Rafalko supervised the march to a nearby cafeteria, where everyone took a tray and lined up for lunch. Mr Abda stood in line with them, but only bought a glass of ginger ale, which he carried upstairs, alone, to the balcony tables.

Twiller grabbed a table by the window. Crutch sat with him. A bum was going around in the revolving door and the manager was waiting for him to come around again so he could throw him into the street. Lily was sitting with Dominick Panaro. Mr Kherlacombe was with a friend who'd met him at the bus stop, looking like a duke or an earl too, in even fancier clothes than Mr Kherlacombe's, and walking with an egg up *his* ass, a soft-boiled one.

The center of each table held a raised little carousel of all different relishes and dressings. Twiller turned it slowly. The cut-glass bottles were like the glass city outside. He used every bottle and turned to the window. He wanted to be outside, grown-up, alone, walking through the towering canyons and maybe talking to a beautiful woman in a little dress up over her knees.

He ate his sandwich and drank a glass of funny-tasting water. The pies and cakes were in the wall, locked in little glass safes. "I think I'll have one," he said, like a regular Broadway customer, and walked over.

He dropped a coin in the slot. The handle wouldn't turn and the little safe didn't open. He worked it a few times, and then backed away, hoping no one saw how he couldn't get it open.

"Did you lose your quarter?" called Mr Kherlacombe.

"No."

"I thought I saw you put one in."

An old woman left her table, walked to the cake window,

and turned the knob with his coin in it. She opened the safe and took his cake.

◇ ◇ ◇

The balconies curved one after another below him, down and down toward the distant stage, where the dancers floated around to the music, leaping and spinning in brightly glittering costumes, like tiny people seen through the wrong end of a telescope.

He turned and looked along the dark aisle. Lily and Dominick were sitting awfully close together. Beside them, Crutch's bum leg stuck out over the balcony railing, and a little further down Mr Kherlacombe and his friend were sharing a pair of pearl opera glasses. Miss Rafalko and Mr Abda were beside each other, and Miss Rafalko was holding his hand. She looked very happy. Mr Abda's hat was over his eyes and he was snoring.

◇ ◇ ◇

Mr Kherlacombe led the school through the crowd, to a big dressing room backstage, where the dancers were talking and laughing, and drinking from thin-stemmed wine glasses.

"Miss Chouteau will sign your program," said Mr Kherlacombe, standing beside a fairy princess. Twiller moved toward her, feeling he was in a dream. Her neck was long and white, and a rainbow seemed to shimmer off her costume. He got his program out, along with his special ball-point pen shaped like a baseball bat, Compliments of Mid-Valley Machinery.

She took it from him, her slender wrist moving in quick graceful strokes over his program. Her smile was bright and wide, and her painted eyes like huge butterfly wings. His heart turned into a melted jelly bean.

◇ ◇ ◇

He stepped onto the bus, weak inside from loving Miss Chouteau. He would study ballet his whole life and learn everything there was to know and then one night he'd come back and leap through the air in front of her, wearing a wonderful costume.

Who are you? she'd ask, and he'd unroll the wrinkled, faded program and hand it to her, and she'd suddenly remember.

"Move it, move it along . . ." The bus driver waved him down the aisle. Mr Kherlacombe and Miss Rafalko were still on the sidewalk, and Miss Rafalko was looking up and down the block, craning her neck over the passing crowd.

"One missing," said the bus driver, as he reached the back.

"Our piano player," said Crutch.

The driver looked out the window and then went back down the aisle. He stepped off into the street and stood with Mr Kherlacombe as Miss Rafalko kept looking around.

"He won't be coming," said Crutch, stretching his bum leg across the empty seat, and Twiller knew it was true. Mr Abda had gone forever from the Kherlacombe School of the Dance, had faded into the crowd somewhere, hands in his pockets, hat down over his eyes, a cigarette dangling from his lips.

The bus driver tapped the face of his watch. Mr Kherlacombe said something to Miss Rafalko, then took her gently by the arm and led her up the steps. She turned on the top stair, still looking out over the crowd, and then she was coming up the aisle, trying to smile at the Star-Spangled Girls, her mouth trembling and her eye makeup running down her cheek.

◇ ◇ ◇

His hazatska costume was bright green, with billowy gold-

106

en sleeves, and the Masonic Hall was filled, he could hear the audience from his position in the wings. The other cossacks were lined up beside him, waiting for the fairy ballerinas to finish their number. If only Miss Chouteau could see him now.

The fairies twisted and turned in their tinfoil wings, some of them wandering aimlessly on stage, one of them crying with her fairy crown dangling down around her neck, but the audience didn't mind. It was a full house and Mr Kherlacombe said it was a tribute to the school but it was relatives.

"*Places, everyone,*" whispered Mr Kherlacombe, and Twiller shifted in his galoshes. They didn't look so hot, but Mr Kherlacombe had insisted that every cossack wear boots, adding that the type of boot would not be visible from the audience. His own were higher than anyone else's, and had shiny zippers up the sides. Twiller's had big metal buckles up the seams and it felt like he was walking in old rubber tires.

"This way, dear, don't cry . . ." Miss Rafalko led the sobbing little ballerina off stage; the other fairies followed, tinfoil wings crinkled, bent, and drooping, and the audience was applauding. The Star-Spangled Girls joined the cossacks in the wings and Lily stepped in front of Twiller, smoothing down his shirt front. She was in her top hat and tights and he loved her deeply for paying attention to him. "*Good luck,*" she whispered, and he swallowed with difficulty, preparing for his big leap.

Mr Kherlacombe raised his riding whip.

The cossacks braced themselves.

The music rang out, the whip snapped down, and Twiller took a running jump, into the spotlight.

The cossacks all joined hands and the ring started to spin, everyone shouting and jumping. He felt an incredible energy shooting through him, making him leap higher than at rehearsal; Mr Kherlacombe squatted down fiercely in the center of the ring, laying his egg, legs shooting in and out with tremendous speed.

Twiller left the ground and came back down, Crutch hanging on desperately behind him, leg sticking out like a wooden clothes pole. His face was twisted with pain, and he clutched at Twiller's shirt. Twiller leapt and his sleeve came off in Crutch's hand, flapping there, as the audience cheered.

Mr Kherlacombe's eyes were closed, but he smiled, hearing the applause, and shot his legs out even faster.

"Hiiiiiiiiii! Hiiiiiiiiiii! Hiiiiiiiiiii!"

Crutch fell over Kherlacombe's outstretched leg and went down, dragging Twiller with him. They hit the floor and the other cossacks jumped over them. Kherlacombe's flying boot heel caught Crutch in the face and knocked him over backwards. Crutch looked up with squinting terrified eyes; Kherlacombe had said cossacks couldn't wear glasses. Twiller got him to his feet and tried to lead him out of the spinning ring, beyond Kherlacombe's flying boots.

Crutch held on blindly, spit running down his chin, eyes glazed, a bootmark on his forehead. He raised his arm as if he were flagging a taxi, and Twiller yanked him along, jumping and dodging each time Kherlacombe kicked, as the circle spun faster and faster around them, the audience applauding and Kherlacombe smiling, eyes closed.

"HIIIIIIIIII! HIIIIIIIIIIII! HIIIIIIIIIIII!"

◇   ◇   ◇

Twiller waited in the alley alongside the theater, his hazatska costume in his gym bag. Crutch had gone to the hospital to have his knee X-rayed. Mr Kherlacombe said the show was a brilliant success, especially the hazatska, which had received such an ovation, and he hoped they'd all continue their studies with him.

The stage door opened and Lily came out, Dom Panaro

beside her. Dom had received two curtain calls for his tap dance up the stairs to nowhere.

Twiller quickly opened his gym bag and pretended to be straightening out the dashing costume inside it, carefully folding the green-gold sleeves and breeches. Dom and Lily stepped together into the summer street, a faint green-gold ghost following them, dashing, swirling, touching Lily's hair.

Chapter 19

Physically Strong, Mentally Awake,
and Morally Straight.

◇ ◇ ◇

"We're happy to have you with us, fellows." Scoutmaster
Ramsey gave Twiller and Crutch the official Boy Scout
Handshake, then nodded across the room to the hallway,
where Spider was talking to several Eagle Scouts. "Pronka
seems to know a few of the older fellows already. That's good,
he'll receive plenty of scouting pointers from them."

The assistant scoutmaster handed them their membership
cards. "Pronka's family is . . . on relief, I believe?"

"Yessir," said Crutch. "His old man's in jail."

The assistant scoutmaster turned toward Ramsey and
spoke in a low voice. "We'll arrange for his uniform, Ben."

Twiller already had his uniform, had repeated the Scout
Oath from memory, had told how in an emergency you get in
touch with the doctor, the police, or the sheriff, and
described the harm to a live tree that comes from hacking it
with an axe or other sharp tool.

"I'm glad you fellows brought Pronka along," said Scoutmaster Ramsey. "I know scouting will be good for him, and for you. It'll give you a pride and confidence you can't acquire anywhere else." He raised his hand in a sharp three-fingered salute.

They saluted back, turned about-face, and walked across the meeting room, into the hallway, joining Spider and the Eagle Scouts.

"I'll give you a buck for it," said one of the Eagles, pointing to the little blue hotbook Spider was fanning slowly under his nose.

"A deuce," said Spider, "or stop wastin' my time."

The Eagle opened his Official Boy Scout wallet, with the emblem of scouting on it, and laid out two bucks. Spider folded them neatly and handed him the hotbook.

"I'll buy as many as you have," said the Eagle.

"The supply is limited," said Spider. "The next one might cost more."

"You're a real prick, aren't you, Pronka." The Eagle rolled the hotbook up in his pocket.

"I'm just passin' through."

Bandages were being wrapped on one side of the room, and artificial respiration was being given on the other. Twiller sat with the knot-tiers in the center of the big church basement, and fumbled with a sheepshank, coming up with something that looked like a handful of overcooked spaghetti. He tried again and tied his thumb up inside the sliding loop.

"Don't tie your prick in there, Twiller." Star Scout Crocker could tie knots like lightning. Twiller watched Crocker's fingers fly over, under, and around. "OK, patrol, try it again. Twiller, you come with me."

Crocker led the way across the room to the hall, where the Scouting Library was. He ran his eyes along the books, took

111

one down and flipped through the pages to an illustrated section on knots. "Want to see a picture of my girl?" he asked quietly.

"Yeah." Twiller knew it would be no ordinary picture. Crocker had his Photography Merit Badge, had his own darkroom where he could develop any kind of picture he wanted.

"Come on." Crocker led him down the hallway to the lavatory. They stepped inside and Crocker took out his wallet.

"You'll have to show me something," he said, slowly opening the wallet.

"I've got one of Spider's hotbooks at home."

"Yeah? What's in it?"

"I'll show it to you next patrol meeting."

"If you want to see my girl," said Crocker, "you've got to show me something *now*."

"I don't have anything on me, Crocker."

"What's in your wallet?"

"Nothing."

"You're holding out on me, Twiller."

Twiller quickly opened his wallet, showing Crocker his I-Am-A-Catholic-In-Case-Of-Accident-Call-A-Priest card, and his bubble-gum cards of Alvin Dark and Ferris Fain.

"OK," said Crocker, "tell you what. You show me your dick, I'll show you my girl."

Twiller could feel her waiting in Crocker's wallet, in a hot pose, taken in the woods maybe, or in Crocker's bedroom when nobody was home. He stepped over to the urinals and took his prick out.

Crocker looked down. "You do a lot of pulling, Twiller."

Nervously, Twiller zipped up his fly. "OK, let me see your girl."

"Sure . . ." Crocker opened his wallet to a picture of a girl on a porch rail, just sitting there, completely dressed with nothing showing, not even her knees.

"Hey . . ."

"What'd you expect?" Crocker laughed, snapping the wallet shut and walking out.

Twiller stared at the door, as the urinals flushed themselves behind him.

◇ ◇ ◇

"Alright," said Crutch, "here are the flags. Spider, you send the message and Twiller will receive it."

Spider took the semaphore flags, jammed them in his belt and walked across the field.

Crutch knelt beside Twiller, with a writing pad on his knee. "Signal him that you're ready to receive."

Twiller wig-wagged to Spider. Spider raised his own flags, sending the first letter. Twiller studied it, then called it out.

"F . . ."

"Got it," mumbled Crutch.

". . . U . . ."

Spider paused, looked at his Scouting Manual, and continued with the signal.

". . . C . . . K . . ." Twiller squinted at Spider's flags.
". . . Y . . ."

"Yeah, ok, got it."

". . . O . . . U . . . end of message."

"Signal that the message was received and understood."

Twiller sent *understood* and Spider signaled back, with his middle finger.

Their shoes scattered the autumn leaves on the sidewalk and crushed them underneath with a steady scuffling sound of fifty scouts strong. The night was sharply cold, and they marched briskly, their breath visible before them.

"Column right, *march!*" The voice of the drillmaster swung them rank-by-rank across the avenue, and through the gates of the School for the Deaf and Dumb. The big rolling lawn was dark on both sides of them, but the school was lit like an old stone castle, at the top of a winding drive.

They marched beneath old-fashioned lampposts and were brought to a halt before a basement entrance. Scoutmaster Ramsey led the march from there, through double doors and down a brightly lit hallway, into the school's gymnasium. It was decorated with paper streamers and balloons. The troop fanned out along the length of it, and came to attention.

On the far side of the gym, seated on folding chairs, were the deaf and dumb kids, making excited hand signals to each other. Scoutmaster Ramsey and the director of the school stood together in the middle of the floor, talking quietly. One of the deaf and dumb girls let out a croaking groan that sent a shiver through Twiller, but the girl was only smiling at her friend alongside her, and the wild twisted sound died away while her fingers kept moving in speech. She was pretty, with short red hair and a fantastic figure, and every eye in the troop was on her now, as her fingers danced.

Scoutmaster Ramsey faced the troop and saluted. "Fall out, men, and enjoy yourselves."

The ranks dispersed, the director of the school turned on a record player and the music began.

"They can't hear it." Crutch nodded toward the deaf girls.

Twiller watched Crocker and a couple of other big shots cross the floor, medals jingling. They stood before the girls, and asked for a dance. The girls rose in a confusion of little hand signs, to each other, to the scouts, to no one in particular. Crocker had the redhead, was already holding her in his arms. A misshapen groan came from one of the deaf and dumb boys seated further down the row.

Twiller saw Spider gliding along the far edge of the gymnasium, and then out through the gym door into the hall, where he disappeared into the shadows.

"Spider's casin' the place."

114

"Better not say anything."

Twiller turned back to the dance floor, to the redhead's spinning skirt and the little bit of fluttering slip beneath it, as Crocker sent her whirling at the end of his arm and reeled her back in with a quick snap that brought her full against his medals. She melted there, her arms around him and her hands extended behind his back, making a little comment to a girlfriend dancing just beyond her. Her girlfriend answered with a quick reply on her own fingers, before her Eagle Scout twirled her away.

"We're trained dancers," said Crutch. "We should be out there, showin' them the fuckin' hazatska."

Twiller bent down to tie his shoe, trying to spy out a bit of panty as the girls spun by. He wanted to dance with the redhead, wanted to signal *I Love You* with his semaphore flags. But he'd only learned how to signal *Fuck You* and *Eat It, Mac.*

He looked toward the hallway again; Spider was nowhere in sight, but Twiller could feel him moving along his thread, somewhere deep in the building.

The first dance ended, and another wave of high-ranking scouts took the floor. Crocker came off and walked over to his patrol. "Why aren't you dancing, Twiller? Don't you like girls?"

"I don't like dancing."

"It's fun." Crocker reached out and adjusted the slip knot on Twiller's neckerchief, pulling it so tight against Twiller's throat it choked him. "I'll teach you how sometime."

He swaggered off, giving horse-shit little touches to other uniforms in the broken rank, and Twiller bent down to his shoes again, still trying for an eyeful of panty. Scoutmaster Ramsey and the director were talking near the record player, and some of the other scouts were sitting with the deaf and dumb guys, showing them knot-tying, semaphore, and first aid. The deaf and dumb guys smiled and tried it, but their

115

eyes kept going back to their girlfriends on the dance floor, slow-dancing now, with Star Scouts, Life Scouts, and Eagles.

Spider came back through the doorway, his uniform blending immediately into the crowd, until he emerged a few moments later, at the heart of the patrol.

"Where you been, Spider?" asked Crutch softly.

"Right here, fucknose," said Spider, whipping out a piece of rope, "tying a motherfucking bowline in case anybody asks."

◇ ◇ ◇

The basement of the church was silent, everybody at attention. Scoutmaster Ramsey paced back and forth, slapping the attendance book against his leg. He hadn't bothered to fill it in, hadn't begun the meeting with a story of scouting as he usually did, had just brought them up sharp and held them there, as he passed, looking them over one by one, disgust in his eyes.

"Two watches, three rings, and a hearing aid. Stolen from afflicted children, from those we'd gone to cheer up." He spun on them, and his words came coldly:

"There's a thief among us."

The ranks didn't breathe, didn't dare to even blink. Twiller felt his chest tightening, his pulse speeding up as Ramsey passed his patrol a second time, and turned, back to the center of the room. "I've already paid for the stolen objects, out of your treasury. The watches and rings, the hearing aid, will be replaced. But what cannot be replaced, what cannot be so easily bought—"

He slammed the attendance book on the floor with a crash that made them jump. "—is our ruined honor! That we can never buy back. But by God, we're going to try."

◇ ◇ ◇

116

The troop was spread out around the school, raking leaves, pruning dead branches from the trees, cleaning out around the hedges. Scouts dangled on the sides of the stone building, trimming the ivy, emptying the rain gutters, washing windows. Twiller carried a basket of trash toward the bonfire in back, Crutch beside him, pushing a wheelbarrow.

Drillmaster Billy Lance was tending the fire, a cloud of smoke around his freckled face. Crutch dumped the wheelbarrow, and Lance stirred the fire with a long stick. "I wouldn't want to be in Spider's shoes today." He poked at the little pockets of flame.

Twiller shook out his basket and marched off again with Crutch, back to the rear of the building. "Think Spider'll rat on us?"

Crutch bent over another pile of trash. "*We* didn't steal the fuckin' watches."

"But we knew he was gone. We knew he was robbing the place."

The back door opened and Tenderfoot Marvin Ulbadini stepped out with a bucket of soapy water. He tossed it in the concrete gutter alongside the building, and lowered his voice. "*Crocker's takin' a shower with the redhead.*" He looked quickly around behind him.

"Where?"

"On the second floor."

Scoutmaster Ramsey came along the edge of the building, the assistant scoutmaster beside him. "Alright, men, break it up and get back to work."

"This is the last load of trash, sir."

"Then join the clean-up crew inside. Ulbadini, show them where to go."

Ulbadini led them to a basement washroom, and the head of the mopping squad issued them buckets, mops, and rags. "Upstairs, front hall. Keep the water clean."

They started at the front of the building, below the old

stained-glass windows at the entranceway. Twiller splashed his mop out beside Ulbadini. "Where's Spider?"

"They got him out by the back road. Fox Patrol is holdin' him. He was carryin' his rod."

They mopped along toward the front staircase and Twiller started mopping up it, leaving wet steps behind him. He could hear the sound of the shower running on the second floor, and imagined how the redhead was splashing around in there with Crocker, her body slippery with soap as Crocker rubbed her down.

He mopped across the landing and worked up the next flight of stairs, to the top step. The Wolf Patrol was at the far end of the hall, scrubbing the same bit of floor, over and over. Just beyond them was the shower-room door.

He mopped down the hall, toward it.

"Hold it right there, Twiller."

"I'm supposed to mop the floor."

"Mop the other way."

"I need some clean water." He pointed toward the sound of the running shower.

"Get lost."

He turned around and mopped the other way, saw Scoutmaster Ramsey coming up the stairs. The Wolf Patrol shifted nervously, but held the blockade in front of the shower-room doorway. Ramsey came to the top stair and looked down the hall toward them. "You're doing a thorough job, men." He started along the hallway, examining the work area, and the Wolves spilled a lot of soapy water on the floor in front of him, scrubbing madly. Ramsey smiled and spoke gently. "It all comes out in the wash, doesn't it?"

A long low moan came from the shower room. Scoutmaster Ramsey shook his head sadly. "You men are not to disturb any of these children in their daily routine. Just let them go about their business and you go about yours. Is that clear?"

They nodded, the leader of the Wolf Patrol giving Ramsey

a sharp salute. The scoutmaster turned and headed back down the stairs.

◇ ◇ ◇

"Troop—*dismissed!*"
They marched down the long winding drive and out through the main gates, then separated on the avenue and circled on back to the dirt road behind the school, where the Fox Patrol was holding Spider.
They spread out along the road, taking off their belts and forming two lines. Spider was led to the mouth of the lines and pushed in between them.
"Alright, Pronka, run."
"I ain't runnin'."
"OK, don't run." The Fox leader wound up, snapped his belt across Spider's ass, and Spider ran, down between the lines, one belt after another cracking behind him. Twiller faked it as Spider came by with his eyebrows pinched together and his teeth clinched, an arrow in his back again.

◇ ◇ ◇

"Hey, Meatball, knock it off will you, we're tryin' to get some sleep."
Meatball Macbean chuckled softly, his bunk going silent for a few minutes. Then . . .
Squeak squeak squeak
Twiller lay in his sleeping bag, listening. Scoutmaster Ramsey's voice drifted into his half-dream, with the squeaking of Meatball's bunk: "*Hundreds of scouts will share the fun of Bear Lake with you, learning skills that will help you to serve the community and the country of which you are a part . . .*"
Hundreds of scouts were in their sleeping bags, in tents all around him, and their bunks were squeaking too, you could

119

hear it, along with the croaking of the frogs and the singing of the crickets.

A counselor's flashlight was coming along the path, from tent to tent. It flashed through the doorway, lighting up Meatball's bunk. "That's enough of that."

Meatball stopped, chuckling softly again, and the flashlight passed on.

Squeak squeak squeak

◇　◇　◇

"What class you got today?" Crutch rolled his sleeping bag into a ball and laid it at the end of his bunk.

"Axe-throwing." Twiller's new axe was already on his belt. "How about you?"

Crutch took a shovel out of his pack. "Latrine duty."

"With the rest of the assholes." Crocker lay on his bunk, hands behind his head.

"Up yours, Crocker."

"I left a big one in there, sweetheart, just for you."

Crutch walked out through the tent flaps, and Twiller followed him, onto the path. "Some fuckin' vacation." Crutch shouldered his shit shovel, turned and walked up the path toward the latrine. Twiller went the other way, taking a trail through the woods to the axe-throw.

The class had formed, and scouts were already throwing. The axes glinted in the sunlight, arcing end over end, then quivered for a moment as they buried into a hardwood stump. It was the height of a man, the instructor explained, and pointed out the vital areas for striking. "Here you would hit the chest, here the neck, here between the eyes."

Twiller lined up, happy to be learning a skill that would help the community and the country of which he was a part.

◇　◇　◇

"I won't do it," said Ulbadini.

"You'll do it," said Crocker, "or I'll beat the living shit out of you."

Ulbadini jumped toward the tent flap. Meatball Macbean tripped him with a semaphore flag and dropped on top of him. "Go on," said Meatball in a kindly voice. "Give Crocker a blowjob. It won't kill you."

"Fuck you guys. I ain't doin' it. I don't care what you do to me."

Meatball and Crocker slipped the chains off their footlockers.

"Hey," said Ulbadini, "this is some fuckin' deal, hey fellas, gimme a break."

"We'll give you a break, you little bastard." Crocker whipped the chain around Ulbadini's neck.

"Hey, Crocker, what're ya . . ."

"I'm gonna chain you down and shit in your mouth."

Ulbadini looked around, eyes pleading. "Hey, come on, I thought we were buddies."

"Sure, Ulbadini . . ." Crocker tightened the chain slowly. ". . . we can be good buddies, but you've got to stop being a snob."

"I'm not a snob," whimpered Ulbadini. "I just never gave no blowjob to nobody, that's all."

"And now you're going to." Crocker tightened the chain another link.

"O . . . K . . ." gasped Ulbadini. "I'll . . . do it. On . . . one condition."

"Yeah?" Crocker loosened the chain. "What's that?"

"You wrap your dick in cellophane." Ulbadini reached into his footlocker and brought out a sandwich. He unwrapped it slowly, smoothing the cellophane on his knee.

Twiller edged slowly toward the end of his bunk, ready to dive outside. Crocker was after him too, was going to make all the new guys blow him.

121

"Leave him alone, Crocker." Schank, the Eagle Scout in the tent, sat up slowly in his bunk.

"Fuck you," said Crocker.

"Yeah, hey Schank," whined Ulbadini, "make him leave me alone,"

"Schank isn't going to do shit." Crocker walked to Schank's bunk and lifted up the end of it; he dropped it back down with a crash and stood there, waiting.

Schank closed his eyes. He had a big mouth and bragged a lot about his IQ, but he didn't say anything now, and Crocker walked away, grabbing Ulbadini by the collar.

"It's time for a little prick-licking."

Ulbadini struggled, but Meatball held onto him while Crocker lay down on his bunk. "Come on," said Crocker.

Meatball pushed Ulbadini between Crocker's legs, and Ulbadini hurried with the cellophane, as Crocker forced his head down.

The cellophane started crackling.

"Not bad," said Crocker, "not bad at all."

Twiller watched Ulbadini's head going up and down, and reached under his pillow for his axe, glad now for the practice he'd had throwing it this afternoon.

"Ah yes . . ." Crocker sighed as the cellophane crackled faster, "that's good cocksucking."

"A dick sandwich," said Meatball from the other end of the bunk.

The cellophane crackled like a campfire, and Crocker stiffened, raising his hips.

Ulbadini's head bobbed sharply upward, then down again, and Crocker twisted on his sleeping bag. Ulbadini's head went faster and Crocker reached out, grabbing him by the hair. "OK, ok, that's enough."

Ulbadini brought his head away and looked around, dazed, a piece of cellophane stuck to his nose.

"Nice, Ulbadini," said Crocker, "very very nice."

Ulbadini peeled the cellophane off his nose. The opened

sandwich was still on top of his footlocker. He picked it up and threw it at Crocker.

Crocker ducked away, laughing. "Next time, you won't need cellophane."

Schank's voice came from the corner of the tent. "You're going to get yours someday, Crocker."

"Come here and say that," said Crocker in a movie-star whisper.

The camp bugler blew taps over the waters of the lake, and the lanterns were extinguished. Meatball started sending on his Morse-code set. Twiller followed the dots and dashes buzzing out through the tent flap.

ULBADINI BLOWJOBS
YOU SUPPLY CELLOPHANE

◇ ◇ ◇

He floated, staring up into the late afternoon sky. Floating that way, with his ears submerged, he almost felt as if he didn't exist. It was a feeling he'd had a lot lately. He raised his head. "Hey, Crutch . . ."

Crutch was standing in water up to his chin, his eyes like two oysters. "Yeah, whattya want, I can't see you too well."

Twiller doggy paddled over. "Sometimes I get this feeling like I'm not really here."

"Yeah, where are you?"

"I dunno. It's like I'm nowhere."

"Yeah, well that makes two of us, because this whole fuckin' camp is nowhere." Crutch held his nose, submerged in place, and walked slowly away, underwater. He walked underwater every day, trying to perfect the technique. He surfaced, gasping. "Some prick up there—" He pointed to the staff tent on the hill. "—has it in for me. I drew latrine duty again."

Twiller rolled over on his back, looking up at the blue sky.

123

The feeling hit him again, that he was cut off from the world, that other people existed but he was fading, or that maybe he was some kind of mistake.

Crutch's head came along again, just under the surface. "Crutch, hey . . ."

Crutch came up, choking and beating the water away from his face. "Yeah, what?"

"You never feel like . . . like the world isn't real?"

"Ever stick your head in a latrine four hundred guys have been shitting in all week? That's real."

"I think there's something wrong with me."

"There's nothin' wrong with you. It's this place. It's like a motherfucking jail."

The whistle sounded, *all out of the water.*

"Whistles, bugles, a guy can't take a piss without a whistle." Crutch submerged again, walking underwater toward shore.

◇ ◇ ◇

It's a long way to Tipperary
It's a long way, I know . . .

Mr Snow, the gray-haired old veteran of World War I, led the singing in the mess hall. The tables had all been cleared, and now four hundred voices filled the air, singing the songs of the doughboys.

Twiller sang with the others, and saw the doughboys marching, across the lonesome fields of no-man's-land. Outside the windows, in the shadowy pines, he thought the spirit of a doughboy might be listening, called by the singing, and waiting for the story that Mr Snow would tell, like he told each night, of courage on the battlefield of long ago.

The song built toward the end, the scoutmasters all singing too, leading their troops to the rousing finish.

* * *

124

. . . it's a long way to Tipperary—
but you can tell them I'll be there ere long!

Cheering filled the hall and then died away as the lanterns flickered and Mr Snow sat on the edge of the homemade stage, feet dangling, addressing them in a strong, quiet voice.

"Boys, scouting is the finest life there is, a life of sharing, of learning, of giving. In the First War, one could always tell who the scouts were, for they were manly, brave, and quick to grasp what was needed in an emergency. Our commanding officers knew this, and when new recruits fell in, the first question they were asked was—*Are there any Eagle Scouts in the ranks?* When an Eagle Scout stepped forward, it was a wonderful thing to see, for he wasn't a slouching, confused greenhorn. He was a trained soldier already. And that Eagle Scout was given special consideration from the moment he stepped forward. In a very short while, he was commanding troops of his own. I remember one night . . ."

The story went on in the lamplight, a wonderful story of sacrifice and heroism, as the voices of the doughboys spoke through Mr Snow, and the mess hall seemed to dissolve in shadow, changed to a dark open battlefield where the smoke of campfires drifted and ghostly soldiers kept a silent watch. Twiller saw the barbed wire and the trenches, heard the footsteps of the sentry, and the sky over Bear Lake seemed to listen too, and speak, thunder rumbling softly like the cannons in the tale. The attack was made, the doughboys fell, but an Eagle Scout got through, leading a charge that was doomed to fail, leading it across the hell of no-man's-land, with four hundred dreaming scouts beside him now in the phantom moonlight, charging through the mud and wire into the devastating fire of the enemy. They fell, without a thought for themselves, and gritted their teeth in the trembling darkness, waiting for the end to come.

Mr Snow's voice finished almost in a whisper, with a

prayer for his lost comrades, and a lantern was hung in the window of the mess hall. From the edge of Bear Lake, the bugler blew taps, long, low, and mournfully over the water.

Their footsteps were soft as they left the mess hall, and their voices hushed as they walked along the path, each one caught in the spell of the story. The true spirit of scouting was clear to Twiller at last. He walked along humbly in the darkness, hoping that he could become such a scout himself someday, filled with those qualities that separated the Eagle from all other men.

Ahead of him, scouts were going quietly into their tents, and all of the lanterns were low. Everybody was feeling it like he was, a sense of quiet comradeship and sharing, a feeling that came only with the uniform and all it stood for.

He went up the steps of his own tent and pushed silently through the flap. Schank lay face down, hands and feet chained to his bunk, a lighted candle sticking out of his ass.

Crocker stood over him, grinning. Schank growled, a khaki Boy Scout sock stuffed in his mouth. He struggled to free his hands, and the candle cast a flickering halo of light on his bare ass.

"Relax, Schank, you're not going anywhere," Crocker walked over to his own bunk and undressed. "Come here, Ulbadini, and bring the cellophane."

"Ah, Crocker . . ."

"Do you want a candle up your ass?"

Twiller listened to Ulbadini opening his footlocker and unwrapping another sandwich.

A heavy footstep struck the wooden stair. "Alright, men, extinguish that light."

Meatball leaned over Schank's bunk and blew out the ass-candle. Twiller climbed into his sleeping bag and watched the little curl of candle smoke drift up past the moonlit door-way.

The cellophane started to crackle.

◇ ◇ ◇

The tent was damp, silent, asleep. Twiller moved carefully out of his sleeping bag, emptied his footlocker, and rolled up his pack. Crutch looked up in the darkness, pink-eyed and squinting. Twiller pointed at his pack, and then at the road that led out from Bear Lake.

Crutch slipped out of his bag. Twiller tiptoed over to Schank's bunk and pulled the candle out of his ass. Schank nodded stiffly, and Twiller turned back toward the door. Crutch was shouldering his pack and moving through the mosquito netting. Twiller followed him down the stairs, putting his feet where the planks wouldn't squeak, and they stepped off together onto the moonlit path.

"What about Schank?"

"I pulled the candle out of his ass."

"Yeah, but maybe we should unchain him."

"Crocker and Meatball'll wake up and beat the crap out of us."

"We'll take him bed and all." Crutch limped back up the stairs and Twiller went after him, into the tent. They crept across the plank floor, keeping low. Meatball's bunk started squeaking, but they knew Meatball was just jacking off in his sleep. He sighed and rolled over, and the squeaking stopped.

They crawled on by him, to Schank's bunk, going one to each end. They lifted, the bunk swayed for a moment, and then they walked, through the snoring.

Meatball's bunk started squeaking again; they could see his hand going up and down in his sleeping bag but the beat was off. They moved by him slowly, toward Crocker, who was in his fancy monogrammed pajamas, one arm hanging down to the floor, and then suddenly he was sitting up, staring at them.

He reached out as if he were putting his arm around someone, and sank back down, hugging himself. They moved on, through the mosquito netting and down the steps.

The moon was colder now, and farther away, high over the pines. They worked their way along the path, to the big open beach, and set the bunk in the sand. Twiller took the sock out of Schank's mouth. Schank's mouth stayed open in the shape the gag had forced it into.

They axe-hammered his chains and threw them in the lake. Schank bent his legs back and forth slowly, rubbing the joints, and then stood up stiffly, bare-ass in the moonlight.

"Can I borrow your axe?" His voice was hoarse and choked.

"So you can go back there and murder Crocker?" Crutch took him by one arm and Twiller took the other. "You don't want to do that, Schank. You want to come with us, out of this fuckin' place."

He walked between them, legs trembling like a shell-shocked doughboy. They led him up the path to where their packs were stowed, and then on past the rows of tents to the dark, deserted mess hall. Crutch slipped through the back door and Twiller waited with Schank on the gravel walk outside.

"Fuckin' Crocker . . ." Schank's mouth was still twisted from the sock, and tears of rage filled his eyes as he picked the candle wax off his ass. "What a fuckin' no-good prick."

Crutch came out the door, carrying a pair of aprons and a chef's hat. "This is all I could find."

Schank put the aprons on, one in front and one in back, and jammed the hat down on his head. They walked along the Bear Lake road, to the empty highway. "It's late for a ride," said Twiller.

"I don't care if I have to sleep in a tree." Crutch limped along, pack on his back. "We pulled the candle out of Schank's ass and tomorrow I won't be cleaning toilets."

"You guys are alright." Schank adjusted his chef's hat. "I won't forget this."

They marched along, singing, "*It's a long way to Tipperary . . .*" and sang down the winding highway, around the bend, and over a low concrete bridge. The stream that fed Bear Lake was below and Crutch pissed in it, singing

"*. . . to the sweetest gal I know . . .*"

A rumbling sound came from somewhere back along the highway. They crossed to the far end of the bridge and lined up on the shoulder of the road, ready with their thumbs. "Get out there, Schank," said Crutch, "where they can see your white hat."

The crest of the hill grew brighter, and then a truck came rattling over the top of it and down toward them, headlights blinking. The gears shifted, the brakes squealed, and they were running after it along the road.

The driver's belly was up against the wheel, a cigar glowing under his nose. He looked at Schank. "Who the fuck's this, Chef Boy-ar-dee?"

They climbed up beside him, and he threw it in gear, moving on down the highway.

Chapter 20

Model S for Those Under Five Feet Tall

He shaped the crown of the cap, so the RR was plainly visible, and then checked the whole uniform out from the side.

RUBBISH REMOVAL

The big red letters curved across his shoulders. A fine pinstripe ran through his cream-colored shirt and pants, down to his red and white socks. He fielded a ground ball in the mirror, and whipped it to first.

◊ ◊ ◊

"I didn't know you were in the Little League." Lily sat on the playground swing.

He stared at the tips of her sneakers. It was a break, finding her alone like this. "Where's Steve tonight?"

"How should I know?" She kicked at the ground. The

swing creaked and she stretched her legs out, kicking higher.

"You and Steve have a fight or something?"

"Aren't you nosey." She swung on by him, higher, legs out. He didn't want to cut in on Steve Zuba, as Zuba had been helping out at his father's gas station lifting tires and was developing arms like an orangutan.

"You're not waitin' for him or anything?"

"I never saw anybody so nosey." Her bare legs angled up past him, her voice rising into the evening sky as she took the swing as high as it could go.

He fixed the peak of his Rubbish Removal cap. "Wanna go to the movies?"

The evening sun streaked her curls with yellow light, as she glided on by him. She glided out, and back, and touched her toe to the ground, dragging the swing to a stop. "OK," she said, stepping off.

She walked with him through the playground gate. Other Little Leaguers were ahead, blue caps and socks showing brightly on the avenue. "You see the game tonight? We beat Industrial Forklift." He nodded toward the defeated players, and brushed a little dirt off his knees, hoping she'd ask him about who slid home with the winning run.

But she was looking on the other side of the avenue, where the gas stations were.

"Steve helpin' out tonight?" He pointed a thumb at Zuba Sunoco.

"Don't ask me," she said, tilting her nose in the air.

"You worried about him seein' you with me?"

"Why should I worry," she said, and suddenly took hold of his hand.

It was an incredible feeling, Lily's fingers snaking in between his own. If Steve saw it, he'd be out with a grease gun.

But a Rubbish Removal shortstop can't back down. Especially if he's training with the Joe Bonomo Delux Muscle-Worker, Model S for those under five feet tall. To build Pep, Personality, and the Physically Perfect Male.

"Next time, Zuba, you'd better think first before you start shooting off your mouth at me!"

"Oh Jack, you're wonderful . . ."

"That supervisor's job is yours, Jack. You've made yourself into a real comer."

"Why don't we cut through the alley here," he said, tugging her away from the gas station. "It's a good shortcut."

"No," she said, "let's go this way," and she pulled him across the avenue, toward Zuba Sunoco. He glanced nervously at the grease rack. It was Saturday night, and Steve would definitely be in there, pretending to be a mechanic, wearing a filthy Sunoco jacket and throwing heavy batteries around.

"Hey, Lily, I think we might be late for the show, whyn't we jump on the trolley, here it comes . . ."

She started fooling with his cap as they passed the gas pumps. "Why don't you wear it like this?" she said, tipping it down over his eyes.

"Let's jump on the trolley, ok, here it is . . ."

She twisted his cap sideways, the gas pumps behind her and the trolley car sputtering on past and down the block.

You can kayo your enemy with one clean scientific wallop. The experts who prepared this deadly Judo book want to make a "big man" out of every small one. If not satisfied, return within 8 days for immediate refund of full purchase price.

"What number do you have?" She turned him around, standing on the concrete island at the pumps, so nobody could possibly miss her. "Number three . . ." She traced the big red number on his back with her finger as he looked toward the bright flame of a welding tool in back of the station. The flame got longer and sparks started shooting off a fender. He saw spots in front of his eyes for a second and then

Steve Zuba appeared in the middle of them, in the garage doorway.

Lily turned away quickly, tugging Twiller by the hand. *"Come on,"* she said loudly, *"we don't want to miss the show."*

Twiller kept his eye on Zuba, but Steve just stood in the doorway, looking sort of numb.

"Where do you like to sit?" asked Lily, even louder. *"In the balcony?"*

She dragged him along, past the gas pumps and on past the high Sunoco fence. He realized that she'd fallen for him, and wanted to let Zuba know it.

This was the most perfect night of his life.

"Yeah, the balcony," he said. "I always sit there," though he didn't, the balcony was just for making out.

They walked along the avenue, past the other gas stations and the Dairy Farms ice cream parlor. His teammates were all in there, talking about the game and insulting the girls, just like he'd be doing himself, except here he was on a date, his very first one.

"It's a double feature tonight," he said, relaxing, no longer worried about Zuba kicking the shit out of him. Zuba Sunoco was dropping out of sight behind him. Lily turned, checking it out too, but they were completely safe, you couldn't even see the high Sunoco sign.

"I've changed my mind," she said, and took her hand out of his.

"Huh?"

"I said I've changed my mind. I don't feel like going to the movies."

"Well, we could go for a soda at the drugstore."

"I don't want to," she said. "I think I'm going home."

"I'm going that way myself, I'll walk you."

"No—" She pushed her hair back with both hands and fluffed it out on the sides. "—I'd like to go home, alone."

133

He looked at her hair, the way all the little curls spun the setting red of the sun, and then he looked down at his Official Little League sneakers. "Yeah," he said, "ok . . ."

"Maybe we can go to the movies some other time." She turned toward the hill to her house.

"Tomorrow night?"

"No."

"Yeah ok. Well . . ." He straightened his Rubbish cap. Another trolley was coming, and he ran in behind it and jumped onto the bumper. He hung there, riding along in the wind, and watched her climb the hill. His first date hadn't worked out too well, hadn't even gotten started really.

Chapter 21

.... In Which the Question Is Asked,
"Can this girl from a mining town in the west
find happiness as the wife
of a wealthy and titled Englishman?"

◇ ◇ ◇

From the dugout he could look across the field, and up into
the bleacher seats where she was sitting with Zuba. She was
wearing jeans and a white shirt, with a blue scarf tied at her
throat, and she was holding Zuba's hand while Zuba talked
and joked in his paper mechanic's hat; his pants were half-
eaten away by battery acid and he was making sure everybody saw.

"Dussnock, you're on deck. Twiller, you're up after Dussnock . . ."

He had to stop watching her. Baseball was a thousand
times more important than some stupid girl.

He took a mouthful of water, spit it out and climbed the
dugout steps toward the bat rack. Dussnock was just ahead of
him, picking out a bat and whipping it around.

A blue scarf waved from the bleachers.

Is she waving at me?

He turned toward her and then something hit him in the
head with a tremendous *bonnnnnnnnnnnnnggggggggg*.

He looked up at Dussnock standing over him, the bat hanging from Dussnock's hand. ". . . you walked into me," said Dussnock, and then everybody was standing around him and gongs were echoing over the field, over the fence, over the distant houses.

He tried to stand because he was supposed to be on deck, but he was back down on his knees, with the field spinning beneath him.

". . . take him by the arms, that's it . . ."

He heard the manager's voice, and felt them lifting him up. He looked around at the crowd, and the faces were blurred and edged with wavy lights. There was a wet cloth against his head, and he felt water dripping into his uniform. He looked for *her*, knew she'd be making her way through the crowd toward him.

"I've got to go to him, Steve. I just realized he's the one, he's my shortstop."

◇ ◇ ◇

"For a wash that's deep clean, sparkling clean, use deep cleaning Oxydol. Oxydol is deep cleaning, deep cleaning, deeeeeeeep cleaning . . . "

The organ music came on, giving him a sad feeling.

". . . and now—time once again for Oxydol's own Ma Perkins . . ."

He turned toward the radio, careful not to disturb the bandage on his head. He could hear dogs barking and chasing around outside, and some girls went by the house, talking and laughing, and then the organ music returned, taking him to organ land where it always hurt a little, white sheets blowing there, on the line.

"Well, today Ma's going to ask Evvie and Willy a question she hates to ask. We know how reluctant Ma is to interfere in other folk's affairs, but for months now all of us have been wishing that Ma would do some interfering . . ."

136

He stared at the radio. It seemed that all Ma *ever* did was interfere in other folk's affairs, but he liked her anyway, it made the time go by.

He touched at the bandage, feeling the lump very gently. Under the lump was the fractured skull. He'd felt like a hero at first but now he felt like shit, after a month in bed.

He thought about jacking off, but he could probably wait until *The Romance of Helen Trent.* There was only so much jacking off he could do in a day and he had to space it out. And Helen was younger than Ma Perkins, he didn't feel like she was spying on him to see if he *was* jacking off. With Helen Trent he could just lie back and stroke in peace.

"*. . . and so Evvie does what Sylvester told her to do, she lies to Ma . . .*"

He looked at the slim papered body of his Piper Cub hanging from the ceiling and thought of winding it up and sending it out the window with a firecracker in its tail. But then that'd be the end of it and he wouldn't have it anymore.

"*You know I guess a lot of you ladies are having trouble with those halfway soaps for dishes. I mean bar soaps because they don't have real speed . . .*"

He heard the faint crack of a bat coming from the field. Rubbish Removal was practicing.

"*. . . and now—Our Gal Sunday, the story of an orphan girl named Sunday, from the little town of Silver Creek, Colorado, who in young womanhood married England's richest, most handsome lord, Lord Henry Brinthrope—the story that asks the question, can this girl from a mining town in the west find happiness as the wife of a wealthy and titled Englishman . . .*"

His chemistry set was nearby but his latest experiment had eaten the veneer off the dresser, and Dad wasn't too happy about it.

Is that the doorbell?

He heard bells a lot these days, the doctor said he would for a while, but it sounded like somebody was on the porch, maybe it was Dussnock, he said he'd bring over his ukulele.

"Come on up!"

The downstairs door opened. Quiet footsteps came through, and stopped in the hall.

"Up here!" He switched off the radio, and the footsteps came onto the stairs, slowly and softly, a girl's footsteps. It must be Lily! He knew she'd come and visit him.

He jumped out of bed, rushed to the mirror and adjusted his pompadour, then made a dash for his robe.

The footsteps turned at the landing and came up the last few stairs.

"Down here," he said, twisting into his robe and stumbling toward the armchair, where he sat quickly, trying to look like Lord Henry Brinthrope of Black Swan Hall.

The footsteps came quietly near, and then Floyd Flynn appeared in the doorway. "I brought some books. May I leave them with you?"

Bells went off again as he stood and went to the dresser, where Floyd was laying out the books on the disintegrated veneer. "I thought maybe these . . ."

Shortstop Shadow, Race for the Pennant, Southpaw, Doubleplay . . .

"They're not due back for four weeks. I'll return them when you've finished."

The bells drifted away; he touched the smooth library bindings and thumbed the pages. Floyd stood beside him, twisting his umbrella. "Like to play some checkers?" He pointed to the open board by the bed table.

They set up the pieces.

"Chocolate cigarette?" Lord Henry took the package from his pocket.

"Thank you," said Floyd.

Chapter 22

... In Which Doctors Unanimously Agree
That Abstinence from Sexual Intercourse
Before Marriage
Is in Keeping with Good Moral
and Physical Development.

The lunch hour crowd was scattered over the schoolyard. He walked slowly, avoiding the groups that were horsing around, as the doctor said pressure on the brain could result from any sort of push or shove. He found Spider in a card game on the back basement stairs, playing for cigarettes, the cards snapping off his fingertips. Everybody from North Side Junior High knew Spider, and Twiller wished his own father were in jail because it seemed to make a person more popular.

The clock crept slowly toward 3:25. Spider was in the seat behind him, jacking off in a book, Twiller could hear the pages softly rippling. The student who got the book next year would have a wonderful time getting the pages apart.

The minute hand jumped to the five, and Mr. Trojano nodded to him. He stood, forced to leave early to avoid the crowd in the locker room and possible pressure on the brain. Feet came out all down the aisle, tripping him, and somebody jabbed him in the ass with an ink pen. They did it every day, but he couldn't fight back; one blow to the head could kill him the doctor said. He stumbled out of the aisle and took a spitball in the face. The girls were snickering, and even Mr Trojano seemed to have it in for him, maybe because the lump had gone down, and you couldn't actually see the fracture.

He opened the door and stepped into the empty hall.

Floyd Flynn sat at the far end of it, in a hall-guard chair. He looked up and waved. Twiller walked toward him slowly, at the snail's pace the doctor had given him.

"You'd better hurry," said Floyd. "Here comes the stampede."

The bell rang and thunder started to roll out of every room. Twiller descended the stairs slowly, like walking through a dream where you want to go faster but can't. The roar of voices and footsteps swelled and broke, spilling all around him. Locker doors flew open, guys pushing and shoving toward the exit. He turned the dial on his combination lock. Spider stepped in alongside him to his own locker, but didn't bother with the combination, just kicked the wooden slats out of the bottom panel and threw his books in.

"Hey, Spider, wait up . . ." He tried to get Spider to run interference for him, but Spider was already threading through the crowd at the door.

"Come on, move it up there." Somebody gave him a jab in the back, and he couldn't get out of the current rushing for the door. Elbows and fists were rocking and socking him on both sides, and a sudden *thud* got him square across the top of the head, a book, somebody'd nailed him with a book, didn't they know, didn't they understand about his fracture?

"My fracture!" He spun around. The cover of the book came at him again, *splat* across the forehead.

He fell backwards, against the crowd. "Who did that!" he shouted, trying to get his balance.

140

"Come on, move this fuckin' line . . ." The crowd rolled him along out the door, and dumped him on the sidewalk. He stood up slowly, amazed that he wasn't dead of pressure on the brain. He'd been hit with a geography book, one of the big volumes. He felt the top of his head, and then felt his forehead where the fracture was.

"What's wrong?" Crutch was coming in alongside him.

"I just got hit on the fracture."

"Yeah, you got a lump again."

"I feel alright though." He tapped the fracture with his fingers. "It doesn't even hurt."

"Yeah, you're ok." Crutch swung his books over his shoulder. "Let's get away from this fuckin' dungeon, there goes Tootsie."

They moved in behind Tootsie, who'd done it with fifteen guys down by the coal breaker, and then later on a moving motorcycle with Drainpipe Drobish. Twiller loved her. He walked along, watching her big swinging hips, and feeling his head. "I'm not going to leave class early anymore."

"I wouldn't care if I was number fifteen on line." Crutch stared through his goggles at Tootsie.

◇ ◇ ◇

"Hey, Spider . . ." Crutch knocked on Spider's cellar window, and it tipped open just a crack.

"Yeah, ok . . ."

The morning was clear and bright, and they tried to get a glimpse of Nancy Pronka getting dressed.

The cellar door opened and Spider came out, Old Lady Pronka walking up the steps behind him, on the way to a cleaning job, her hair tied in a babushka and a cigarette dangling from the corner of her mouth.

"And don't you skip no school today . . ."

"Alrigh'," said Spider, "keep your shirt on."

141

"You're fuckin' bums," she said, going past them, smelling like rags and furniture polish.

"How about a quarter?" asked Spider.

"I'll give you a quarter," she said, and just kept on going, up the block.

They started down the hill, toward the river. "Another day in fuckin' jail." Crutch swung his books against a telephone pole, cracking the spines.

"Somebody oughta just knock off the principal." Spider squeezed his trigger finger at the air.

"All we'd get is half-day off maybe. Remember when Saurlempe fell into the buzz saw in wood shop? The ambulance came to patch him up and we still didn't get one fuckin' minute off." Crutch swung his books again, splattering them against a mailbox. "A piece of Saurlempe's nose was hangin' from the ceiling, and we were sandin' our tie racks."

They turned onto the avenue. The smoke stack from the button mill was going, and the coal breaker was pounding. They headed toward the narrow bridge across the river.

"I'm skippin'." Spider cut around the bridge, onto the embankment. "You mudfucks comin'?"

He moved down to the water's edge, looking both ways over his shoulder, and Twiller could feel the whole long passage of the river, past the junkyard and the factories and the iron foundry, the river winding for miles through the valley.

Spider looked across the river, toward the railroad tracks and North Side Avenue. He raised his arm to the distant windows of North Side Junior High, and gave it the finger.

Then he was gone, out of sight.

A horn sounded behind them. An old Hudson was pulling in at the curb, Mr Trojano at the wheel. He signaled them to get in.

Twiller took the back door handle in his hand, but the door wouldn't open.

"Up front." Trojano motioned him toward the other door.

They went around the car and climbed in front with him. Twiller looked over his shoulder into the back seat. A rope stretched from one door handle to the other, holding them shut; the doors rattled open a few inches as the car started up, and continued rattling. Trojano unfolded a morning newspaper and held it in front of him at the wheel.

"Tell me if anything gets in the way." He began turning the pages.

They watched the road as Trojano steered with two fingers on the wheels, his eyes on the newspaper.

"Red light, Mr Trojano."

He put the brakes on, humming to himself as he read the editorial page.

"Green now."

He drove on, making a left onto the next block, eyes glued to the Letters to the Editor.

"Lady coming . . ."

He blew the horn and the lady scampered, surprised to find a car coming down the wrong side of the street.

"You're in the wrong lane, Mr Trojano."

He touched the wheel lightly as he turned the page, and brought the Hudson back to the right side of the road, holding a steady course, eyes on the sports page.

The Hudson started up the long winding slope of Fuel Street; Trojano seemed to know the turns by heart and went on the sidewalk only once, with the obituary notices.

"Some guys on the road, sir."

He honked and the guys looked up, holding their ground. They were North Side hoods and expected the driver to swerve for *them,* and then, when they saw nothing but an open newspaper at the wheel they jumped, fast, as the rattling Hudson brushed on by them.

"*. . . you son of a bitch!*"

143

Twiller turned, saw one guy pointing at the toe of his engineer boot, which Trojano had run over.

◇ ◇ ◇

SEX - MARRIAGE - PREMARITAL INTERCOURSE
. . . a relationship expressed in premarital sexual intercourse has nothing to recommend it. As well, light and heavy petting can affect our faculties of judgment, and have deleterious effects on the health. And—nothing can cheapen a relationship faster than extra or premarital "love-making."

Doctors unanimously agree that abstinence from sexual intercourse before marriage is in keeping with good moral and physical development. However, in our new, more "modern" day and age, this sound of warning is too often ignored by young people, who plunge headlong into the confusion, conflict, and debilitating health practice of premarital intercourse. How much more sweet and tender their lives would be, if they but waited until marriage, thereby building a life together based on mutual respect and understanding.

If and when you are faced wth the decision of whether or not to satisfy the sexual urge premaritally, remember—by following this dangerous urge, you are going to encounter a lowering of your standard of decency, and possible venereal disease. . . .

He looked up from *Guidebook for a Healthy Life*, horny from reading it. If only he could *find* someone to lower the standard of decency with. He turned toward Tootsie, who favored see-through blouses; the one she had on today was almost completely transparent and it was producing the "dangerous urge" which would soon be satisfied in the lavatory, slumped back on the toilet.

144

She bent down to straighten her loafer, and Twiller ogled the view through her blouse, of soft skin bulging up over the lacy edge of her bra.

His hand went into his pocket. He wouldn't even make it to the lav. His health, he knew, would be deleteriously affected, along with his jockey shorts, but he couldn't help it. He stroked quietly, in premarital intercourse with his thumb and index finger, as Tootsie ran her fingers through her hair, giving him a gorgeous view of straps and flowered cups.

MASTURBATION
Individuals who indulge in this practice often develop serious emotional problems and feelings of inferiority. A good way to solve the problem is through engaging oneself in a hobby.

He shifted in his seat, groaning inside and crossing his legs. The problem was his hobby was masturbation.

They stood on the bridge, looking down at Snake's Junkyard on the riverbank below. "Now there's a good bike." Crutch pointed to a twisted pile of scrap with a pair of handlebars sticking out of it. "Snake said he'd give me a buy on it."

"It looks pretty fucked up."

"It's the bike Benny Zick put under a trolley car." Crutch kicked a stone off the edge of the bridge. "Tootsie might really go for me on a bike like that."

Twiller looked at his buddy. They had three years to go before they could even license a bike, they were still under five feet tall, and the closest either of them would get to Tootsie was one-handed in their own pants. But he felt the same dream, of tearing away on a hot bike, Tootsie hugging on behind him. He leaned further over the rail. "Yeah, it could probably be fixed up . . ."

"Right, the trolley just dragged it a little, before it ran over the motor."

"The fenders look like they're in the gas tank."

"The right tools," said Crutch.

Twiller nodded. They had no tools, and only last week Crutch had almost electrocuted himself with a screwdriver in shop class.

◊ ◊ ◊

The air was cold and the sky overcast. Lily and Wanda Locomovitz were ahead, swinging their books. Their long scarves trailed down over their shoulders. Wanda turned, saw him, and shrieked with laughter, as she usually did when she saw him looking at Lily.

He dodged quickly into the A&P parking lot, over the icy, jagged surface, the ice trapped in swirls of gray, ridged and treaded where the produce trucks had come through.

The wind blew up the driveway, rattling the corrugated doors above the loading platform. Floyd Flynn's high voice came from the other side of the supermarket; the wind whipped it away for a moment and then it came back, babbling and excited.

Twiller crept around the edge of the building. Floyd was moving into the tall weed-trees beside the lot, Bruno Valvona beside him, in a black leather jacket. Floyd extended his umbrella, holding the branches back as he entered the grove. Bruno followed him, his heavy engineer boots crunching on the ice.

Twiller went up the back wall of the parking lot, and crawled along the top of it, until he could see down into the grove. The wind was carrying Floyd's voice over the trees.

"Anything for you, Bruno . . ."

Floyd bent over, spreading his coat on the snow. Bruno

146

drew his leg back and gave Floyd an engineer boot in the ass.

Floyd sprawled face-first into the snow, as two other motorcycle hoods came out of the trees, running toward him for the kickoff.

Floyd spun around, opening his umbrella with a smooth *pop* and defending himself with it, but they knocked it aside and booted him back down.

". . . oh . . . oh . . . help!"

"Here come the cops!" Twiller jumped up on the wall, pointing toward the A&P drive. Bruno and his pals took off through the grove and up the wall. They scrambled over it and bounced down off the trashcans on the other side, shadowboxing, feinting and laughing, throwing lefts and rights, and then disappearing between the other stores.

Twiller climbed down into the grove. The wind was blowing the umbrella over the ice and he grabbed it. Floyd stood slowly, holding his ribs. Twiller handed him the umbrella.

"Thank—you," said Floyd, in a pained whisper.

"You should get one that turns into a sword."

The band was in place below the apron of the stage, and Mr Karey came down the aisle in his pink shoes, baton in hand. He was wearing his gold-threaded jacket and shiny black pants, his hair done in a wild ducktail and he seemed out-of-it as usual. The school gave him a big hand. He waved his baton at them, and took his position in front of the band. The school anthem was struck up and everybody stood to sing. Twiller lifted his voice and went down suddenly, kicked from behind in the kneecaps by Spider. Mr Karey sang as he conducted, his voice rising above the others, but he seemed to be singing in some other language, nobody knew what.

The anthem ended in a crescendo, and Principal Cones came out of the wings, his bald head shining in the spotlight.

147

He walked to the center of the stage, raised his hand for silence and got it, because if he didn't get it, there'd be no show.

"It's time once again for the Annual Talent Contest, and as you know, every year a fine array of gifted classmates come up here on stage and perform for us, and this year is no exception. They've been preparing for a good many weeks and I for one . . ."

Cones liked giving speeches, and was laying it on, spurred by an occasional round of applause tossed at him to keep him going and kill the morning. He complimented the assembly on their school spirit, and gestured toward the wings.

". . . and now, let's have the first of our talented contestants . . ."

A girl in a blue dress came out, rolling a handkerchief in her fingers. She waited, as Mr Karey fumbled with the sheet music, looking for her tune. When he found it he smiled at her, and gave the downbeat. She looked at him as the music poured forth, then looked at the audience, and stood in silence, as if praying. Karey waved his baton happily through the number, during which the girl didn't open her mouth.

They gave her a hearty round of applause as the number ended and she walked off the stage.

Principal Cones appeared again, explaining that there'd been a mix-up. Mr Karey was informed as to which piece of sheet music was required, and he obliged with a little wave of his baton.

The girl was introduced again, returned to the stage, and sang her number.

"Yes, a brave trooper." Principal Cones bounced back into the spotlight. "Let's give her a special hand." He called her back out and she appeared at the edge of the curtain, still twisting her handkerchief. "Very good, thank you so much, we all love the old favorites—and now an exhibition of fancy tumbling by a group of fellows who call themselves the Gymnastics. Gentlemen, the stage is yours . . ."

148

The acts continued, singers, a trumpet solo, a comedy skit, a guy juggling plates, all of which he dropped and broke, ending the act in a pile of broken china and receiving the biggest hand so far.

"Very well," said Principal Cones, "we'll have a few minutes' wait while the dishes are being swept up. Perhaps Mr Karey has a song we all might sing . . ."

Karey flipped through his sheet music, followed by the members of the band, who found the indicated piece and began. Principal Cones smiled and gave little shakes of his bald head, and the audience clapped time and stamped their feet, the stamping growing dangerously loud, like a herd of cattle coming closer every second; Cones raised a nervous finger, signaling Karey, who nodded, waving his baton faster.

Rummmmmmmmmmmmmmmmblerummmmmmmmmmm-mmmblerummmmmmmmmmmmmmmmmmble

Twiller looked overhead and saw the balcony shaking above him, plaster splitting off the base. He crouched, ready to jump, but Karey brought the tune to its conclusion, hair falling in his eyes, baton raised triumphantly.

"Very good, Mr Karey, a most rousing rendition, and will the seating monitors please provide me with the room numbers of those spirited students in the balcony. And now a group of young ladies known to you all, great favorites I'm sure, and the winners of last year's talent show—the Zonkas Sisters!"

The foot stomping began again, along with shouts, cheers, and whistles, as Tootsie, Tomato, and Rita Zonkas came on stage in gowns that squeezed their knockers halfway into the front row. Principal Cones stood beside the American flag, rocking on his heels and tugging at the lapels of his jacket. Mr Karey played for them on his Hawaiian guitar, and the Zonkas sisters sang from the edge of the stage, pouring out their souls.

* * *

149

"Laa-laa-laa-laa laa-laaaaaa
ladda-ladda-ladda laa-laaaaaa . . ."

A spotlight bathed them in blue, their gowns shimmering
as they sang, holding out their arms in unison. A penny arced
through the air, glistening in the spotlight and falling at their
feet. Their voices wavered; Principal Cones whirled around
on his flagpole, flashing his gold teeth with a terrible leer. A
bone-chilling vision of his paddle filled the auditorium immediately. The paddle was three feet long, made for him in
wood shop; he'd let you sign it before he hit you with it; he'd
even let you carve your name in it. Many names were carved
in it now, and when he blasted you with it, it left *Skavazza*
spelled backwards on your ass.

". . . we saaaaaaiiiiiiiidddddd . . .
Laa-laa-laa-laa laa-laaaaaaaaaa . . ."

Septo Kanapka let off one of his inhuman farts, and Twiller was caught directly in it, unable to escape. He leaned
back, holding his nose. Mr Trojano, on the other side of Septo, gave Kanapka a dirty look, but Septo just gazed straight
ahead, smiling. He could clear the entire candy store in 30
seconds.

". . . ladda-ladda-ladda laa-laaaaaaaaa . . ."

Tootsie, Tomato, and Rita sang on, throwing in some syn-
chronized rotations, and when they finished the applause was
tremendous. They bowed, giving everyone a clear shot down
the tops of their gowns. Principal Cones rose up on tiptoe,
holding to his flagpole.

"A wonderful rendition of a popular favorite, thank you so
much, girls, we sincerely appreciate that lovely ballad."
Cones bent and pocketed the penny. "And now for the last

contestant in our Annual Talent Review, Herbert Wron-kee."

Wronkee came out and stepped into the spotlight, picking his nose. The orchestra struck up a dramatic drum roll, and Wronkee began.

"Drink to me only with thine eyes,
and I will pledge with mine . . ."

Twiller knew him from electric shop; he ate his own snot. When he wasn't eating it he was rolling it back and forth in his fingers, making little balls, or laying in a supply of it under the workbench, which was covered with dried green boogers that could be activated in times of shortage.

II

Persons attempting to find a moral will be banished.

—*Mark Twain*

Chapter 23

Hand Me a Half-inch Socket, Will You?

◊ ◊ ◊

The block and tackle swayed and groaned, and the engine rose slowly. The iron cable dug into Twiller's palms, and he heaved again, beneath the high wooden tripod of two-by-fours.

"Keep it comin' . . ." Scuduto stood on the fender, directing the operation, a socket wrench in his hand. The rest of his tools were all neatly arranged in a big upright tool chest just beyond Twiller: he had tremendous admiration for Scudsy, who *knew* what was happening inside cars.

". . . easy . . . not too fast . . . ok, raise 'er . . ."

Twiller strained against the weight, Crutch beside him, pulling on the cable. Metal scraped against metal; he wished some chicks would come along to see this; he was covered with grease. Casually, he wiped a filthy hand across his forehead.

". . . hold it right there . . ."

The motor swung free and they lowered it to the ground. Scuduto gave it a kick. "What a hunk of crap that was.

155

Nothin' but heartache." He undid the hooks and released the chain. "Let's put a real motor in." He nodded toward the shined-up engine, the professional nod of someone in his third year of Automotive at Manual Trades High.

They hooked onto the new engine and raised it up, Scuduto guiding the chain. Twiller wiped his hand across his pants, which looked like he'd been cleaning axles with them.

". . . let 'er down . . ."

If he performed only moderate bathing, grease would still be clinging to him tomorrow, giving his fingernails that handsome mechanical look.

Yeah, we tore out a motor yesterday and slapped in a new one . . .

The motor clanked into place and Scuduto leaned in over it. "She'll burn up the competition." He undid the chain and reached for his other wrenches. "It's one fucker of an engine."

Twiller peered down at the mysterious animal. He'd never understand cars, because he was attending Anthracite Academic, studying science, which he didn't understand either.

"Gimme that half-inch socket . . ."

It passed by him, down into the weird coils and wires and valves.

"It's going to be fast," said Scuduto, "and clean. Doesn't burn a drop of oil. Gimme that vice-grips."

Vice-grips, wrenches, Scuduto had it all, could fix anything on wheels.

"A motor like this is a fuckin' find . . . hold it, Crutch . . ."

Twiller listened to the ratchet teeth of the wrench clicking with that cool sound he longed to make, but he couldn't even take out a sparkplug. The only time he'd tried, his shirttail had gotten caught in the fan belt and he'd nearly strangled.

". . . it cost me a lot of bread, but I'm not gonna be eatin' dust anymore." Scuduto took a wrench and crawled under

156

the car. "Somebody come down here and give me a hand."

Twiller crawled under, took hold of some unknown part of the car and held it in place. Flecks of genuine automotive dirt sprinkled down on him. He continued holding, as a car approached in the alley and came to a stop alongside him.

"*It'll never fly.*" A car door opened and he saw Steve Zuba's acid-eaten *Sunoco* pants, and then beside them a pair of legs he'd know anywhere.

"Alright'," said Scuduto, sliding forward, "don't let it drop." He wriggled out and went above. Twiller stayed below, arms overhead, dirt falling in his face, listening.

"Steve, how's it going?"

"Where'd you get the machinery?"

"Vinny Ventura."

"This is from the car Vinny rolled? You got somethin' then."

"You better believe it."

"You see Vinny in his wheelchair? He's got a hot little electric motor on it."

Twiller's arms began to ache, as Scuduto worked the wrench above, and Lily's legs moved around to the far side of the car.

He tried desperately to think of something to say, so she'd know it was him underneath, slapping in a motor.

Hand me a half-inch socket, will you?

"Hey, we'll catch you guys later."

"Right, Steve, hang loose."

Two car doors slammed, and Steve's wheels peeled away down the alley.

Crutch's face appeared above the motor. "I'd like to check *her* fuckin' oil."

"Steve gettin' any, you think?" Scuduto leaned in beside him.

"Come on, he's got to be . . ."

". . . hand me that half-inch socket."

157

The engine idled with hardly a tremor. Scuduto stepped back. "That's it, motherfucker. We're ready to *burn*."

They slammed the hood, slapped a few tools into the trunk, and climbed in. Scuduto pumped the gas a little, revving it up. "Listen to that . . . listen to *that*."

He popped the clutch and they screeched toward the avenue. Scuduto whipped the steering wheel, straightening out, and floored it. A trememdous explosion shook the hood, the car shuddered, seemed to float, and then stopped dead. Smoke poured from the hood, enveloping the windshield.

Scuduto jumped out and flung up the hood like the lid of a frying pan. A billow of smoke blew around him and then Twiller saw the motor cooking, blue flames leaping from it, wires twisting and melting.

"Sand! Get some sand!"

He ran to the ballfield, filled his shirt with sand and ran back. A customized Chev pulled up, some guys jumped out, yelling, "Piss on it," and Twiller threw his sand.

The fire spread with a swift roar, burning along the wires, licking through the floorboards and the dash. He saw the steering wheel peeling, heard a bottle of beer explode. The flames leapt up, devouring Scuduto's seat covers.

"It's gonna blow."

"I saw one blow last year at Hinkle's garage. Sent the gas tank right through the ceiling."

Scuduto raced to the trunk and yanked out his tools. A jet of water erupted from the radiator. Smoke rolled out from under the fenders, followed by curling flames. The tires blew and sank.

"It's Vinny Ventura's old motor."

"No shit? Must be a curse on the motherfucker."

"We just slapped it in there about an hour ago."

"It's cooling down. I don't think it's gonna blow."

The gas tank blew and Twiller ducked flying metal and

158

glass, tripping backward as the huge bloom of fire leapt up to the telephone wires. Flames spilled along the street and he saw the backseat come down in a tree, springs and stuffing hanging out of it. He got up again, jumped over the burning stream of gasoline and made it to the field. Little kids were dancing around, screaming and waving sticks. The sound of fire engines clanged in the distance. The neighbors were gathering, and he stood in the crowd, letting his grease-covered hands hang out, casually.

Chapter 24

Here Come the Cunt!

◇ ◇ ◇

"No one's home at my house tonight," said Floyd, joining them at the corner. "Let's get some good Scotch."

Spider pulled his knife out of the telephone pole. "Fugazzi's Grill has sneaky-pete wine for half-a-buck a gallon."

Floyd straightened his crisp white cuffs. "Has it got *joie de vivre*?"

"It drives you nuts."

"Sounds good." Crutch dug into his pocket for some dough, and Twiller tossed in what he had, hoping tonight would be the night when he'd finally get tanked and barf like a hero, but booze tasted so bad he wasn't sure he could get enough down to do the job right.

Spider counted the money, and pocketed it smoothly. Floyd turned toward his house. "I'll go and get some sort of buffet started."

"All we want is pussy." Spider took out his little black book and slipped it to Floyd. "Make some phone calls."

"There're nothing but sluts in here." Floyd held the black

book away from him like it was a dead mouse and walked up the sidewalk to his house.

Crutch limped along. "You think any of your girls'll come, Spider?"

"I dunno, maybe we'll pick somethin' up on the way."

"Yeah, gum on our shoe." Crutch put his hands in his pockets and slouched over. Twiller felt the same way. Spider talked a lot of pussy but when it came down to actually producing it, there was none.

But—there was always the *possibility*.

They crossed the avenue, onto Scenic Street, and started down it. Trailers and bungalows lined both sides of it, rusty and rotting at the sills. A mine cave-in below the street had rocked them all lopsided. A man was sitting on his porch chair on such a steep angle it looked like he was going to slide off through the porch rail; but he was smoking a pipe and gazing out peacefully, slantwise into the air.

"You sure Fugazzi's will sell to us, Spider?"

"Yeah . . ."

"You know them, do you?"

"My old man robbed the place."

They moved into Drain Court and continued along it, to the edge of the river, past Snake's Junkyard. They walked slowly, checking out the cars. "I've got my eye on a '40 Chrysler in there," said Crutch.

"How much's Snake want for it?"

"Fifteen bucks. It needs some work."

"What's wrong with it?"

"It's underwater. But the motor's supposed to be good."

"It's underwater?"

"Yeah, that's it, there," Crutch pointed to a banged-up black Chrysler, the front of it submerged, water spilling and splashing through the windows, foam churning around the doors. "Haul it up, clean out the sand, and you'd have something."

They walked along to the end of the junkyard, and then

161

cut off, onto the dirt streets that spread out around the river. The houses were falling apart from being flooded every year, and the smell of the river hung heavy in the air. "I knew a pinhead chick down here," said Spider. "She gave blow-jobs."

Crutch's goggles lit up. "Let's give her a call."

"I think they took her away or somethin'," said Spider.

Crutch slouched over again. "The good stuff always gets by me. I never get a fuckin' break."

Fugazzi's came into view, alongside the railroad trestle. Far up the tracks a freight was slowly chugging along, smoke rising in the dying light. They crossed the potholed street, toward the bar. The neon sign was buzzing, several letters no longer lit. Spider led the way around to the rear.

The backyard was filled with stacked-up beer barrels. They stepped onto a rickety porch and opened the door, into a hallway filled with empty cases. Twiller could hear voices ahead, in the barroom, and Spider pushed through the doorway.

A few men stood at the bar, hunched over their drinks. They looked up bleary-eyed, as Spider fished out his dough.

The bartender wiped his hands in his apron and scooped it up. "How's your old man?"

"Still sewin' mail bags."

The bartender counted the money. "What'll it be?"

"Twenty-five quarts and some of the red stuff."

One of the men, in railroad cap and overalls, came up out of his hunch. "You boys are hard drinkers."

Twiller swelled his chest out and put a foot on the bar rail. He *had* to get loaded tonight and puke all over himself.

The bartender lined the quarts up on the bar. "Cold ones." He dug back down under the bar and came up with three unlabeled gallon jugs. "And the red stuff."

The sound of the freight train got louder and the barroom

162

started to vibrate. The old railroader pulled out his pocket watch and checked it with a nod. "Right on time . . ."

The bottles on the wall began to bounce and everyone held their glasses. The roar was deafening, the whole place shaking; the hanging lamps swung back and forth, tin shades rattling, and then the freight was on by, caboose wheels clicking.

"Enough to give a man the shakes." One of the drunks raised a trembling hand.

"Have one on me, Ned." The bartender tipped the bottle.

"Much obliged . . ."

Twiller knew that this would one day be *his* bar, where he'd get served anytime he wanted without having to come in the back door. The good days were ahead.

"Hey," said one of the bar-props, staring at him over his drink, "ain't you shortstop for Certified Concrete? Up the Junior League?"

Twiller nodded.

"Give that ballplayer one on me." The bar-prop waved a floppy arm and swiveled on his stool. "He scoops 'em up the way I did in the old days." He bent down to the floor for a ground ball and collapsed in the sawdust.

The old railroader leaned over and helped him up. "Settle on your stool, Mike, don't rush yerself . . ."

". . . the St. Patty's nine . . . never been a team like 'er sinct . . ." The retired shortstop adjusted his sleeves and lowered his elbows back to the bar.

The bartender pushed the bags toward Spider. "You guys better shove off."

"Right," said Spider. "We'll catch you later."

"Be good, boys," called the shortstop.

"Oh, they're good boys alright," said the railroader.

◇ ◇ ◇

Floyd hurried to let them in. He'd put on a satiny smoking jacket and was using a long cigarette holder. "Now listen, we must try not to break anything." He gestured with his cigarette holder, toward the little tables and knickknacks and spindly antique chairs that filled the house. Twiller followed him toward the kitchen, the wine jugs in his arms. The rooms were all spotless, and hung with thick drapes, everything in its proper place, faintly gleaming with polish.

". . . careful, careful . . ." Floyd directed traffic into the kitchen. "Mother will have a fit if we disturb anything. Set the bottles down there—"

"Did you call any pussy?"

Floyd pointed to a little alcove, where Rider Wendorf sat with the telephone and Spider's black book.

"Rider, you have any luck yet?"

"I'm workin' on it . . ."

Floyd poured the wine. "It smells like shoe polish."

Twiller took a glass and put it to his lips.

A sophisticate, at last.

"God . . ." Floyd wrinkled up his face. "It *tastes* like shoe polish."

Spider drained his glass and refilled it. "Old Lady Fugazzi makes it herself."

"Where, in her armpit?" Floyd set his glass down, unfinished.

Twiller wandered back through the house, glass in hand, dreaming of the bachelor pad he'd have someday. There wouldn't be so many little chairs all around, he'd rather have a pool table in the living room, and maybe a pinball machine.

He stopped, examining Mrs. Flynn's wallpaper. It was very thick, the flowers made out of some kind of fuzzy material. He'd paper his own pad with full-page pictures cut out of *Sport* magazine, you couldn't beat that for color.

"What're ya lookin' at, fucknuts?" Spider came by, carrying a jug of wine and a glass. The walls in the Pronka apartment, Twiller recalled, were decorated with newspaper photos of Old Man Pronka being handcuffed to a radiator by the police.

The front doorbell rang, and Floyd hurried past them, straightening his ascot. He paused at the door for a moment, drawing himself up and clicking his heels like his own butler, then turned the knob. "Leo, Leo . . . *do* come in."

Leo Bodell came through, carrying his accordion. He was growing a successful mustache. Twiller ran a quick check in the mirror on his own mustache—a few scraggly hairs that looked like they were pasted on.

Leo took a glass of wine, knocked it back with one gulp, and then took hold of a quart of beer. Twiller felt Leo was an important addition to the gang, a guy who could really drink, *and* grow a mustache and play the accordion.

"Give us a tune on the box, Leo."

Leo chugged back some more booze, lit up a cigarette, and opened the straps of his accordion, while Twiller watched on, feeling the way he always felt when Leo played, like the chicks had to arrive at any moment to hear the kind of gang they had—talented guys, and unusual too—like Rider Wendorf, who'd get drunk and ride around the room in circles, bent wrist still holding the reins, a guy who'd really adjusted to a serious handicap in life.

Great fucking wonderful guys.

Twiller felt the love swelling in his chest, as Leo started to roll with "Lady of Spain." The smoke curled up from Leo's cigarette, and he squinted his eyes in a really cool way, looking sort of like a sleazy Mexican bandit.

"He plays divinely." Floyd sat in a gilt-trimmed chair, legs crossed, a quart of beer in his hand. "He should be on television."

Twiller nodded. Leo was definitely going somewhere. They all were—Crutch wanted his own car wash, Floyd was going to be an actor, Spider would probably go to Alcatraz, Scuduto was going to race at the Holiday Drag Strip.

165

You guys are the best, he said in his heart, and took another swallow of Mrs. Fugazzi's shoe polish. A warm glow spread through him, and he almost felt like crying.

Leo swung into some classical stuff, his fingers whizzing up and down the keys.

"Gershwin," said Floyd, and dimmed the overhead chandelier.

"Here come the cunt!" Crutch stumbled toward the door. Twiller whipped out his comb, giving a fast one to his pompadour. Crutch opened the door and looked out. "Wait a second, wait . . . I was wrong, it's just Scuduto."

"You fuckin' scumbag." Spider put his thumbs on Crutch's Coke-bottle glasses. "Get a new pair."

"I thought it was Gina Gabooch." Crutch wiped his glasses off. "Her brother's got a Ford like Scudsy's."

"Her brother's an asshole."

"Angelo Gabooch is a tough motherfucker, Spider."

Spider pulled out his rod. "I'll part his fuckin' hair."

Floyd pointed his cigarette holder at Spider. "There's to be *no* shooting in this house."

The door opened and Scuduto came in, like a greased skunk, white stripes down his black peg-pants, his hair shining with Wildroot Cream Oil.

"Gimme five." He laid out his palm and Spider slapped him down, after which Scuduto went to the living room mirror and checked himself out.

Every hair was in place, his ducktail swooping around over his ears and tucking together in a perfect seam in back of his head. "Where are the cunt?" He turned in the mirror, checking each angle.

"They're coming, Scudsy." Crutch tipped a quart of beer to his lips. "They said they couldn't wait to see you."

"I'm ready for them." Scuduto slowly rolled up the sleeve of his Hawaiian shirt, flattening his bicep against his side until it spread out into something resembling a muscle. "Look at this fuckin' definition."

"Looks good, Scudsy, looks *very* powerful."

Rider Wendorf came through and handed Spider the little black book back. "I made fifty-two calls."

"And . . ."

"Nobody's comin'."

"You fuckin' loser." Spider slapped the book back into his pocket. "Don't you know how to talk to chicks?"

"I mentioned your name, Spider, and a couple of them got sick."

Floyd tapped a long cigarette ash into Scuduto's cuff. "It's a bachelor party. There's nothing wrong with that."

"Ah, shit . . ." Crutch flopped down in a chair. "It's gonna turn into another dick-measuring contest."

Twiller emptied his glass and started a second one. The warm glow had spread all over him. It was the best party he'd ever been to and he didn't care who came. He was on his second glass of wine and going strong. He sipped another mouthful and returned to listening to Leo, who was shaking the bellows, smoke in his eyes, fingers flying.

"Work it on out, Leo . . ." He felt he was a *good* listener, who could be counted on to mutter a few authentic phrases at the right time.

The door opened and Schunkenfeld came through, smiling his moron's smile. " 'Lo, fellas. Havin' a party?"

"Yeah, Schunky, grab a seat."

They poured him a glass of wine and he smiled into it. "I seed Bunny and Wanda at the playfroun'. I tolt dem come, they said ok."

"They're coming?" Crutch jumped out of his chair. "Bunny and Wanda are coming?"

"Yeah, comin' along behint me."

Scuduto spun back to the mirror, checking his ducktail again, and Twiller tried to stand, but his legs were suddenly rubbery and the hinges were gone from his knees. He sank back into his chair and picked up a big metal ashtray in which to check out his hair. His reflection was warped, his pompadour looked like an opposum was riding sideways on his head.

"Bunny and Wanda . . ." Crutch was limping excitedly back and forth and Rider started riding around the dining room table. Leo got up and rode behind him, playing the Lone Ranger's theme. Twiller struggled to his feet, into the vision of Bunny and Wanda that now filled the room. He downed his glass of wine and poured a third round for himself; he'd be good and ready when they arrived, maybe he'd even have the blind staggers.

Rider rode on by, Leo behind him, and Twiller joined the dance, around the long antique table. What a wonderful party, with his wonderful pals, everybody joining now—Spider and Scudsy and Floyd and Schunky—everybody riding around the table, shouting and screaming. Floyd took a flying ballet leap, his smoking jacket flapping. "Oh god, I'm pissed already . . ."

Floyd's mother would be happy, Twiller thought, to see her son enjoying himself with his friends, hanging from the curtain rod.

They rode faster, Leo speeding up the tune, accordion bouncing on his chest. Twiller could feel a special magic coming into the air—Rider tossed a beer bottle against the wall and caught it on the first bounce, a *difficult* catch, foam spilling all over the wall, the rug, and Rider's cowboy shirt.

". . . this fuckin' box . . ." Leo shrugged off his accordion, tossed it into a chair, and clicked on the big upright radio.

. . . Uuuuuuuuuuuuuuuuu-wha,   uuuuuuuuuu-whaaaaaaaaaa   Uuuu-uuu-uuu-uuu-uuuuuuuuuuuuuuuuuuuuuuuuuuuuuuuuu-wha . . .

The beautiful words broke over them, *their* tune, a deeply meaningful sound that brought the tears to Twiller's eyes as he rode hard to the beat, waving his wine glass over his head.

This was forever, this was the gang, the gang that would never die.

Leo jumped onto the dining room table and began to dance.

"Go, Leo, go!"

He had a quart of beer to his lips and was guzzling it, fingers snapping, the contents of the quart sinking slowly.

"Do it, Leo, do it, baby . . ."

Twiller circled with the others cheering Leo on. Heavy drinking like this could make a gang famous. He whistled and shouted, and Leo swallowed the last bit of foam, face screwing up into a really cool nauseated shudder, and then Leo let out a scream, his feet flying into a flurry of dance steps, as everybody clapped time. Twiller downed his third wine and started a fourth, wishing he could dance like Leo, like a spastic chicken.

Leo's hair fell into his eyes, his body freakishly twisting to the beat, as if he were being screwed down through the table top. He froze, arms contorted, knees knocked, and then tore his shirt off with a demented cry, buttons popping across the room. He bent down, reared back, and took a flying leap toward the window.

Rider and Scuduto caught him mid-flight, but he tangled in the drapes and brought them down around himself, onto the floor, the rod bending across his head. He was wet as a snail and babbling.

"Well," said Floyd, looking at the heap on the floor. "Mother *will* shit her pants over this."

Twiller picked up the wine jug and put the whole thing to his lips, chug-a-lugging the sneaky-pete straight down. He gurgled and slobbered, spilling it all over himself and making a terrific nauseated face.

"Way to go, Twiller . . ."

He lowered the jug with a proud smile, and casually passed it on. He took hold of his shirt and prepared to rip it off, but his fingers weren't working right, everything was starting to

169

spin, and he was falling on the floor. He heard Floyd shouting, "He needs air, loosen his trousers!" and then everything went black.

◇ ◇ ◇

He woke in a puddle of barf.
He'd done it, he'd puked like a hero.
He smiled and rolled over.
The guys were standing around the dining room table. Floyd was moving along with the tape measure.
Twiller tried to rise, but someone had fastened his shoes to the molding.
Or am I glued to the floor?
He felt terribly weak all over. "Hey, where are . . . the chicks?"
Spider looked down through the smoke. "Fuckhead is awake."
"Did . . . Wanda and Bunny make it, Spider?"
"They gave everybody a handjob, except you."
Crutch called from the other end of the table. "Don't worry, nobody came." He pushed Floyd's hand. ". . . watch the fingers when you measure . . ."
"I was *just* trying for *accuracy*." Floyd's smoking jacket was hanging off him, pockets ripped apart, sash dragging the floor. "Anyway, Leo's clearly the winner again." He pointed with his broken cigarette holder.
Scuduto grabbed the tape measure. "Gimme that fuckin' thing. You missed a half-inch of *root* . . ."
Twiller looked up at the ceiling. The floor was whirling again, and he grabbed at it, calling for help, but it was too late, he was going under.

◇ ◇ ◇

He woke outside, toes dragging, arms stretched like a scarecrow over Crutch and Schunky.

170

The toes of his blue suede shoes were getting badly scuffed, he might never get the sheen back into them. He tried to navigate, but his shoes were on the wrong feet, were pointing out instead of in, he could see them trying to walk in two different directions.

"This is your house, Twiller, there's your front door. Can you make it?"

He staggered across the sidewalk toward the porch. The stairs were on ball bearings and started to move sideways. The house turned upside-down, and he puked in the hedges, collapsing over the top of them. He hung there, head down, retching painfully, but nothing more came up.

The dry heaves, he'd heard about them. You had to be pret-ty cool to get into *that* scene.

Chapter 25

. . . In Which Lord Henry Brinthrope
Composes Himself.

He stood by the window and watched his parents' taillights
disappearing, for the weekend. He was in charge of the house
now, a grown-up son who could be trusted—a thoughtful,
conscientious son a mother and father could count on to
watch over things.

He went to the telephone.

"They're gone."

"*We're on the way.*"

He hung up the phone and walked down the hall, wishing
he owned a smoking jacket like Floyd's.

He walked to the kitchen and stared out the back window
into the valley, its dark slopes lit by soft Christmas lights, the
whole valley flickering with elves on the rooftops, and rein-
deer, and Santa's sled, and beyond all these, burning bright
as always, the great slag pile, coal-gas flames dancing around
to the very top, where the rotten-egg fumes were curling and
drifting off toward the twinkling houses.

172

A monocle would complete his wardrobe, along with a trumpet.

He opened the old man's liquor cabinet, under the sink, and poured himself a Scotch on the rocks. Then he walked to the window and studied his reflection in the glass.

Lord Henry Brinthrope of Black Swan Hall.

All I need is a thundering concerto in the background.

Lord Henry took a sip of Scotch. The flames hit his throat and he choked, backfiring the drink up his nose. Burning snot flew out of his nostrils and he clung to the sink.

The doorbell rang and Lord Henry composed himself, sinuses blazing. He walked back through Black Swan Hall, to the front door.

Spider, Crutch, and Leo came in, and Lord Henry led them to the kitchen sink for a gentlemanly toast to the coming new year. "We can't take too much or the old man'll get wise." He poured a round for each of them, and they raised their glasses.

"Up yours." Spider tipped his down, and Lord Henry and the others followed, Lord Henry managing to swallow most of his drink, coughing only a small portion of it up behind his eyebrows. He clung to the sink, gasping. ". . . smooth . . . very smooth . . ."

A roar split the darkness, fiery exhaust burning into the driveway. He went to the door again as Scuduto and Floyd slid into the front yard on Scudsy's new motorcycle. Floyd's polka-dot bow tie was twisted and his hair was hanging in his face, but every wave on Scuduto's head was still in place, locked in grease. He came in, carrying his portable radio, tuned to *their* station, the one that played the finest sounds.

Did-a-liddle-liddle-liddle-lit-yea-ah
did-a-liddle-liddle-liddle-lit-yea-ah . . .

"We stopped by the liquor store." Floyd opened his um-

173

brella, and several dozen brandy samplers fell out onto the floor.

"There are glasses in the kitchen," said Lord Henry, and excused himself for a moment, to the bathroom, in order to complete his preparations for the evening by painting his nose. He picked up the bottle of pimple cream.

> "I WAS ASHAMED OF MY FACE . . .
> *until Viderm made my dreams*
> *of a clearer skin come true . . ."*

Lord Henry covered the pimple completely with pink cream. He now appeared to be wearing, for the Christmas season, a pink berry on the end of his nose.

He returned to his guests and found them pooling their money on the coffee table. "Alrigh'," said Scuduto, scooping up the dough, "I'll make the run."

"I'll come with you," said Lord Henry, in need of a little air after imbibing Scotch through his nasal passages.

They went into the yard and he climbed on back of the shining bike. Scuduto revved it up and they skidded out onto the bare pave. It was freezing cold, and Scuduto gunned the engine, bending over the handlebars, the wind in his face, every hair still holding around his head, which gleamed with grease. Lord Henry clung tight, drinking in long gulps of air as the Christmas lights went by in streaks of blue and red and green, twisting, tangling, breaking free again, looping porches, shrubbery, and chimneys.

They dipped down Scenic Street, past the sinking houses. Santa Claus smiled from a cockeyed doorway, and strings of lights hung from the upended porch rails.

Scuduto cornered and gunned the big bike again, toward the river. Lord Henry shivered on back, as the river lights went by in a blur. Scuduto peered back over his shoulder, looking like Marlon Branflakes, and made the turn toward Fugazzi's.

174

The bike bounced along the potholed street, Lord Henry going up and down in back. Scuduto whipped the bike into Fugazzi's drive and hit the brakes; Lord Henry shot forward into Scuduto's ducktail; grease plugged up his nostrils and he fought to get his breath.

"Watch it," growled Scuduto, his comb coming around in a flash, the sharp teeth raking Lord Henry's noseberry.

They climbed off the bike and walked over to the back door of Fugazzi's and into the dark hallway. Low voices came from ahead, and then stopped as they entered the barroom.

"Merry Christmas, boys." The bartender gave them a friendly wave. The mirror behind him was decorated with faded sagging streamers and a couple of dead-looking wreaths. "What'll it be?"

"Quarts."

"And three gallons of the red stuff," said Lord Henry, knowledgeable now about such matters—Mrs Fugazzi's own home brew, a young little wine for the worst headache of your life, lasting three days.

"You're good for twenty quarts." The bartender counted their money into the cash register.

"Only twenty this time?" The old railroader was in the same place at the bar he'd been a month ago, looking like he hadn't moved once during that time. "They bought twenty-five last time. The boys are slippin'."

The retired shortstop beside him peered over his glass. "Yeah, but there's only two of them this time . . ."

The bartender pushed the quarts over the bar. "Twenty cold ones, three gallons of the red stuff, and you don't know where you bought it."

They gathered up the bags and headed for the door, as the bar began to vibrate, the dusty Christmas wreaths trembling on the mirror. They walked through the hall and out the back door, into the roar of the passing train. Scuduto gunned his bike and they jumped forward, Lord Henry grabbing tightly

175

onto the four sweaters Scudsy was wearing to make himself appear muscular.

The train cut along through the dark and they raced it, pulling steadily ahead, Lord Henry huddling, the booze cradled in his lap. Scuduto's shining ducktail was before his eyes, the waves like pieces of chiseled coal dipped in Crisco.

They turned away from the tracks, leaving the train to curve away into the dark valley. Scuduto leaned them onto Scenic Street again, Lord Henry leaning with him, as they followed the sloping path of Christmas lights. The headlamp of the bike bounced a crazy beam over the broken-up pavement, Lord Henry's kidneys shaking out of place, and then they shot over the top.

The trolley clanged frantically as Scuduto knifed in front of it. Lord Henry closed his eyes and hugged tighter to Scuduto's four sweaters. They slipped on by, and leaned into the turn toward Lord Henry's manor. The familiar houses were a single streak of light, lasting only a second, and then the big bike was biting at the gravel in the driveway. Lord Henry stepped off nonchalantly, and threw up in the bushes.

"What's wrong with you?" Scuduto picked up the fallen packages and Lord Henry indicated by a faint gesture that it was nothing to be concerned over, he would remain here in the bushes, retching, for a moment longer.

". . . arrrrghhhhhhh . . . ahhhhhhhhhhgggggg . . . oh goggggggg . . ."

"I'm goin' in." Scuduto went up the back stairs, toward the kitchen, and Lord Henry went into the cellar, groping his way toward the laundry sink, where he proceeded to freshen up a bit and wash the supper out of his nose.

". . . snnnnnshhhhhhh . . . snissshhhhhhhh . . ."

Having cleared his nasal passages, he sweetened his breath with a few squirts from his pocket atomizer of Lavoris.

"And now . . ."

176

He walked toward the cellar stairs and climbed upward, into the house.

Gina Gabooch was standing in the kitchen, a most incredible sight, a live chick attending one of their parties. Looking around quickly, he noticed signs of more chickies from Gina's gang, in the other room.

He was giving *the* party of the season.

Leo Bodell bopped through, shirt already in shreds, and pulled Gina into some spastic dancing. She sneered and glided with him, her steps slow, owing to the enormous engineer boots she was wearing.

Lord Henry loved her. Her eyebrows were two black threads, and a white skull was painted on the back of her jacket, with white roses around it, dripping blood.

"How about some red stuff?" he asked with a debonair flourish. She ignored him, fascinated as she was by Leo's Mexican mustache and his shirt hanging off in casual pieces.

"He even ate the buttons," said Crutch.

Lord Henry shook his head sadly. How could he compete with that?

He poured himself a glass of wine, and continued to gaze at Gina's black jeans, the zipper on her back pocket stretching as she bent her hip out with Leo. Leo screamed like a ruptured monkey and tore off what remained of his shirt. Lord Henry studied the move, wondering if he'd ever achieve such spontaneous sophistication.

Crutch pushed his glasses back on his nose. "If she kicked you with those boots . . ."

Lord Henry nodded. She was carrying steel toes around, and could easily shatter your shinbone.

She turned their way as she danced, and her black eyes gave Lord Henry a chill. She was tough, and her brother Angelo was tougher. Lord Henry hoped Angelo would not put in an appearance at the party, as it would undoubtedly result

177

in somebody getting decked, probably himself, in his role as host.

Crutch chewed a fingernail. "I hear Angelo fuckin' near killed a guy at the B-Z Lounge last month."

Lord Henry took his eyes off Gina. Angelo had hung one of Gina's dates upside-down from their second-floor apartment, causing comb and car keys to fall to the sidewalk below.

"I'm gonna check out the other chicks."

"They're all from Gina's gang." Crutch started on another fingernail. "A bunch of ballbreakers."

Lord Henry walked into the living room. Four more motor-cycle mamas were there, bopping with each other. Scuduto was eyeing them, and flexing his sweaters.

"He's going to do something violent," said Floyd, sipping brandy in the easy chair.

Scuduto put the wine jug to his lips and started guzzling. Trickles of red ran down the corners of his mouth, and one of the chicks said, "Go, daddy . . ."

Scuduto lowered the jug, and then turned, head down. He charged across the room past the chicks and drove his head into the wall.

Bouncing back, every hair in place, he rolled his shoulder padding. His eyes were glassy from a severe blow on the head, but he managed a sneer.

"Lookin' good, baby . . ." The chickies bopped on.

Scuduto lowered his head again and charged the other wall. He hit like a battering ram and his head disappeared into the plaster.

"Hey, how a-bout that . . ."

His body dangled limply against the wall. The rest of the party gathered to look at him. "Right through to the stud-ding . . ."

"Yeah, look, that's wiring by his ear."

Lord Henry began loosening the plaster around Scuduto's head, then pried apart the broken laths. Scuduto fell out,

178

onto the floor. There was plaster in his ducktail, but every hair was in place.

"Loosen his trousers."

"We should tie him up," said Crutch.

"We can't tie him up," said Lord Henry, "he's a pal."

"Well," said Crutch, "let's roll him in the rug."

They carried Scuduto to the end of the rug and tucked it around him. Then they rolled him in it, across the room, and stood him up in a corner.

"That's good," said Crutch, "he's out of the way, but he can still enjoy himself." Scuduto looked out from the top of the rug, smiling dizzily.

The front door opened and Steve Zuba and Lily came through. Lily's eyes met Lord Henry's; their memories crossed through the smoke, to the afternoon long ago, when he'd welcomed her to his birthday party and she'd come in with Band-Aids on her knees. He started to speak, but Leo raced into the living room, in his underpants.

"He ripped his chinos to bits," said Floyd, holding one of the pockets in his hand.

Leo's jockey shorts had gotten pink in the washing machine and there were holes worn in the rear, a nice little touch of disdain chic, reflected Lord Henry, making a mental note to fray his own underwear with a hammer at first opportunity.

"Let's BOP!" Leo began bouncing around on the furniture. His bare chest was scrawny, and his mustache now made him look like an undernourished Mexican jumping bean, but Lord Henry could see that Leo's uninhibited dancing style was attracting glances from the chicks; his leap from footstool to sofa was especially impressive; the sofa sagged down with a creak and a spring came up between the cushions with a *boinnnnngg*, as Leo sprang off the top of it, onto the easy chair.

"Rockrockrockrock . . ." Leo bounced away, back through the hall to the kitchen.

179

Steve Zuba pointed toward the drive. "Whose bike is that?"

Crutch nodded toward Scuduto. Zuba walked over to him. "Hey, Scudsy, lemme have a ride on your bike."

"Get me outta here, Steve. I'm rolled up in a fuckin' rug."

"Don't let him out," said Crutch. "He'll put his head through the wall again."

"Hey," said Scuduto, "that was just for laughs."

"Here, Scudsy . . ." Crutch put a quart of beer up to Scuduto's lips, and Scuduto guzzled, head back.

Twiller stepped in beside Zuba. "Here are the keys to the bike. Scudsy won't mind."

Zuba went out the door and Twiller went over to Lily. "How've you been . . ."

A motorcycle exploded out of the drive and burned up the street.

"You have wild parties." She had her hands in her jacket pockets. Her eyes were dark with makeup, but he saw the little girl in her eyes, in back of the silver-blue shadow.

He pointed toward the closet. "Do you remember?"

"Wasn't that the post office?"

"It still is." He snuck his arm around her waist, edging her into the shadows of the hallway. She moved with the touch of his arm as if they were dancing, and raised her lips, her eyes slowly closing as he drew her to him.

"Help!"

Floyd appeared on the stairs just above them. "They're trying on your mother's jewelry!"

"What?"

"And her lingerie!" Floyd panted down the stairs, his bow tie flopping. "It's scandalous . . ." He wiped his forehead limply, and sank onto the bottom step.

Lord Henry turned to Lily. This was the sort of high excitement that might add to his image. "Excuse me a moment . . ." He ran up the stairs to the bedroom, and burst through heroically.

All the bureau drawers were open. Gina Gabooch was looking at herself in the vanity mirror, a string of artificial pearls around her neck. "Relax, honey." She spoke to his reflection in the mirror. "We're just havin' a little fashion show."

"Hey, get the fuck outta here." Lord Henry advanced cautiously, toward Gina's girlfriend, who was slightly smaller and did not, so far as he knew, have a dangerous brother.

She had his mother's nightgown up against herself. She lowered it slowly, drew a switchblade, and murmured softly, "*Back off . . .*"

He backed off, out into the hallway and closed the door behind him. Floyd was standing there, sipping brandy. He handed it to Lord Henry, who downed the sweet drink, taking new courage.

"Where's Spider?"

"In your bedroom."

Lord Henry ran down the hall and plunged into the darkened room. There was a pile of black leather on the floor, and two shadowy figures in the sheets. Spider's ass was going up and down.

"Spider, give me your rod."

Spider's ass froze and he looked around over his shoulder. "You stupid fuck, I'm in the saddle."

"Hey, Spider, this is an emergency."

"In my pants, on the bedpost."

Lord Henry fished out the rod and raced back into the hall. Floyd opened the door to the parental bedroom with a little bow. Lord Henry ran through, and fired.

The bullet came out sideways as usual, but the girls didn't know that, and fell on the floor screaming, as the wall three feet to the right of them opened with a tiny puff of plaster.

Gina removed the artificial pearls very slowly. "Don't do

anything bad, honey . . ." She dropped the pearls alongside her on the floor.

"Move out." He waved the warped blackened gun barrel and they moved, crawling through the doorway, into the hall. He stepped quickly after them and they jumped up and thundered down the stairs in their heavy boots.

He watched them go, and coolly jammed the gun into his belt. A difficult situation had been handled. Angelo Gabooch would now come by and hang him upside-down out the window.

"That was *marv*-elous . . ." Floyd walked with him to the stairs. "We're not going to let anybody push *us* around."

Lord Henry maintained a steely silence, though inwardly the picture of himself hanging upside-down out the window persisted. He descended the stairs, and searched the smoky living room for Lily, but she wasn't there. Then he saw the closet door ajar, and realized—she was waiting for him.

Da-da-da-da-doooooooo dough-da
da-dough da-dough da-dough daaaaaaaa . . .

The powerfully moving music swelled around him as he crossed the room, and opened the door.

She had her arms around Leo, her skin-tight jeans pressed against his pink underpants.

A motorcycle roared up the driveway and she slipped out of Leo's arms and on past Lord Henry, into the smoke. He followed her across the room to the window, where she stood by the Christmas tree, looking out toward the driveway.

Lord Henry picked an ornament from the tree—a large one, with artificial snowflakes covering it. He popped it into his mouth and gazed at Lily. She stared back. He bit down, crushing the ornament and chewing it, pieces of broken glass and snowflakes falling from his lips.

"Twiller, for Crissakes . . ." Crutch was on him, holding him from behind.

182

Lord Henry broke away, grabbed an open quart of beer and swallowed, the pieces washing down with surprising smoothness.

. . . du-du da-duuuuuuuuuuu
da-du da-du-du da-duuuuuuuuuuu . . .

Lily was staring at him, but he couldn't really tell if she was impressed. He hauled out Spider's revolver and pointed it toward the open closet. "Everybody out of the way!"

"Hey, Twiller, hey . . ."

"Don't go near him, he's nuts!"

He extended his arm, aiming at the closet. Scuduto, rolled up beside it in the rug, looked toward the barrel, terror in his eyes.

"Twiller, that gun don't shoot straight."

Lord Henry aimed at the lightbulb hanging in the closet, and fired. Three shelves above it, his basketball exploded.

The living room cleared, guests jumping over the furniture and scrambling toward the door.

BLAM!

Pinocchio, hanging from strings in the closet, dropped his head. Scuduto, rolled in the rug, moved his lips silently.

BLAM!

BLAM!

Lord Henry lowered the revolver, feeling that he had definitely become the life of the party.

Except the party seemed to be over. He was standing alone with Scuduto in the pistol smoke, with a Christmas tree ornament in his stomach.

. . . mum-mitty mum-ah
mum-mitty-mummmmmmmmmmmm . . .

The haunting tune echoed through the empty room, as the smoke started to settle around the furniture and glasses. Scuduto had fainted, head drooping over the edge of the rug. Twiller went to the window and looked out.

The motorcycle bounced out of the drive, Floyd bent over the handlebars, long bow tie trailing behind him.

◇ ◇ ◇

Lord Henry woke on the floor in the early dawn, with a terrible pain in his stomach.

The floor was covered with booze and broken bottles lay in every corner, cigarette butts inside them. Scuduto was asleep in the rug, standing up by the closet door. Lord Henry rose and walked bent over in pain through the wreckage, toward the kitchen.

Crutch was asleep on the kitchen counter, one hand in a box of pretzels.

A piece of glass shifted in Lord Henry's bowels, and he collapsed on the floor, drawing his knees up into his stomach.

The glass moved slowly, stabbing its way along. "Crutch . . ." He reached up, shaking Crutch by the arm.

Crutch raised himself and stared at the pretzel box on his hand. "Where . . . am I?"

"In the manor."

Crutch swung his leg around and slipped down off the counter. "We've got to clean up before your parents get back."

The lord of the manor rolled over on his side, elbows pressed into his stomach. "I've got a Christmas tree ornament . . . inside me."

"Come on, get up. Walking is an aid to digestion." Crutch yanked him to his feet and they walked to the living room.

Scuduto looked up from inside the rug. "Hey, let me out of this thing."

"Look at the fuckin' hole you put in the wall." Crutch twisted him around in the rug.

"I've got a head like fuckin' steel."

They lowered the rug and unrolled him. He spun out the other end of it and flopped around on the floor, unable to stand up.

Lord Henry draped himself over a footstool and rocked slowly back and forth, massaging his aching bowels.

Crutch went to the wall, examining the hole. "We're gonna need plaster and paint."

"I spent the night in a rug." Scuduto got up, swinging his arms around. "It's hard to believe."

Crutch picked at the broken plaster, removing the loose pieces. "We shoulda put you in the toilet."

"Hey listen—" Scuduto flexed his knees up and down. "—the old man's got everything we need in his workshop. We can fix that hole in no time."

"Come on, Twiller, on your feet, we're goin' to Scudsy's."

Lord Henry stood, fists balled into his stomach. They went out the front door. Scuduto looked around the hard frozen ground. "Where's my bike?"

"Floyd took it." Lord Henry started to walk, head between his knees.

"Son of a bitch, he can't ride a bike."

"He had it wide open."

"We'll find him in a fuckin' ditch."

They went down the driveway, to the alley. Lord Henry felt his stomach coming up, and held on to a tree, sucking air.

If I heave, the glass might tear my nose apart.

He continued hobbling along, arms pressed into his abdomen. The glass kept moving in waves, and he hung on to telephone poles as they walked. The found Floyd at the end of the alley, in a ditch, feet in the air, motorcycle on top of him.

"Hey, Floyd, hey . . ."

They lifted the motorcycle off him and shook him awake. His eyelids fluttered and he stared up at them dumbly.

"You fuckin' maniac . . ." Scuduto prowled around the bike suspiciously. ". . . look at the scratch on this fender."

"Oh, blow it out your ass." Floyd got slowly to his feet. Twiller crawled toward the bushes. An incredibly wicked shit was coming out of nowhere, *at once.* He dove in the bushes and dropped his pants. "Anybody got any tissues?"

Crutch stood outside the bushes and handed some in. "The jack-off artist is always prepared."

Lord Henry rocked and moaned, as the ornament started to slice through.

"Did you eat the little wire hook too?"

"No, just the ball." Sweat broke out on his brow and he started trembling, the broken glass jabbing and scratching his frightened asshole. He began to sing. "Oh little town of Bethlehem," as he grunted and pressed.

"You can always get a job in the circus," said Crutch.

◊   ◊   ◊

". . . and this!" His father pointed to the broken spring in the couch, sticking up through the cushions.

From the top of the stairs, his mother's wailing voice sobbed out: "There's a bullet in the bedroom wall!"

"Do you know what you are?" asked his father coldly.

Lord Henry looked down at the rug, his gaze traveling along it toward the kitchen. At least the kitchen looked ok. Crutch had even waxed the linoleum.

"You're an animal."

His mother's slow stunned footsteps came down the stairs. "Everything smells of beer . . ." She stood on the last step, drawing herself up dramatically as her eyes swept across the living room. ". . . and the *wall.*" She pointed to the beautiful patch Scuduto had labored over. "It's ruined." She broke down, sobbing. "I just can't believe what's happened . . ."

"Bums." His father paced the floor. "No-good rotten bums."

186

"Crackers . . ." His mother pointed to the rug, where Leo had done some interpretive dancing, on a package of saltines. "It'll never be the same. It's permanently stained. Our brand-new rug . . ."

His father swung around toward him. "Do you know how much it costs to get a rug cleaned?"

"No."

"You're going to find out."

His mother sank into the easy chair, her blond hair falling tragically over one eye. The other eye was brimming with tears. "There's beer on the ceiling."

"You've come to the end of the road, mister." His father spun around again, finger pointed. "This I-don't-give-a-damn attitude of yours is over with. From here on in, you're paying your own way."

"What do you mean?"

"Never mind what I mean." His father paced away toward the other end of the room.

His mother stood, dabbing at her eyes. Her voice had taken on a tone that weighed like a stone. "I have to lie down. I'm not feeling well . . ."

She walked back toward the stairs and started slowly up them. His father nodded toward her bent, climbing form. "You've upset your mother terribly." His voice implied dark organic disturbances. Twiller struggled with the mountainous guilt rising in him. "It was just a party, Dad."

"Son . . ." His father used the word like a vile poison flowed inside it. ". . . you'd better straighten yourself out—in a hurry. That's all I can say."

The old man sighed, and sank down onto his sofa. The broken spring stuck up alongside him. He looked at it, looked up at his son, then shook his head sadly and bent the spring over. Holding it bent, he arched his back around it and slid into nap position, face to the wall.

"Dad . . ."

"Don't talk to me now." His father's voice was muffled in

the cushions, and he sighed again, deeply. "I've been beaten down . . . by my own son."

The mountain of guilt doubled in size. The gray December day was made of lead. Lord Henry stood numbly in the center of the living room.

"*Oh my God . . .*"

His mother's voice shot down again from the bedroom, and then her slow heavy footsteps came back onto the stairs.

Lord Henry listened as she descended, and looked up as she stepped in front of him. Her eyes were like cast iron, and the already unbearable atmosphere grew still more ominous and terrible, with signs of vast untold continents of guilt appearing. "*Your friends—went through my drawers.*"

The whole hideous world of guilt blossomed inside him, her words hinting at motives so unspeakably evil he couldn't begin to respond. The worst crime of the century had been committed, right here, in this very house.

"I can't believe that a son of mine could be part of this . . ." She opened her hands to show him the nail wounds in her palms.

He pulled his stomach in tight, the last pieces of artificial snow and glass still working around. His mother turned away slowly, toward the kitchen. "Our lovely home . . ."

"*Your mother's heart is broken,*" muttered his father, into the cushions.

Lord Henry turned back toward the window, and looked out again on the lead-lined, lifeless afternoon.

". . . *oh god . . .*" His mother's voice wrapped a final shroud around the day. ". . . *they waxed the dirt right into the floor.*"

"I'll clean it, Mom. I'm sorry."

"*Being sorry's not good enough.*" His father's voice was deep in the cushions.

His mother came back to the living room. "How . . . how could you do this?" She gazed out through strands of disheveled blond hair, and he realized she was about to deal him the ultimate guilt-blow, one she reserved only for the highest occasions of state. "I . . . carried . . . you . . . inside . . . me."

His father shifted on the couch, the spring wedging against his back. "Alright, that's enough now. I don't want to hear any more about what your son has done." He reached behind him and bent the spring away. "I've got to get my rest."

Lord Henry turned toward the stairs. Things were going to be hairy around the manor house for a while, until the Democrats did something new to undermine the city.

Chapter 26

Lots of Nooky.

The jukebox bubbles circled slowly, deep inside the Shack. Cigarette smoke curled at the windows and drifted out into the darkness. The parking lot was filled with hot-looking cars, and spring was in the air, the night seeming to promise a punch in the mouth.

He leaned against a fender. Crutch leaned beside him, chewing his fingernails down to nothing. "Lots of nooky tonight."

Twiller eyed the open doorway, as the chicks bopped by, dancing with each other. Beyond them was the slapped-together board counter where sodas and hot dogs were being hustled; a bunch of hoods sat at the counter, skulls and other motorcycle emblems on their jackets, but Twiller knew none of them had bikes, they rode revolving stools. One of them gave the signal, and they picked up and moved out through the doorway, as if heavy machinery awaited them, and then they just faded, on foot up the sidewalk, chains clanking.

"When I finally get some wheels," said Crutch, "everything's going to change. I'll be beating off chicks with both hands."

"You might just be beating off."

A deep rumble started in the center of the lot, and a mean V-8 edged forward, dual mufflers boiling. Conversation stopped for a moment, as the big vehicle rumbled across the lot. It leapt suddenly, spraying rocks and dirt behind it, and peeled off toward the railroad tracks.

Conversation resumed around fenders and bumpers, while the jukebox bubbles continued to circle.

"Let's check it out." Crutch pushed off, and Twiller joined him. They sauntered toward the Shack, engineer boots crunching the gravel. Twiller dug the weight of his new boots, kind of like having lead pails on his feet; if trouble came along he could jump out of them and run with a tremendous feeling of lightness.

"Lots of *bad* nooky." Crutch climbed the steps toward the chicks, and Twiller squirted a quick shot of Lavoris into his mouth.

The windows of the Shack were strung with colored lights, and their soft candy glow played along the rough boards of the doorway. Twiller went through loose, but not too loose; he didn't want to look like he was trying to prove anything, but at the same time he had to make it look like he was nobody to fuck with. It was a fine line and on each side of the Shack was a row of sagging booths filled with guys toeing the same line.

He scanned the place quickly, looking for Angelo Gabooch, whose presence would be the signal for immediate departure.

Angelo was not present. He straightened up a little, and let a bit of sneer hang from one lip.

Shoooooom-boom da-doom-ba
shooooooom-boom-bitty-boom-na . . .

191

A beautiful ballad was coming from the box, and a hush had fallen over the Shack, everyone deep into the words which so clearly spoke their feelings.

. . . shooooooom moooooooom mutta mooooom mutta mutta mutta mmmmmmooooooooooooooo-oom . . .

"What a fuckin' tune." Crutch leaned up against the wall and Twiller slid along over to the jukebox and scanned the other tunes. The glow of the box enveloped him, bright gases flowing through him, melting him down. When you had the right music behind you, you could do anything.

. . . yum-mum-ta ta mumbaaaaaaaaaaaaaaaaa doughhhhhhhhhhhhhhhhhhhhhhhhhhhhhhhhhhhh.

The song finished with that incredible ending it had, and he punched up a couple more goldies, tunes that would show the chicks how he felt about things. He moved away toward the window and struck a thoughtful pose, shoulders rounded, thumbs hung in his belt buckle.

A huge old Cadillac was smoking down the hill toward the railroad tracks. He watched it coming, as did the other hot-rods, everyone in the lot cheering as it hit the tracks full tilt and flew into the air, all four tires leaving the ground. It came down with a screech and shuddered forward, making a long skidding sweep into the parking lot.

The door opened and Floyd got out from behind the wheel. Spider slid out from the other side. They came across the lot, Spider giving easy fingers to guys he knew, and Floyd strolled on ahead, all in white, his pants tight, his shirt sleeves billowing.

Drainpipe Drobish looked up from his booth, where he was

192

sitting with a few of his boys, cutting up the stuffing. "Here comes the ice-cream man." Drainpipe pointed a stubby gorilla finger at the doorway.

Floyd stepped through, smoothing down his long collars. He looked around nervously for a moment, until he spotted Twiller, then started across the room. One of the girls moved out and began chattering the way girls sometimes did with Floyd, like he was one of them. Twiller looked on, wishing they'd come over and talk to him, but they were ignoring him; when their eyes came his way they passed right on by, giving him the feeling he was a part of the wall, a doorknob or a coat rack maybe, but Floyd was doing ok, he had two chicks talking to him now.

"How does he do it?" Twiller turned to Crutch.

"He don't look too happy about it . . ."

Floyd's eyes were still darting nervously, toward Drainpipe Drobish, who was tearing more stuffing out of the booth and giving Floyd a look that said *you-are-my-punching-bag.*

The girls were moving to the jukebox, and Floyd stepped with them, out of Drainpipe's range. They pressed a tune up, and took Floyd's hands.

He pulled back, but they hung on and hauled him out onto the little dance floor. He glanced around, shrugged his shoulders, and started bopping.

Twiller's boot heel marked time on the tune, but he didn't have Floyd's feeling for it, Floyd was a great dancer, smooth and fast, and the girls liked dancing with him, he knew all the splits, the turns, the fancy steps. He twirled them under, two at a time, and slid between them, oil in his joints, hips snapping, shoulders shaking.

Twiller saw Drainpipe's hairline lower, brow creased with growing thoughts of violence. Floyd was whipping off some lightning love-bumps, pelvis moving in and out like rubber, first at the one chick, then the other. Twiller kept his eyes on Drainpipe: he had the battle plan already mapped out—

they'd pile chairs in the way and jump out the window. He wished it always didn't come down to this kind of shit, but Floyd seemed to attract knuckle sandwiches.

"Hey . . ." Noises came from Drainpipe's mouth, dark noises, terrible noises. Twiller prepared to leap out of his engineer boots.

Spider walked in and sat down beside Drainpipe. Drainpipe grunted and Spider took out his new line of dirty playing cards, flicking Drainpipe the joker. Drainpipe's mind fogged, and Twiller settled his feet back into his boots.

"Close fuckin' call." Crutch lowered his leg from the windowsill.

"Why don't we collect Floyd and shove . . ." Twiller nodded toward the lot.

"Fuckin' Floyd—" Crutch gestured at the broken-down counter and the falling-apart stools. "—This is *the* place. This is where the action is. I'm hangin' in *and* I'll be ready for Drainpipe." He slid an empty soda case under the windowsill, and raised his leg up to the window again. "Yeah, ok, that's better."

Twiller turned back to the dance floor. The tune was ending and Floyd was spinning both girls toward the corner where the other chicks were standing, their jaws moving some heavy loads of gum. Floyd let go and drew away, joining Twiller. Crutch was looking out the window at the line-up of cars. "How's your Caddie runnin', Floyd?"

"I carry a case of oil in the trunk."

"It needs a ring job."

"*I* need a ring job. If only I could find someone to give me one." Floyd cast a melancholy gaze across the parking lot, off into the darkness. "*Well,*" he said, nudging Twiller, "look who's here."

Twiller followed Floyd's gaze, to the edge of the lot, where Gina Gabooch was walking in with a couple of her girlfriends.

194

"Go ahead." Floyd gave him a little push. "Eat a taillight for her."

Twiller hesitated. He'd heard she was interested in him now, since he'd taken a shot at her, but what about her brother Angelo?

The picture flashed in his mind again, of being hung upside-down out a window. A thing like that could ruin your confidence.

"Take a *chance*." Floyd shoved him again.

"Alrigh', alrigh' . . ." He rounded his shoulders a little more and slouched toward the doorway.

. . . shuuuuuuuuuu-mup shuuuuuuuuuuu-mup mup-mup-mup-mup shuuuuuuuuuuuuuuuuu-mupp-pp . . .

The jukebox was *not* playing one of his favorite tunes, but he hooked his thumbs behind his belt buckle and tried to feel it anyway; background music was everything in a move like this.

He went down the steps, onto the gravel. Gina was talking to Noosh Fanatta alongside Noosh's homemade motorcycle. It had a lawn mower motor mounted on it, and Noosh had to start it with a pull-rope. It didn't go very fast, and the motor stuck out sideways, which forced Noosh to always hang off the other side to balance it, but he was dressed like Death and Danger anyway—a winged helmet on his head and a jacket with so much metal on it he looked like he was wearing a tin can. He adjusted one of his zippers, a biker's scowl on his face as he spoke to Gina. Twiller walked along the edge of the shack and stepped beneath a window where Gina could see him—but the colored bulb overhead turned his hands a weird shade of orange. He moved on to the end of the Shack, and took out his Lavoris.

"Hey, hotshot—" Her voice nailed him as he squeezed the

195

atomizer and he squeezed too hard, sending the Lavoris down his throat. "—where's your pistol?"

He choked in the shadows, Lavoris burning its way into his windpipe. Noosh tried to get Gina's attention back; he yanked his lawn mower rope and started up, but she was looking toward the Shack now. Noosh snapped his visor down and blasted off, leaning sideways, his mower put-putting into the road.

Twiller clung to the edge of the Shack, coughing. She came toward him slowly in her big boots. Little bells were jingling, down around her cuffs.

He wiped the Lavoris from his cheek and turned slowly, thumb in his belt, left shoulder in a really deep hang, like he was attached to the side of the Shack by a hook.

The jingling stopped and she was looking right at him. He looked coolly past her, toward Noosh riding sideways in the moonlight, his mowercycle moving slowly over the railroad tracks.

Gina raised her hand, firing a thumb-and-finger pistol shot. "Where you been keepin' yourself?"

He tried to speak; the mouthwash had dried his throat terribly, and an extremely puckered sneer was the best he could manage. But the jukebox was playing one of *his* tunes now:

Wahm wahm waaaaaaaaaaaaaaaaaaah wahm waaaaaaaaaaaaah-waaaaaaaaaah-wahmmmmmmmm-mmmmmmmm . . .

Gina leaned toward him, crinkling up her nose. "What've you been drinkin', honey?"

"Lavoris."

"You're far out, you know that?"

"Ever walk . . . back that way?" he gasped, still dry, and pointed toward the scrubby end of the parking lot, where the cars were nosed into the high weeds.

She fell into step beside him, her bells jingling as she

196

danced a little to the music coming through the gray warped boards of the Shack. They moved into the dark part of the lot and the music came more softly. He took a chance and stepped closer to her; if she kicked him with her steel-toed boots it was all over.

But her bells just jingled as she danced a few more steps, faint streaks of light from the Shack touching her hair. It was time for him to make his *move*.

From the front of the Shack, mufflers rumbled, an exciting sound, the kind of soundtrack he needed. He raised his hand to the long curving lock of hair that laid along her cheek. He moved it aside, uncovering faint scars of acne.

Headlights swung along the edge of the Shack, and moved up toward them, gravel crunching under the whitewall tires of a custom Ford, and then Drainpipe Drobish was leaning out from the steering wheel, right beside them. "Go for a ride, Gina?"

A cigarette dangled from Drainpipe's thick hanging lip. His sleeve was rolled up, showing the tattoo of a steam shovel on his arm. In the back seat of the Ford were other heavy shapes, looking bad.

Twiller lifted one thumb out of his belt, and lowered his shoulder some more, to give an I-don't-scare-easily look.

Gina glanced at him, perhaps curious to see how he'd handle five guys jumping up and down on his chest. He lowered his shoulder a last little bit, so that he seemed to be casually dangling in the air—and then he curled his lip up slightly. *That* should show her what he thought of the whole situation.

"See you later then," she said, and stepped toward the car.

"Sure," he said, "take it easy."

The car door opened and she climbed in beside Drainpipe. He gave Twiller a so-long-shithead look and floored the gas.

Twiller nonchalantly ducked the flying gravel, and then

197

walked back to the front of the Shack. Crutch and Floyd were coming out.

"Did you get any?" asked Crutch.

"Smell my finger."

Crutch sniffed over the knuckles. "Smells like Lavoris."

"That's what I got."

They climbed into Floyd's Cadillac and smoked off over the railroad tracks.

Chapter 27

. . . In Which Ashcan O'Houlihan Is Suckerpunched.

◇ ◇ ◇

He stood at the fence, looking in at the chicks playing miniature golf. The night was warm and the chicks were wearing
shorts. Crutch, in a huge white golfing cap, was following
them to the ninth hole. They played it through and exited at
the gate, toward Hamburg Heaven. Crutch followed, tugging
the enormous brim of his cap; it stuck out over his head like
the bill of some gigantic platypus who was trying to swallow
him. Twiller looked into the dark recess beneath the brim.
"How was your score?"

"I asked them to autograph my balls."

A customized Olds screeched into the lot and Scuduto
leaned from the window, greased head reflecting the glow of
the floodlit golf course. A chick was walking past the parked
cars and Scuduto gave her his Rudolph Vaselino look. "Hey,
what's happenin', baby?"

She ignored him and he pulled up alongside Twiller and
Crutch. Twiller saw a huge figure in the seat beside Scuduto,
crushing a beer can in his fist.

Twiller turned to Crutch. "Who's that?"

"Ashcan O'Houlihan. He's bad news."

Scuduto parked and Ashcan climbed out, trouble written all over his smiling Irish mug. Twiller noticed the weird gaze in Scuduto's eyes—he'd been drinking a lot of protein shakes lately, trying to become a giant fullback. He swaggered toward them, like someone much larger. "We're hittin' the dance at the Social Club. Who's goin' with us?"

"Downtown pussy," said Crutch, nodding inside his golf cap.

"Alright, me lads," said Ashcan, "we just stopped here for a little pee." He leaned against a car, opened the gas tank and dropped his hose inside.

"Way to go, Ashcan," said Scuduto, laughing and faking a few punches, then dancing away as Ashcan tried to piss on him. Ashcan swayed along between the cars, zipping his fly and singing. They climbed into Scuduto's shitbox, Ashcan riding shotgun and cracking his knuckles like an automatic rifle.

Scuduto popped the clutch and they laid rubber across the lot. "I'm goin' to beat the crap out of somebody tonight," said Ashcan, matter-of-factly.

Twiller cracked the knuckles of his first two fingers; the others wouldn't crack, he could never get them to.

They spun out onto the highway, toward the bridge into town, Scuduto steering by radar, his eyes never leaving his reflection in the rearview mirror, into which he made Rudolph Vaselino expressions. Dangling from the mirror was a pair of large foam dice that swung back and forth as Scuduto whipped the wheel, lining them up for the run over the bridge. "Nobody's fuckin' with us *tonight*, motherfucker."

The girders of the bridge sped by, and they rolled off the other end, into town, Ashcan pounding on the roof, his hand like a slab of sirloin. The streets were crowded with Friday night traffic, and Scuduto edged forward impatiently, Hollywood mufflers crackling, then exploding with a tremendous backfire. Twiller felt the blood rushing to his head. Anybody fucks with us tonight, that's *it,* motherfucker.

Crutch had an open can of protein shake in his hand, and was sipping it through a straw. There was a case of protein shake on the floor, at his feet.

Ashcan threw an empty beer can toward a sidewalk full of shoppers, adding a few threats and challenges, and concluded with a sausage-thick middle finger jabbing the air. Scuduto jumped the car forward through traffic, opening it up at the intersection and screeching across it. He cut hard, into a No Parking zone, and kissed the curbstone outside of the Diesel Street Social Club.

Twiller yanked the door handle, feeling like he needed to punch somebody's lights out. He was far along in his mail-order judo lessons, had been studying all summer and was ready to get down and *rumble.*

Scuduto danced out onto the sidewalk, smoothing his ducktail back with his palms and waiting for his man Ashcan to emerge; the front door flew open, there was a slight pause, and then Ashcan climbed out, crushing another beer can and flipping it into the gutter. He was big, and meaner than a junkyard dog, and Twiller watched the guys at the doorway of the club drawing back.

That's right, motherfuckers, we're bad, and we're coming in.

He went through the doorway, Scuduto alongside him and Ashcan bringing up the rear.

The music came from the second floor, floating down over the heads of the mob gathered on the stairs. Twiller pushed forward, elbows out, until he noticed the crowd was no longer fading at the sight of him. He turned quickly around, and saw Ashcan way back at the doorway, talking to some guys.

He tried to get hold of Scuduto, but Scudsy was still acting large, padded shoulders rolling. From the mob gathered at the foot of the stairs, a single figure emerged, like a rhinoceros from the bush.

Scuduto pushed by him, head down, fists balled. Angelo Gabooch stuck a hand out and yanked him back, over the stair rail. "Where the fuck you think *you're* goin'?"

With one violent shake from Angelo's arm, Scuduto's concrete ducktail fell apart, collapsing around his ears. He might have spoken but Angelo was choking him.

Twiller stepped forward, knowing he couldn't win but at least he had some fighting technique down now, at least he wouldn't be fucking humiliated. "Hey, Angelo—"

Angelo reached out and grabbed him; he countered with a quick pivoting of his feet, turning at the waist and getting his shoulder up under Angelo's arm, preparing for a Major Hip Toss. He bent and lifted.

Angelo felt like a pile of manhole covers.

Suddenly the hallway was going by in a blur, Angelo driving him head-first through the crowd, Scuduto in Angelo's other hand, eyes bulging, arms waving. The doorway cleared and they went sailing through it, across the sidewalk and into the gutter, Twiller sprawling flat-out on the pavement, Scuduto bouncing and rolling to a stop against the bumper of his car, hair hanging in his face. He made a quick move for his comb.

Ashcan and Angelo squared off in the doorway. "You can't do that to me mates," said Ashcan.

"Yeah, but I just did."

Twiller feigned unconsciousness, attempting to look like a fireplug. The raw vicious force that'd just bowled him through the doorway was like nothing he'd ever even considered.

"Let's go into that lot." Ashcan pointed toward the dark empty space beside the Social Club. "Just you and me."

Angelo followed him. Nobody else moved. One of the Great Moments In Sport was going unwatched but Twiller wouldn't have budged out of the gutter for all the nooky in town tonight; the other heroes and hotshots seemed to feel the same way, nobody moving from the sidewalk, where they strained their ears to hear something from the dark lot.

There were no sounds, no shouts, no signs of battle. Music floated out of the Social Club windows and shadowy figures danced above, in the red light of the ballroom. Scuduto combed and arranged his hair. Angelo came out of the lot, tucking his shirt back into his belt. Guys faded left and right, and he walked back into the club.

Ashcan appeared after him, walking slowly, shiners on both his eyes. "Fair fight," he said to the crowd, "fair fight."

His mates got off the ground and they climbed into Scuduto's shitbox, Ashcan slamming the door hard and bringing his fist down on the dashboard as they peeled out. "Drive to South Side. We're getting Hammer and Tony and Bongo." The glove compartment fell open and he kneed it violently back in place. "What's tonight, Friday, they'll be at the Shamrock. You drive to the Shamrock Grill on Boiler Avenue, you'll see some good men come runnin'. We'll cream that guinea whoormaster."

"What'd he—suckerpunch you, Ash?"

"He coldcocked me while I was tyin' me shoelace."

"Alrigh' . . ." Scuduto spun the wheel toward South Side. ". . . we'll fix *his* motherfuckin' wagon."

Twiller looked out the back window, trying to spot Crutch in the crowd, but he'd disappeared.

I'm alone with these two gum-heads.

"Hey, Scudsy, you can let me off here."

Ashcan turned in the seat and pointed a finger. "You're not goin' anywhere, son."

"Yeah, right. I just had to buy some handkerchiefs."

Ashcan tipped another beer to his lips, then laid the cold edge of the can against his eye. Twiller bent down and opened a protein shake.

"Angelo Gabooch," said Scuduto. "He's playin' for Drumville High now. Plays right tackle."

203

"He'll be playin' right fuck when we get done with him."
Ashcan rolled down his window and tossed out the half-empty beer can. "Bongo, me, and Hammer. And Charlie Saparito." Another can popped, beer spraying onto the window. "Those lads can *go*, do ye hear what I'm tellin' ye?"

Twiller heard. Ashcan was sounding more Irish every minute, as if a punch in the head brought out the old sod in him.

"Good enough, there's the Shamrock, pull up . . ." Ashcan's door was already open and he jumped out, moving with long loping strides, his big shadow dancing along behind him.

Scuduto made a few more adjustments to his damaged ducktail. Twiller sipped his protein shake.

Say So Long To Being Skinny. Super Formula 77 will put on the pounds, enabling you to excel in all sports through the rapid development of Super-Muscle tissue. Used by OLYMPIC CHAMPIONS!

"*No*body else is going to fuck with us tonight, motherfucker." Scuduto slipped his comb into its case, and threw a couple of light jabs at his foam dice.

Use Super Formula Daily. Safe for the entire family, growing children and women. Also available in tablet form.

The door of the Shamrock opened. Ashcan came out alone, carrying a bag of quarts. "Eddie said they're over at the Landmark." He flopped the quarts in and slammed the door. Scuduto peeled out; Twiller felt the protein shake gurgling in his stomach. Faintly nauseous, he opened a second one.

"Bongo, me, and Hammer . . ." Ashcan opened a quart, handed it to Scuduto, and opened another for himself. "How about you, Handkerchief?"

"I'm fine," said Twiller, holding up his shake.

"You're alright," said Ashcan. "You were in the action."

A warm glow spread around Twiller's heart. Anybody else fucks with us tonight, they're in trouble.

Scuduto pulled in at the Landmark. Ashcan set his quart on the floor and crawled out, his massive frame filling the car door, then gliding away, toward the neon glow of the bar.

Send for our free catalog of Body Building Supplements. Vitamins, Minerals, Wheat Germ Oil capsules—for Stamina and Drive.

Twiller stared out the window into the dark alleyway beside the bar. Faint sounds of shuffleboard came from the back room, iron quoits clicking against each other.

Scuduto flipped on the radio. "*. . . for Schoop and Bonnie, Marge and Tommy T, and for all the guys at Dino's Upholstery . . .*"

Ashcan came out, smiling, his two black eyes glowing.

"Do you know where they are?" He swung the door open. "They're down at the dance." The door crashed shut. Scuduto floored it, quart to his lips. Twiller set another empty can of protein shake back into the case; the contents were washing around inside him, rapidly developing muscle tissue. *Anybody punches me in the stomach, motherfucker, they're going to have to step back in a hurry.*

"Ain't that a fuckin' situation?" Ashcan flipped the empty quart out the window and watched it shatter on the pave. "They were at the dance all the time. Me good pals were right there . . ." He drummed his fingers on the dashboard. "We'll go into the dance easy. Anybody asks you, say we had us a fair fight and we're not lookin' for no more trouble. Then I'll round up the boys and we'll stomp that guinea fuck to death."

Twiller pulled the seal on another Formula 77, raising the thick, sweetly sickening formula to his lips. Scuduto ran the red lights along Diesel Street, while Ashcan bellowed and beat the side of the car with his fist.

"Hey, look at these guys comin' up behind us," said Scuduto. "They want to go."

"Go with them, *go!*" shouted Ashcan. "We'll smoke those cuntlappers!"

Twiller turned his head and watched the car behind them moving up, closing the gap. Scuduto threw his shitbox into second and tromped it.

"Wind it! Wind it all the way!" Ashcan stuck his head out the window. "You cocksuckers! *Here* . . ." He wired a foaming quart at them, shattering it on their hood. The car swerved, fenders kissing against Scuduto's.

"Pass! Pass and cut them off the map!"

Scuduto rammed it down into high and cut across in front of them, forcing them into the curb. Tires screeched and Twiller saw guys flying against the windshield. Scuduto eased into the curb, laughing, as Ashcan jumped out to finish the job. He charged their door, yanking it open so hard it sprung a hinge and hung there, frozen. "Crawl, you honky!"

Twiller jumped after him, yanking at the back door of the car and opening it for Angelo Gabooch, who climbed out and punched him into the pavement. He rolled toward the back tire, assisted by a kick that sent him under the bumper, where he remained, gasping for air. It was a Great Moment In Sport, and gave him a ringside seat at another Great Moment, as Angelo drilled Ashcan again, right between the shiners. Ashcan went down, holding his nose and Angelo kicked him a few times in the chest.

"Hey, Gabooch," said Scuduto, "give him a break, you've got him down."

Scuduto went down, punched into the front wheels and clutching at his ducktail.

Twiller crawled further underneath Scuduto's shitbox. Ashcan's heavy breathing came from the gutter, and then car doors slammed, as Angelo and his pals drove off.

Twiller looked out from under the fender. Ashcan was hanging onto the bumper. ". . . fuck . . ." He gently touched his swollen nose. ". . . that . . . rotten . . . whoormaster . . ."

Scuduto got up, combing. "You ok, Ash?"

"He kicked . . . me ribs in . . ." Ashcan got to his feet, holding his side.

"He's one bad-ass mother . . ." Scuduto brushed off his leather jacket, which had been seriously scraped along the pavement.

"He'll hear from me . . . the dago cocksucker . . ." Ashcan checked out his black-and-blue face in the side mirror, and Twiller wearily opened the back door. An empty can of protein shake rolled out at his feet.

If you want to build your body the way Olympic Champions do, then start today—chocolate or vanilla—

Chapter 28

Can You Blame the Girl Who Confesses,
  "I hate to go out with a fellow
  who has blackheads"?

◊ ◊ ◊

He looked in the mirror, and rubbed a little more Suave into his hair. With enough of it plastered on, it was possible to make a nest of curls all around his head.

He twisted curl after curl in his fingers, each curl secretly interlocked with the one beside it, to produce a devil-may-care appearance, which would nevertheless resist any kind of dishevelment caused by wind, water, or a punch in the mouth.

He stepped back and struck a careless pose. All the curls slowly pushed up against the grease, uncurled, and lay down flat again.

The horn blew outside. He went to the window. "Yeah, just a minute . . ."

He returned to the mirror. His hair now looked like it had been ripped off a dead weasel and ironed on with oleomargarine.

He began with the fingers again, trying for a few strategically placed waves on the side.

The waves held for a moment, and collapsed.

The horn continued blowing. He'd have to settle for the usual—part on the side, with a hump in front. The hump was trying to say something, he wasn't sure what, but he had to go with it. He ran his comb through it fifteen times to get it perfectly balanced, and then studied the overall effect.

The shirt, something about the shirt doesn't make it.

He stripped quickly, went to the closet, and took out his good old gaucho shirt—elastic waist festively colored, and a deep slit collar to show the two hairs growing on his chest.

He slipped it on, closing the bright buttons on the sleeves. If his mustache would only come in, the gaucho shirt would really take off.

He studied the scraggly fuzz on his upper lip. It wasn't growing and neither was he, as a result of jerking off so much; his growing power had gone down the drain in a wad of Kleenex, and he'd probably have to get elevator shoes.

The horn blew again.

The shirt looked ok, but it cried out for his gray pegged pants with the black stripe down the seam.

He quickly pulled off his jeans, went back to the closet and took out his gray pegs, with the tightest cuffs in the city. Complete with hidden buttons to make the cuffs still tighter, a pair of pants that couldn't be cooler if they tried.

But the suede shoes would have to come off first, as his super-tight pegs did *not* go on easily, he could hardly get them on over bare feet.

He bent down to remove his shoes, and his carefully molded hump of hair fell forward, around his eyes.

"*Hey, Twiller,* LET'S GO!"

He got the pegs on and went back to work with his comb, smoothing the hump into position. It resembled a greased doorknob, but it was all he could come up with on short notice.

He sat down, hauling on his suede shoes without bending over, and buttoned the pegs tight around them.

The horn blew again, a long string of blasts, and he knew the old man would be getting pissed about all the noise interfering with his evening nap.

But the gaucho shirt didn't seem to be *making it.*

"HEY, TWILLER, WHAT'RE YOU DOIN' UP THERE!"

He quickly slipped it off, went back to the closet, and took out his black shirt with the iridescent stitching on the pockets to match his black-striped pants.

With the addition of a simple pink tie the outfit would be impossibly cool.

Footsteps creaked on the stairs, to the first landing. "The bums are waiting for you."

"Yeah ok, Dad, I'm just putting on my tie."

He resumed his combing, fifteen more fast ones over the hump, and noticed a new pair of pimples forming, one near each ear; he couldn't cover them, he might get pink pimple cream in his sideburns.

And holy shit here are some more unsightly blackheads on my nose!

I wonder why we're not popular, Sis.
Ask your friend Tom.

Tom, why don't Sis and I get invited to proms and parties?
Frankly, Jim, it's those ugly blackheads.

He bent his nose with his fingers and studied the situation. The blackheads were right in the crease, a very tough spot to work on.

Can you blame the girl who confesses, "I hate to go out with a fellow who has blackheads"? If he's careless about that you're sure he'll embarrass you in other ways too.

210

* * *

He wondered about the other ways he might embarrass a girl. He suspected there were a great many of them.

He reached for his Vacutex.

NEW! SCIENTIFIC! VACUUM ACTION!
In seconds you are rid of those ugly blackheads
that clog the pores and give others such a wrong
impression of you.

That was certainly the problem—others had the wrong impression of him. If only they knew what he was really like.

VACUTEX creates a gentle vacuum pressure around
the blackhead and extracts it—quickly!—without inju-
ry to tender skin tissues.

Fucking Vacutex isn't working. It must be one of those blackheads with roots on it.

Aren't you glad we heard about Vacutex, Sis?

My nose is getting swollen—come out of there, you sonofabitch . . .

That's it, one with roots on it. Look at the grip that mother had.

"HEY, TWILLER!"

He couldn't go digging at the others, his nose'd get too red. He'd extract the rest of them tomorrow.

Thank you, Vacutex.

He studied himself in the mirror. His hump of hair was already sagging.

But if he put one more gob of grease on it, his head would be too heavy to lift. Fuck it, I'll just go natural.

He went back to his room and took a look at his jackets. The black leather might look alarmingly sharp with the pink tie.

The horn blew again. Crutch and Leo started beating on the fenders.

He slipped into the leather jacket and came at the mirror slowly.

The pink is lost behind all the zippers.

Maybe the three-quarter-length car coat with the tremendously padded shoulders is what I need to put the entire ensemble *out there.*

"THAT'S IT, TWILLER, WE'RE SPLITTING . . ."

The mufflers rumbled. He knew they wouldn't split without him, as he was the only one with any gas money.

This car coat makes my head look too small.

He took it off and returned to the closet.

It'd have to be his reversible yachting jacket, with the monogrammed pocket and phosphorescent cuffs, to match his casual life-style.

He put it on, studying himself in the mirror from all angles.

He'd found the right combination. The outfit looked unbelievably cool.

He switched out the light and went quickly down the stairs to the living room. "So long, Dad."

His father rolled over. "You look like a bellhop."

"Could I have a coupla bucks?"

"No."

He checked himself out in the hall mirror, flipped his collar up, and made a sophisticated exit.

"Twiller, you cunt, we've been waiting a half-hour."

"Alright, so let's get it on."

"You're fucking-A, it's out there, *happening.*"

"Where're we goin'?"

"I dunno, how about the Texas Weiner, play a little pinball."

212

"Sounds good."

"OK by me."

The car jerked forward, exhaust coming up through the floorboards.

Chapter 29

A Telltale Lump of Excrement

◇ ◇ ◇

Anthracite Academic was different now, at night, the familiar corridors of fear buried in shadow. The stairs went upward into darkness, and the principal's office was just a dead empty doorway.

An usherette in black dress and white corsage showed him down the aisle to his seat. He stepped over white bucks, and sat down in the midst of Ivy League suits. Anthracite Academic was very button-down collegiate, and his pegged pants and padded shoulders didn't fit in at all, but they were his *vines*, the kind he was comfortable in. The outfit he was wearing tonight, for example—electrifying. All black with heavy white stitching down the pants leg. Matching white stitches on the suit jacket, and shoulders out to here. A neon-blue shirt with gold bubbles on it. And of course, a pink tie.

The seats squeaked down in back and in front of him, one after another, and the spring night came in through the doors and windows. He took out his atomizer, palmed it, and squirted mouthwash, quietly. There were familiar faces all around—class officers, school heroes, honor scholars, dressed and groomed alike, moving on the same social level. Poise and confidence filled the rows in all directions. He put his atomizer away. The house lights were flickering.

Slowly they began to dim. Gradually, his suit and tie began to glow in the dark. He felt like something out of a Batman comic book.

The curtains opened invisibly and then a spotlight came up on Lily, seated at an old-fashioned desk on stage. She was smiling to herself, and writing something in a notebook, as she spoke.

"I remember . . . Mama's sisters . . . my sister Christine—and the littlest sister, Dagmar. Beside me, there was our boarder, Mr Hyde. Mr Hyde was an Englishman who had once been an actor, and Mama was impressed by his flowery talk and courtly manners. He used to read aloud to us in the evenings. But first and foremost, I remember Mama . . ."

The spot dimmed, leaving her only faintly visible, as the lights came up on a family gathered in their kitchen. Floyd Flynn entered, hair colored gray, and wearing a gray mustache. Mama asked if he was going out.

"Yes, dear Madame, for a few moments only . . ."

He sounded *exactly* like the Late Show. Twiller watched, amazed, at Lily and Floyd so magically transformed. Lily rose from where she was seated; she was wearing old-time clothes and black stockings that shone in the spotlight as she walked.

". . . Mr Hyde reads to us . . . a beautiful story . . ."

The family gathered around Floyd and he started reading the story, his hands moving gracefully in the air. The light faded slowly as he read, and then he and the family were covered in darkness, with Lily remaining alone in her circle of light at the edge of the stage.

"Tonight Mr Hyde finished Tale of Two Cities. *The clos-*

215

ing chapters are indeed superb. How beautiful a thing is self-sacrifice. I wish there were someone I could die for."

Twiller scrunched down further as the play rolled on, and lost track of what was happening; he was dreaming of the spotlight that'd one day be on *him*—at a night game in the big leagues. Out at shortstop, with thousands of fans in the stadium. Or maybe it'd only be the minor leagues, maybe he'd only get that far, but still—it was a long way up the ladder. Somebody'd spot him one of these days—a scout would come through and see him hustling, and that'd be it.

A rumbling noise came from the stage and the set started to rotate on a turntable. Spider was coming on stage, in an undertaker's costume. He wore a little black mustache and a bowler hat and came on sideways, checking to see if anybody was following him. He hammed it up, got a few laughs, and revolved out on the turntable, looking back over his shoulder, shiftily.

◊ ◊ ◊

The night had turned cooler; the crowd was moving off in groups. He went along the sidewalk that led to the back of the school. She'd be coming out that way, from backstage. The doorway was lit by a single bulb; he opened the door and went inside. Voices came from the other end of the building, and she turned the corner; he pulled back into the shadows, to wait. She came down the long hall, talking with other people from the play, all of them gesturing as if they were still on stage.

He wished he had flowers to hand her, without a word, like a mysterious admirer.

"*Hey, fuckhead* . . ." Spider's voice came softly from behind him in the corridor, and then Spider stepped out and waved him into the shadows.

He went quickly, melting with Spider into a doorway.

216

Floyd moved aside, and they stood there, waiting for the people in the hall to pass.

Spider brought a key out of his pocket, and held it up. The voices faded, going out through the basement into the street. The building was silent. Spider moved from the doorway, and led the way up the darkened hall.

◇ ◇ ◇

SPRING PLAY ROBBERY

Receipts totaling over three hundred dollars were stolen last night . . .

He read the newspaper nervously in the living room, the evening edition spread out on the floor before him.

Several members of the Anthracite High School Drama Club said they saw a suspicious person in the halls of Anthracite immediately following the performance of I Remember Mama. *Alfred Wuznack, stage manager for the play, said the unidentified person appeared to be in the uniform of a Western Union messenger, delivering a telegram of congratulations to the cast.*

Detective Inspector John J. MacKinnon is handling the case, assisted by Detective Stanley Velensky and a crew of police lab specialists called in to examine a tell-tale lump of excrement deposited on a desk in Room 101 of the school. It was found shortly after nine o'clock this morning by Miss Geraldine Peck, when she entered the room to teach her first math class of the day.

Miss Peck's report of the soiled desk led to a quick check of all rooms in the school and it was then the robbery of the spring play was discovered.

Miss Peck has been a teacher at Anthracite Academic for 37 years, and it was the first time in her memory

217

*that such an act had ever been committed. Following
her discovery, she was forced to undergo treatment by
the school medical nurse. Detective Velensky told re-
porters that Miss Peck's desk drawers had also been
soiled. A complete investigation is now under way.*

He laid the paper aside, and walked upstairs to his room.
He opened his closet and took out his striped peg pants and
jacket, his neon shirt with the gold bubbles, his pink tie, and
carried them back downstairs, to the cellar.
He opened the furnace and threw them in.
If only Spider hadn't shit on the desk.

◇ ◇ ◇

The jail door opened and they went through, Spider leading the way, Twiller behind him, their footsteps echoing
down the long hall.
The desk sergeant waved them over to a bench. Nancy
Pronka was already there, a large pizza box on her lap, the
smell of warm cheese and tomato surrounding her.
The yellow walls were high and the windows were barred.
Twiller sat down in his new Ivy League suit that made him
look like a chicken wearing a tie. There was nothing he could
do about it, it was his disguise now, to avoid identification as
a Western Union messenger.
The sound of a clanking cell came to them from down the
corridor.
"Alright," said the desk sergeant, nodding his head.
They went into the visiting room. Spider's old man was
leaning against the wall, hands in his pockets, a cigarette in
his thin lips. He looked them over slowly, his eyes dark and
cagey. He was tall and lean, with a little black mustache like
the one Spider'd worn in the play. "How're ya doin', honey,"
he said, giving Nancy a kiss on the cheek.

218

"We brought a friend of ours," said Nancy.

"What's your name, pal?" Old Man Pronka stuck out his hand and Twiller shook it. Nancy opened the pizza box. The guard at the door rattled his newspaper. Old Man Pronka called to him.

"Lou, you wanna slice?"

The guard folded his paper. "Thanks, Al . . ." He took a slice and carried it back to the door, tipping his head and dripping a string of cheese into his mouth.

Old Man Pronka took a slice. "How'd the play go?"

"You should have seen Spider," said Nancy. "He looked great on stage."

"I heard somebody pulled a little job there," said Old Man Pronka quietly.

Spider tapped his chest with his finger and then pointed across his shirtfront, toward Twiller.

"And your other pal, the fruit, how's he makin' out?"

"He was in the play too," said Spider.

"You and him played it together, did you?"

"We stole the show, Pop." With his back to the guard, Spider slipped his old man a wad of bills that went like greased lightning into Al Pronka's shirt.

"How's your mother?" he asked, turning to Nancy.

"She's good."

"Make sure she gets out for a beer once in a while."

Twiller stared at the floor, running his eyes along the tiles, tracing squares over to the guard's shoes and back, to Nancy's brown loafers. Her legs were smooth and shapely, and he came up them slowly with his eyes, and up along her waist to the rolling hills inside her sweater, but he'd never get any of them, she was already dating Manny Sugar, a forty-year-old gangster with a Lincoln Continental.

"Time's up, Al." The guard rattled his newspaper again. "Take the pizza back to the boys."

Old Man Pronka kissed his daughter on the cheek again

219

and gave Spider a friendly rap on the side of the head. The guard opened the door for them and they started on through; Al Pronka touched Twiller's sleeve, his fingers light as a feather, his voice a whisper *"Don't ever double-cross him."*

"No sir," said Twiller, feeling for his wallet. "I won't."

Chapter 30

... In Which Twiller Gets It Together At Last

The halls of Anthracite were hot, baked by the June sun, but he sweltered through them in his new letterman's sweater, flashing the big gold *A*. At the base of the curving letter was a dark round patch, signifying baseball, and every girl in school was seeing it; they were all dressed in light summer blouses and skirts, and he was lumbering along like a yak in his wool sweater, sweat rolling off him, but there was no other way.

He had to show the letter.

Yeah, I woke with a chill this morning, thought I'd better bundle up.

The sweater was a little big, and flopped like a sack when he moved, but it'd been the last letterman's sweater in town. He was lucky to get it; the fact that it hung to his knees didn't matter.

He flopped along toward the exit and staggered into the street. He noticed a couple of freshmen kids looking at his letter. He'd been like them, years ago, a nobody, but now—now he was somebody, a senior, a letterman, a hero. Surreptitiously, he pulled his sweat-soaked underpants out of his asscrack.

Cars were pouring out of the school parking lot—flashy little MG's, convertibles, custom jobs. He walked to his own car and opened the door. The seats still smelled of the river, sort of a green muck smell, and every now and then sand worked its way out of the floorboards, but it was a set of wheels, his very own '40 Chrysler, stuck in second gear.

He switched on the ignition and jerked into the street, then accelerated to top speed, his arm out the window, gold stripes showing on his sleeve, his cool Chrysler shuddering along at a steady ten miles per.

He guided it down the avenue, toward Manual Training High. Leo was waiting on the corner, and jumped in. "Hit the movies?"

"Right . . ." Twiller wheeled around the block, heading toward town. He opened the side vent, directing a stream of air down the prickly collar of his sweater.

"There's a parking space." Leo pointed to the curb ahead.

"Can't make it, Leo." He had to pass it up, as he had no reverse gear, and needed a parking place big enough for a moving van.

He stopped for a traffic light, then edged forward in second gear, the Chrysler shaking violently.

"Can't . . . you . . . fix . . . this . . . thing?" asked Leo, his head jerking back and forth.

"Scudsy said . . . jumping up and down . . . on the bumper . . . might pop it loose." He pulled into the railroad parking lot and circled around until he was facing the entrance, in a spot that would let him roll straight forward later on, when he was coolly pulling away.

They hopped out, slamming the doors. Lumps of river mud fell from under the fenders.

All the schools had let out and the street was filled with girls. Leo was looking very cool in a black T-shirt with the sleeves rolled up, while alongside him your Varsity A man adjusted his wool blanket.

"Aren't you hot in that sweater?"

"The movies are air-conditioned, Leo. I have to keep my throwing arm warm. Your throwing arm catches cold, you're finished."

They walked along through town, giving the chicks the eye. Steam came out of Twiller's collar. The big gold A flopped at his knees. He had it together at last.

NOW SHOWING

REBEL WITHOUT A CAUSE

They ducked under the marquee, bought their tickets and entered the lobby. Cool air was circulating.

Lucky for me I happened to have my sweater.

◊   ◊   ◊

They came out mumbling, the spirit of James Dean with them. Twiller felt it all through his body, his true identity. Leo hunched along, making significant faces at the crowd—tormented brooding faces that showed people where it was at. Twiller shuffled beside him, tormented too, a terrible rash starting on his neck where his ten-pound sweater was rubbing him raw. Society was against them—nobody understood. Twiller adjusted his nose bandage, the Rebel With A Pimple On the End of His Nose.

They walked up the avenue and entered the railroad parking lot. A chopped and channeled '49 Mercury, just like the one Jimmy used in the picture, squealed by them. Twiller gave a Jimmy Dean shrug and jumped up and down on the back bumper of his car. Duckweed fell out onto the pave. He slouched to the front of the car and crawled behind the wheel, slime squirting out from under the seat as he settled in. Leo climbed in the other side, mumbling.

223

Twiller turned the ignition over and shuddered forward in second gear.

Leo pulled a paperback out of his jacket and flashed the title.

My Friend, James Dean

He mumbled something Twiller couldn't understand. Leo was talking like a warped record, voice twisted, sentences punctuated by long dramatic pauses that completely distorted what little was being communicated, but by sign language and shrugs it was finally agreed that they should call the author and get more facts about Jimmy, get the whole story, in order that they could shape their own lives accordingly.

◇ ◇ ◇

"He wants me to come and see him." Leo hung up the phone and crawled under the dining room table. He often stayed there nowadays, cramped into a ball, emulating Dean's posture and smoking moodily.

"Hey, that's great. You've got to go." Twiller answered upside-down from the staircase, which he favored for Dean impersonations, his head hanging off the lower step.

"You've got to come with me," said Leo.

"He didn't invite me."

"He didn't realize . . . that you . . . that we . . ." Leo plunged back into dark mutterings, his voice lost in the table leaves.

Twiller inched down backwards off the step, until his head was touching the floor and his feet were locked in the banister. It was an authentic pose, and he knew—he had to go too, had to meet the author of *My Friend, James Dean*, and gain more precious information.

"We'll go tomorrow," he said spontaneously, and went

spontaneously out the front door and hopped spontaneously into his Chrysler.

He roared away, toward Lily's house. The role was on him, and he knew he could pull anything off tonight.

He checked himself out in the rearview mirror. His hair was exactly like Dean's, now that he'd stopped greasing it. To think that all these years he'd been smearing it with Suave. Well, he'd found himself now—no more grease in the hair.

Of course, his forehead was still secreting enough grease to lubricate the axles of his car, but he'd been told he'd outgrow it.

The Chrysler shuddered across the intersection. The faint smell of burning clutch came through the floorboards. He tried to lock in with the spirit of Dean, going 110 miles per in his Porsche, on the way to Salinas, to a tragic destiny, but unfortunately it was impossible for him to rack himself up with a car that was stuck in second gear and only went ten miler per—unless he parked it on the railroad tracks and waited for a freight train to crush him to pieces.

He checked his gas gauge. The glass was covered with green scum and the needle was draped in duckweed. He felt like he was riding in a diving bell.

He hung his hand nonchalantly on the gearshift, which would never go down from second. Up there forever. An armrest.

He turned off the avenue, toward Lily's house, and circled the block, bringing the car in on the downhill side; later, when he left, he would just take the brake off and coast downhill without any teeth-shattering jerks, just Jimmy Dean at the wheel of his custom job, left fender tied on with a coat hanger, muck in the dash, gearshift permanently in the two-o'clock position. Something a little different in customizing.

He nosed the Chrysler to the curb and stopped. There was plenty of room for a moody Jimmy Dean departure.

He opened the door. Sand fell into the neck of his letter

225

man's sweater. He slammed the door behind him and started up the sidewalk toward her house. She opened the door as he crossed the lawn.

"Congratulations," she said, looking at the big gold *A*.

He shrugged modestly, sand running down his back.

"Would you like to come in?"

He mumbled and followed her across the doorstep, into the house. The last time he'd come he'd made a fool of himself with a ring that glowed in the dark. But tonight was different. Dean was with him tonight, directing the scene.

She led him into the kitchen, just as if he'd visited many times; her books were open on the table. "I was studying . . ."

He mumbled and stared down at her sneakers.

"Did you want to see me about something, Jack?" She leaned against the kitchen counter, her elbows back, her sweatshirt lifting a little from her waist.

"Yeah . . . ah . . . yes, yes, I did . . ." He looked at her with a tormented expression, the agony of Dean in *East of Eden*, paying Julie Harris a surprise visit in the night, just like this one. Beyond him, a drop of water hung from the kitchen faucet, trembling, and fell, followed by another, slowly forming. He stared at it, his voice coming with the same tortured slowness of the dripping water.

"I . . . wanted . . . to . . . to . . ." He inched it out, Dean-style. ". . . to . . . ask . . . you . . ."

He was Dean, tortured and tormented, talking to Julie Harris at her window. He saw the scene in his mind and felt it taking him over completely, where Dean drives his head forward in frustration, smacking it against Julie's window frame. It was the perfect touch, and he had to do it too, against Lily's kitchen wall. It'd show her the kind of sensitive guy he was.

". . . to go for . . ." He lifted his face toward her, eyebrows squeezed together like Dean's; he threw in a halting

226

little chuckle, half-swallowed in a mumble, and then let his head fall forward, knocking it against the kitchen wall.

Lily came forward with a little gasp, and he felt the power of the moment surging. Yes, he thought, keeping his eyes closed and his head pressed to the wall, now you know who I am.

He pulled his head away from the wall, slowly, and opened his eyes, still very deep in the part.

An enormous grease spot confronted him, in the shape of his forehead, outlined on the pale yellow wallpaper.

He edged in front of it, trying to hide it, but it was too late; she was already staring at the grease blotch, mute astonishment in her eyes. It looked like somebody'd thrown a hamburger at the wall.

What, he wondered, would she tell her mother?

I had Jack Twiller over. You know, the boy who manufactures peanut oil out of his forehead, and he gave a demonstration . . .

He turned away quickly and headed for the front door. He heard her following him but he couldn't turn back, couldn't face her with his greasy brow, now imprinted forever on her wall.

He trotted across the lawn to his car, hopped in, adjusted his nose bandage, released the brake and roared away into the night, in second gear.

Chapter 31

In Breathtaking Color—Adults Only

◇ ◇ ◇

They stood on the highway, thumbs out. "He'll be glad you came," said Leo. "You have Dean's hair."

Twiller warmed inside, could see the author of *My Friend, James Dean* doing a double-take, first at Leo who had *all* of Dean's facial features and then at—The Hair.

Cars and trucks sped by them. He wished he'd been able to take the Chrysler but driving all the way to New York City in second gear might be a problem.

"How many guys would run this down the way we are?" said Leo. "We're gonna get the *whole story*."

"Right, right . . ." Twiller's wool sweater flopped, the big *A* hanging heavily by his knee. It was a boiling hot day and he was roasting to death, but the kind of meeting that was ahead of them—with a famous author—required the proper out-fit.

Oh, I notice you're a letterman.

Yes sir, at Anthracite Academic. It's a major northeastern high school.

Leo had purchased a red nylon jacket for the occasion, identical to the one Dean had worn, and it really completed Leo's act, with the tormented faces, the twisted gestures, the hunched-over walk. A copy of *My Friend, James Dean* was sticking out of his back pocket.

"Lemme see it again, Leo." Twiller took it, reading a few passages aloud as they thumbed along. The author knew everything there was to know—Dean's likes and dislikes, his moods, his actions off the screen. It was the kind of detail that helped you get the part together yourself.

"In his own home town," he read aloud, *"Jimmy was considered an outsider . . ."*

Leo nodded, mumbling and slouching.

"He often stared into space for hours."

Leo's head straightened, eyes going glassy.

Twiller closed the book and stuck it into his own back pocket.

Your hair—there's something about it—yes, it's like Jimmy's, isn't it . . .

◇ ◇ ◇

The lobby was small and clean, just off fabulous Fifth Avenue, where afternoon traffic was rolling by. Leo pressed the bell, and they waited. Twiller smoothed his hair, making sure of the shape. The Big Moment was coming.

The door buzzer sounded and Leo pushed through, your varsity *A* man following, wool sweater weighing a ton in the city humidity. Sweat poured out of him as they climbed the carpeted staircase. A door opened above them and a figure appeared on the landing, looking very Ivy League, with short black hair and an older, sophisticated face.

Leo smiled, waving shyly. "It's Leo Bodell. You said we could come and visit you."

The author of *My Friend, James Dean* waited for them on

the landing. As they turned the corner of the staircase he came forward.

"Didn't I tell you to come alone?"

Leo stopped, laughing uneasily. "Well—my friend read your book too—we thought—"

The author gave an impatient shrug, and opened the door of his apartment. Twiller followed Leo inside; he wasn't wanted, and wasn't surprised. It was the sort of thing he always secretly felt, that the right people would never want him around.

The apartment was one large room, with stark white furniture, carefully arranged, a real bachelor pad. On the wall was a huge framed photograph of Jimmy Dean, light from the window playing on the actor's brooding face.

"You see," said the author, quietly to Leo, "I've only made arrangements for two. We're to go to dinner . . ."

Twiller looked away from the photograph. "Hey, don't worry about me. I'm going to take a walk around the city." He turned to Leo. "I'll call you later, ok?"

Leo hesitated, his face red, but the author stepped between them. "Yes, that'd be fine. You call back this evening sometime." He went to the door and opened it for your varsity *A* man, who went through with a jaunty step, the whole thing just a lark to him. The door closed behind him and he stood in the hallway, waiting for the author of *My Friend, James Dean* to reopen it and invite him back in.

I was just testing you. Come on in, have a seat, take off your sweater. I notice you're a letterman.

◇ ◇ ◇

He stood on Times Square, watching the lights flash against the night sky. The honky-tonk shops blasted their music all around him and the crowds swarmed by.

Alone in New York City. On his own at last. Shown the

230

door by the author of *My Friend, James Dean,* the young shortstop proves he can take it in the big leagues.

He stared at the movie posters.

HOT FUDGE HOTEL
*Starring the Fabulous
Honey Moon!
In breathtaking color
adults only*

He moved along from poster to poster, and walked into the penny arcade. The pinball machines were clanging and he took one, dropping in a coin and applying his special body English to the sides of the machine.

TILT

He walked back out into the street. The Square was pulsating, traffic streaming by, the crowd jostling him. He stopped in front of a cocktail lounge and looked through the door. The crowd inside was older, and wonderfully sophisticated, with fancy clothes and big cigars. They sat at candlelit tables, speaking softly. He wondered if they could see him.

Who's that mysterious guy in the doorway there, with the little bandage on his nose?

Looks a lot like James Dean, doesn't he?

I'm going to ask him to join us. I'd like to know his story.

He walked on, toward the sound of drums up ahead, and pulled in under an empty marquee where two black guys were playing the congas, a cap on the sidewalk in front of them, filled with change.

He felt the rhythm, the excitement, the speed of the night, people rushing, black hands pounding, keeping the beat.

"I usta be with Krupa," announced a bum, coming up

231

beside him, a pair of banana peels in his hands. The bum started slapping the peels together. "They tell me—Larry, they say—you're too old for that fast playin'. But I can't stop. It's in my blood." His peels flapped and snapped, splitting up the middle in his hands. He stared at them, as if his fingers had just exploded. "Larry—they say—Larry—" The peels slipped from his grip and fell onto the sidewalk. "I give it all I got. Played my fingers off. How 'bout givin' an old bum a dime . . ."

"Fuzz . . . here come the fuzz . . ."

The drums stopped, the crowd fanned out, and Twiller moved into a phone booth. A million drifters had pissed in it; he held his breath and dialed.

"Hello?"

"Is Leo there?"

Leo came on, quietly. *"He's going to put me up for the night."*

"What should I do, come by in the morning?"

"Come by early. We'll hit the road."

"OK, Leo, hang in there. Get the whole story."

◊ ◊ ◊

They stood on Route 22, thumbs out. Cars whizzed by them in a steady stream, and Leo wasn't talking. Twiller knew Leo could be that way, moody and silent when the part of Jimmy Dean was really on him, and he tried to be patient. Leo was thinking about Dean. The whole story had affected him deeply; he was staring up the road, lost in thought.

Trucks rumbled by, and buses, and vans, and the sun beat down on the highway, radiating back off it in shimmering waves. "So, did you talk about Dean?"

"A little . . ." Leo's voice was distant and cold. Twiller felt himself getting a little ticked-off. He'd spent the night wandering nowhere and finally wound up on a bus-station bench. A few words about Dean would give him a lift. It didn't seem like a lot to ask from your road buddy.

"Well, what did he tell you about him?"

"Not much . . ."

"What exactly was it, I'd like to know. I had to sleep on a bus-station bench."

"Big deal."

"Come on, what'd you talk about?"

"Nothing."

"Nothing? You were there all night."

Leo turned up the collar on his red jacket. "We listened to records."

"And never mentioned Dean? Not a word? Leo, what're you trying to hand me?"

Leo spun suddenly around, grabbing him by the sweater and hissing his words out over the roar of the traffic. "He said, *Jimmy would have liked you.*"

Chapter 32

Let's Have Some Pussy!

◇ ◇ ◇

They stepped up to the ticket-taker's booth. He looked at them suspiciously. "How old are you guys?"

"Sixty-five." Crutch pushed his glasses back up his nose.

"A wise-ass." The seller took their money and looked it over carefully too. "But I'm gonna sell you a ticket, because you look hard-up."

"Hard-up and fucked-up, mister. When's the next show?"

"Fifteen minutes. Can you wait that long?"

They moved back into the crowd on the carnival midway, and Twiller saw lettermen from all over the city—track stars, fullbacks, tall bony basketballers—the sort of all-star gathering that always ended with somebody getting their teeth knocked out.

He gave the eye to some chicks, who looked through him. It would be the usual sort of evening, ending on the toilet, perfecting his stroke.

"That Lily?" Crutch pointed to a fuzzy halo of curls at the

throwing gallery. Steve Zuba was alongside her, paying for three balls to wire at some wooden milk bottles.

Twiller went over and stepped in alongside Zuba. Zuba was winding up, like the grease monkey that he was, plenty of wrench but no control, his pitch going wide.

Twiller bought three balls and cleared a little space for himself. He was wearing his varsity *A* baseball cap, and it commanded a certain respect from the crowd; here was a guy you knew could throw.

He tossed the ball up and down, getting the feel of it. It felt like lead, a ball you couldn't throw across the diamond if your life depended on it, but he reared back and took three smooth steps as if he was firing on the run from shortstop; a pain shot through his elbow as he brought the ball of lead around; his throw folded, the ball going into the dirt in front of the bottles.

"That's chuckin' 'em in there, Twiller," said Zuba, and fired his other two balls.

"Time for the canary exhibit." Crutch pulled Twiller away, toward the girly tent. "We want to be in front."

The tent was open and the all-stars were pushing their way in. Twiller joined the charge, caught in a quarterback's nightmare, head-crushing linemen all around him, gigantic and crazy, a wall of all-scholastic material—everybody's dream-team and the pride of the community, snarling, farting, shouting, "Let's have some pussy!"

They crowded in around the stage, the press getting tighter as guys kept pushing in from behind. A monster basketballer stuck him in the ribs with an elbow like an angle iron.

"Hey, buddy, take it fuckin' easy."

The basketballer closed his fist and brought it down with a fast conk on top of Twiller's head, shouting, "Bring out the cunt!"

Twiller shook off the blow and kept inching forward, closer to the stage. Crutch was going up the tent pole, rising above the crowd. An overhead speaker buzzed, hummed, and a tune crackled out of it as the flap opened at the rear of the stage and two strippers, a blonde and a brunette, stepped through onto the boards.

"Yeah, yeah!"

"Phreeeeeeeeeeeet-phreeeeeeeeeeeet-phreeuuuuuuuuuuu-uuuuu!"

The blonde smiled, showing a space between her front teeth. She couldn't dance but it didn't matter; she rolled her ass around lazily in the dream-team's face, nothing but a little red string threaded between her cheeks. Twiller had a perfect view, and then lost it as she turned, grinding a pound for the demented shot-putters on the other side of the stage.

He shifted to the brunette; her appendix scar was smiling and she sank toward the floor, knees slowly bending, ankles turned out, black fringe dangling down around her thighs, as she shimmied to the tune.

. . . fum . . . fa . . . fump . . . . . . ah-fump-ah fum fump . . . ah . . . fumppppppppppp . . .

She shook her tassels and Twiller went up on his toes trying to see; it was a classy show, with lots of glitter on the pasties.

. . . fum . . . fum-ah . . . fum . . . crackle . . . buzz . . .

The speaker went dead in the middle of the lovely tune. The strippers looked at each other, shrugged, and walked off the stage.

"WHAT KINDA FUCKIN' SHIT IS THIS?" A fist came down like a hand grenade on the edge of the stage, cracking off a piece of plank.

Twiller stiffened, and the crowd of crazy jocks surged. The shock wave corkscrewed him around and he saw Crutch hanging on to the tent pole, as a pair of lunatic linebackers started to shake it, shouting for pussy.

The wave surged again, twisting Twiller back toward the stage. Some other linemen were lifting the stage by its frame of wooden two-by-fours.

The ticket-seller stuck his head out from behind the tent flap. The stage creaked beneath his feet and he rocked backward. "Now, boys—" He waved his hand for attention. "—it's just a bit of technical difficulty."

"Up your ass with a meathook!"

"BURN THE PLACE DOWN!"

The music started again and the strippers danced in through the tent flap. The stage settled down and the gorillas underneath it crawled out.

"Yeah, take it off!"

"SHOW US YOUR PIE!"

The brunette opened the catch on her G-string and let the sequinned cloth slip down, teasing them with it. She stuck her tongue out, hooked the G-string up again and turned away, grinding her behind.

"WE WANT PUSSY!"

"SHOW US THE OLD QUIM, BABY!"

The blonde came forward lazily, dancing out of time. She shook her cupcakes at them, then ran her hands slowly into her G-string. It bulged and fell open, revealing a patch of curly black hair.

Grunts and slavering moans came from the crowd, and the panting halfbacks, discus throwers, high divers, and muff divers pushed forward.

"Don't crowd me, shitlips . . ."

"Ease off back there, hey, don't fuckin' shove ME . . ."

Twiller's feet twisted beneath him and he was lifted off the ground, suspended in a crush of sweaty armpits. The blonde moved closer, to watch her fans having their ribs slowly broken against the edge of the stage. She pulled her G-string all the way off, her muff in plain view. Twiller felt a sudden spread of long fingers pushing down on his head, as Nazareth Bomboni, top scorer in Class A Eastern Conference basketball, sprang upwards, reaching out the longest arm in the state.

The blonde jumped backwards, but Nazareth had her by the G-string. She screamed, gave him a high heel in the chest, and he yanked her down, into the crowd.

She floated on the surface for a moment, eyes darting fearfully around, and then she disappeared, dozens of hands grabbing at her, pulling her under. Twiller was forced to his knees by the sex-starved all-stars who were climbing over him to reach her, and he went down, into the jungle of stampeding legs.

A space opened in front of him and he saw a pair of bare titties, the nipples like little red eyes staring helplessly at him. Hairy hands closed over the titties and he lost sight of them, could only hear the stripper screaming for her life. Knees and boot heels caught him in the nose, the mouth, the ribs. He crawled madly through the tangle of limbs and Crutch appeared, wrapped around the bottom of the tent pole.

They scrambled upward together, clinging to the swaying pole, surfacing just as the blonde did. She was kicking viciously, her high-heel spikes puncturing the potato nose of Kyril Zyzyk, dream-game fullback. Zyzyk clutched his bleeding potato as she kicked on by him, punching, clawing, and biting. "YOU FUCKING LITTLE BITCHES—" She tore hair, gouged eyes. "—I'LL KILL YOU!"

All-scholastic linemen sank, faces raked with bloody nails. She crawled over their heads, high heels digging and stabbing, breaking the defense to pieces; she scrambled back onto the stage, bare ass, her blond wig twisted sideways.

. . . fump-ah fumpah fum-fum
shooooooo shoooooo dooooooo . . .

238

* * *

She straightened her wig and disappeared into the tent flap, then stepped back out and gave them the finger.

They gave her a big cheer, and the exit flap opened in the rear of the tent, the ticket-seller herding them out with his microphone, calling them a patient and appreciative audience, and inviting them back for the next show, in just fifteen minutes.

Twiller shuffled out onto the open ground of the midway, Crutch beside him, glasses shattered. He peered at Twiller through the webbed, broken lenses. "I'm gonna hang around for the next show."

"OK, I'll catch you near here somewhere . . ." Twiller moved on down the midway, his ribs aching from the kicks he'd taken. He blew a quarter on the wheel of fortune, and saw Gina Gabooch at the next booth, fishing with a bamboo pole over a tank of water, Drainpipe Drobish beside her, elbows on the edge of the booth, talking to a buddy.

Twiller circled the tank until he was facing her across the pond, then bought a pole and tossed in his line. She didn't see him, was trying to hook one of the little wooden fish that lay on the bottom. He glided his line along toward hers until their poles touched. She looked up, a faint smile crossing her lips as she moved her line away.

He followed with his own. She lowered her hook and his floated down beside it. When she pulled back, their lines broke the surface together, beads of water dropping from them and both hooks caught in the same wooden fish.

"We've got a catch," said the fish-pond attendant, pushing back his hat, an old fedora covered with fishing licenses. "Who gets the prize?"

Drainpipe turned around and Twiller moved back into the crowd, taking cover by the Ferris wheel. He bought a ticket with his last quarter, and climbed into a swinging bucket.

It carried him above the fairground. Faintly, from the strip show, the sound of drums started up again, and the wheel circled slowly, around and around, over the midway and the turning merry-go-round, over the fish-pond and the pony ride. In the distance he could see the lights of central city glowing against the dark sky, and he wished something exciting would happen, like in *East of Eden*, where Jimmy Dean is forced to climb down through the bars of the Ferris wheel, to the ground.

His bucket stopped. They were unloading the other buckets, one by one, below.

He looked down through the girders, saw Gina passing underneath with Drainpipe.

He leaned out to the nearest girder, took hold of it and stood. The bucket swayed, and he put one foot out over the top of it.

"*Hey, you fuckin' idiot—*" The operator pointed up at him. "SIDDOWN!"

He sat back down in the swaying bucket, and the wheel turned again, unloading another bucket, and another, his own finally swinging into place above the platform. The operator opened the crossbar, giving him a dirty look, but he ignored it, and walked away, moodily. A skinny little Gypsy kid stuck her head out of a tent alongside him. "Tell your fortune, mister?"

"Naw . . ."

"Suck you off? One dollar."

He searched his pockets desperately, but he'd spent all his money. "How about I pay you later?"

"Hey," said the little girl, "fuck off."

He nodded and moved on toward the refreshment booth, where Lily was eating a candy apple. He was suddenly filled with self-loathing for almost allowing a child to blow him.

Crutch stepped into the midway, navigating slowly from inside his shattered glasses. Twiller joined up with him. "How was the second show?"

"Terrific." Crutch's clothes were covered with mud and he was pulling pieces of straw out of his hair.

They walked along through the phantasmagoria of flashing lights. Twiller pointed with his thumb toward the fortune-teller's tent. "Weird thing happened to me there."

"Yeah, what?"

"A little girl offered to suck me off for a dollar."

Crutch's eyes owled out behind his webbed lenses. "Why didn't you tell me sooner?" He turned toward the tent.

"Crutch, she's only like about nine years old."

Crutch looked back over his shoulder. "My cocker spaniel's only five."

Chapter 33

. . . In Which Twiller Learns the Facts of Life.

◇ ◇ ◇

PROFESSIONAL ATHLETE

Twiller—Monday, Period 7
Guidance Counseling
I have always, as long as I can remember, wanted to be a professional athelete of some kind. Sports, especially baseball, has always been my favorite pastime. I always love to play and when I'm not playing I like to listen or watch a game or read a sporting magazine of some kind.

I realize that some wonderful ballplayers with the makings of professionals have been passed up in the shuffle of countless numbers of boys and men with the same ambition. But that is the chance I am willing to take.

With many boys, a professional athelete seems like a summer daydream but with me it is a very serious business. I play every chance I get in the summer and in the

242

*wintertime I lift weights and work out as much as pos-
sible so as to always be in top condition.*

His counselor stared down at the open folio, Twiller reading along with him, following the looping blue letters. Facing
the page was a full-color picture out of *Sport* magazine, of
Alvin Dark, leaning on a baseball bat.

Mr Malloy looked up from the page. "But is it realistic,
Twiller?"

Twiller lowered his eyes to the page, tracing the final
lines.

*. . . know that the career I have planned for myself
might seem like an impossible dream . . .*

"I hit pretty good this year, Mr Malloy."

Malloy looked again at the career folio, his brow furrowing,
his glasses sliding down his nose. Scattered on the desks were
other career folios—*Business Administration, Mechanical
Engineering, Nursing.* In their midst was Alvin Dark, his
green eyes haunted, wild.

"Twiller, those players who are going on to big-time ball of
some kind—like our fullback Bruno Valvona—have been
scouted and talked to, many, many times already. Has anyone approached you?"

"No, sir."

"You see, that's the—the *problem.* Your career folio isn't
grounded on a solid interest."

"I have a very solid interest, sir."

"Yes, but no one else seems to." Malloy rustled the folio
around. "That's where your thinking goes—a trifle off." He
gestured over his head, indicating clouds, or cuckoo clocks.
"Now here—" He pointed to the other folios. "These are
realistic. They're based on what I like to call the facts-of-
life."

Twiller shifted in his seat, and looked away from Alvin
Dark.

243

"Facts, my boy, the *facts—of—life.*" Malloy tapped slowly on the desk, emphasizing each word. "Now what would you say to a job in the button mill?"

"I . . . don't know, sir."

"There are openings. We've always been able to place a few graduates there."

"Doing what, sir?"

"The ground work, at first. The *heart* of the mill." Malloy made a fist, to indicate good, solid facts of life. There was a rumor going around school that he gave special instruction on the facts of life, in his supply closet, to certain of the senior girls.

Twiller leaned toward the other folios, gazing dumbly down at them. "Is that all that's available? The button mill?"

Malloy shuffled his papers again. "Your grades, Twiller. Your grades present a certain—difficulty."

"Yes sir."

"There's no college in the country would take you." He shuffled the folios again. "Would you be interested in Bird Grooming School?"

"I don't know, sir. I'll have to think about it."

"You do that, my boy. Think it over carefully. I know that together we can come to a good decision *if*—we remain realistic."

He tossed his varsity uniform in the locker-room laundry bin, with the others. The locker-room was nearly empty now, the lockers hanging open, waiting for next year.

But for him it was over.

He packed his gym bag slowly, wanting just a few last moments in the old familiar smell, of linament, and sweat, and the cold ashy aroma of the cinderblock walls.

He breathed it in, to take with him, to remember always.

He'd go on to other things, other places, but this locker-room would always be sacred.

He left his empty locker ajar, and walked slowly down the hall, gym bag in hand.

Then, at Coach Nozollo's door, he paused, staring at the frosted glass.

Inside, sitting among the trophies, was the man who'd shaped him, who'd molded his character.

He tapped on the door and pushed it open, hesitantly.

Nozollo was at his desk, towel around his waist, eating a hero sandwich. He looked up, thick neck slowly turning. "Yeah?"

"I came to say so long, Coach."

"G'wan, get the fuck outta here."

And so the young shortstop and his beloved coach have their deep and fond farewell.

◇　◇　◇

"I'm not sure I can handle this." Twiller paced around the telephone table. Crutch looked at him.

"Put it off any longer and you'll be going to the prom with Floyd."

Twiller paced some more. Crutch stuck him in the back with the receiver. "Go on, give her the horn."

"Alright, I'm doing it."

Click . . . click . . . clickity . . . click click four three six.

"*Hello?*" Voice like a meat truck. Angelo Gabooch.

"Ah yes, is Gina there?"

"*Who wants her?*"

"Just tell her Jack is calling."

"*Jack who?*"

"Just Jack."

"*Go fuck yourself.*"

Clack-hmmmmmmmmmmmmmmmmmmm.

245

He stared at the dead receiver. "I'm not taking that kind of shit."

Click . . . click . . . clickity . . . click click four three six.

"*Yeah?*"

"Lemme talk to Gina."

"*Go fuck yourself.*"

Clack-hmmmmmmmmmmmmmmmmmmm.

Crutch looked at him, and at the dead receiver. "What's going on?"

"Angelo keeps cooling me."

"That cuntlapper." Crutch's voice rose in anger. "What the fuck business is it of his? Call her again. Go right in on past him."

Twiller dialed again, with new determination. He wouldn't stand for that kind of shit from *any*body.

. . . click four three six.

"*Yeah?*"

"Angelo . . ."

"*Go fuck yourself.*"

◊ ◊ ◊

They cruised up the avenue in his new red-hot Buick convertible, converted out of the junkyard for fifty bucks, top permanently down, unless you had three guys to haul up the broken lift mechanism. The body was constructed of chicken wire and plastic filler. One good bounce, it'd all fall away, and there'd be nothing left but a steering wheel and four tires going down the road.

He turned toward Drumville, and moved into it, toward Gina's neighborhood.

"If Angelo answers the door, don't take any shit from him." Crutch whirled the tuning knob on the radio. "Tell him you're selling magazine subscriptions."

The motor started making a fierce tapping noise. Twiller

246

pulled to the side of the road and grabbed a quart of oil from the back seat.

Crutch opened the hood and Twiller leaned in over the motor with the oil. "Drink. Drink deeply . . ."

They slammed the hood down and resumed progress, past Drumville High where Angelo had made a name for himself, along with his brother Nestor, pounding other linemen to pieces. Twiller smoothed his hair down and tried to remain cool. "If he hangs me upside-down over the railing, you know what to do."

"Right, catch your car keys if they fall outta your pocket. Whyn't you just leave the keys with me?"

"Good enough."

Twiller guided the big Buick on past the high school and up the block, toward the Gabooch residence. "I wonder if he remembers the night he kicked me under Scuduto's car."

"Naw, he's kickin' guys all the time."

Twiller pulled in toward the curb and parked. He took his keys out of the ignition and gave them to Crutch.

"Might as well give me your loose change too . . ."

"Yeah, good idea." Twiller emptied his pockets and took a fast glance at himself in the rearview mirror. He worked his comb on through a few times and then added a dash of pink pimple cream to his nose. "I'm ready . . ."

The Scarlet Pimplenose is coming.

He stepped out of the car and jogged lightly across the street. An athlete. In condition.

He went up the sidewalk, happy to see there were lots of thick bushes alongside the Gabooch balcony, to break his fall.

He rang the doorbell.

Silence. Then:

Someone started rolling a refrigerator down the stairs.

The door opened, and Angelo peered out at him "Yeah?"

"Is Gina home?"

247

"No."

"When is she coming back?"

Two huge meatpaws came forward, grabbing the Pimple-nose's lapels. *"Go—fuck—yourself."*

"Hey, man . . ."

"An-gelo!" A piercing cry came from above, and then Gina thundered down the stairs in her engineer boots. She whacked Angelo in the head. "Hey, what's wrong with you?"

Angelo smiled sheepishly and backed off, onto the stairs.

Gina ran a hand quickly along her hair, smoothing it flatter against her cheek. "Beat it out of here, idiot." She pushed her brother again and he turned, going up the stairs, fortunate in that he'd not had to deal further with the Scarlet Pimple-nose, who was now adjusting his lapels. The Pimplenose's shirt seemed to have been stretched in a single instant, five sizes too large. He lounged back inside it, casually, against the porch rail. "How're you doing?"

"OK," said Gina, her gum snapping. "What brings you up this way?"

"I was just rolling by . . ."

"Don't mind Angelo. He's like that sometimes."

"Sure. This shirt was a little small anyway." He fluffed it out, his good old gaucho shirt with the cloth buttons. A lot of shirt. Room for two gauchos in it now. "Angelo doesn't faze me."

"He's an idiot, that's all. He thinks he's a hero." Gina pointed toward the street. "That your convertible?"

"Yeah."

"It looks sharp."

The Pimplenose leaned further back on the railing, in a pose of complete casualness. "You wanna go the Anthracite Prom with me?"

"When is it?"

"Friday night."

"That's not much time . . ."

"Yeah, well, I just found out about it, they just announced it."

"Three days before?"

"Yeah, I dunno, I got the date wrong or something." He stared down at the steps. Above, in the Gabooch apartment, the floor was shaking, as Angelo walked about, perhaps looking for his football shoes, in order to kick a really long one. "I dunno, you wanna go?"

Gina turned her dark eyes toward him. "You send me a corsage or do I buy one?"

"I'll buy you one, that's what I heard, the guys buy it." He put his hands in his pockets. "You hear something different?"

"No."

"OK, I'll pick you up around eight, alright?"

"Yeah, sure." She took a step backward toward the door, and he took two steps toward the stairs. The less time he spent around the Gabooch household the better.

"Right then, I'll see you Friday." He moved on out toward the car, swaggering nonchalantly in his now size-44 shirt.

Crutch looked at him for an answer, and Twiller snapped his fingers. "I'm on."

"Way to go." Crutch handed him back his keys and change. The Pimplenose turned over the ignition and pulled quickly away. "I went right in on past him."

"After he set you back down, yeah, it looked like a smooth move." Crutch clicked on the radio. "So that's you. Now what about me?"

"There's a chick out there for you somewhere."

Crutch sank back in the seat and started cleaning his glasses. He looked up at Twiller with weak squinty eyes. "The only thing I'll be taking to the prom is a pants full of Kleenex."

249

Chapter 34

. . . In Which Eddie Chanooga Plays His Wig Off.

◇ ◇ ◇

A FRANK TALK FROM A GIRL
ABOUT BOYS WHO HAVE PIMPLES
"Having a brother near my age certainly taught me a lot about boys who have pimples. First of all, I want to say that we girls sympathize with boys in this problem. Why shouldn't we . . . we have pimples too. But today, with CLEARASIL *available to all of us, there is really no excuse to let pimples be a social problem."*

He added just a dash and studied the final picture in the mirror. He'd been late in renting his tuxedo, so he'd had to settle for one a size too large. *To be returned within 24 hours to Sabowski & Sons.* It hung down a little low, but his letterman's sweater had made him comfortable with the low-slung look.

He tightened the maroon cummerbund, adjusted his boutonniere, and went downstairs, past the living room. His father rolled over on the couch. "Take my car."

"Thanks, Dad, but really I'd rather take my convertible."

"It shouldn't be on the road, it's falling apart."

"I've got it tuned up pretty good now—"

"—with chicken wire." His father rolled back over, facing into the pillows.

Twiller went out the door and across the lawn. The big red convertible awaited him. He slipped into the driver's seat, onto the cushion necessary to place him comfortably behind the wheel, as the seat was permanently jammed in the back position, a setting suitable for Nazareth Bomboni whose arms were thirteen feet long, but your varsity shortstop required a cushion, discreetly covered in imitation leopard skin, to match the seat covers and steering wheel.

He blasted off. The evening air danced merrily around the open top; below, the frame was so totally rusted from river water running through it at the junkyard there was constant danger of the wheels falling off, but he laughed at danger.

Fuck danger.

He was riding top down, in style.

To Drumville, where there was even more danger, from Angelo and Nestor Gabooch.

But Gina seemed to be able to handle them.

Gina would protect him.

The wind whipped the sleeve of his dinner jacket, and the smell of new-mown grass was in the air. Summer had come, the big night had arrived, and tomorrow he'd be at Bird Grooming School.

He rolled past Drumville High, where Angelo Gabooch drop-kicked opposing players through the goalposts, after which Nestor jumped on their balls.

Nestor and Angelo.

Angelo and Nestor.

Waiting for me to come and pick up their sister.

He turned the corner, nose in his boutonniere. Maybe they wouldn't hit a guy wearing a flower.

He pulled in at the curbstone, switched off the ignition, and looked toward the Gabooch residence.

He tapped the horn, lightly.

She'll hear that, and come down.

He waited, casually, while nothing happened.

Heaving a sigh, he opened the car door and stepped out, about to put his body into the hands of a pair of gorillas; *Gorilla gorilla,* as he believed he'd seen it spelled at the zoo.

He pulled himself together and danced up the stairs to the front porch like the game shortstop he was.

Finger trembling, he rang the bell.

There was a moment of silence and then a refrigerator bounced down the stairs, crunching and splitting the steps, warping the building, shaking the doorframe.

The door opened. He stared at the hulking shape that made Eastern Conference halfbacks shit their pants when they tried to get past it.

"Yeah, come on in." Angelo stepped back, and indicated that Twiller should precede him up the steps.

Smells of strange spicy cooking wafted down the stairs, as Twiller ascended. He waited at the top step and Angelo waved him on through, toward the living room. "Have a seat. Gina's still gettin' ready."

Twiller drew up the creased knees of his tuxedo and went down into the sectional sofa. Angelo sat in a chair across from him. On the tv set were colored photographs of Angelo, Nestor, and Gina, arranged around a vase of plastic flowers wrapped in cellophane.

The floorboards creaked deeply. Twiller looked to his left, and for an instant saw an upright freezer rolling toward him: then his vision cleared and he realized it was Nestor. "How you doin'," said Nestor, rolling on through to the kitchen.

Twiller looked at Angelo. "What's up with football? You got a scholarship, right?"

"Yeah." Angelo lowered his eyes like a shy buffalo. Two

hundred and forty-five pounds of hard-packed salami, at left tackle.

Twiller tried to maintain a friendly conversation. "You guys really dumped Anthracite this year."

Angelo looked up, smiling. "Hey, but you guys did us under in baseball. I saw the game . . ." Angelo interlaced his fingers and cracked his knuckles. ". . . you looked alright out there. You get any offers?"

"Naw, I'll probably play some industrial ball."

"It's a fast league, the Industrial." Angelo hung his arms over the back of the chair, hands dangling like a pair of sledgehammers.

The upright freezer rolled back into the living room. It looked at its brother. "What's keepin' Gina?"

"She's just finishin'." Angelo turned to Twiller. "You in a hurry?"

"Naw, hell no."

"She likes to take her time." Nestor dropped down onto the other end of the sectional, causing Twiller's end to rise. Angelo pointed to the plastic grapes on the coffee table. "Have one." He extended the bowl, but Twiller decided it was not the time to add plastic grapes to his vaudeville swallowing act.

The floorboards creaked again, and Mama Gabooch, a compact model from Westinghouse Refrigeration, rolled in. She raised her arm dramatically, as the whispering of a floor-length gown sounded in the hallway behind her. Gina stepped through, in folds of taffeta and flounce, all of it rustling around the points of two transparent-toed shoes sparkling with rhinestones.

Twiller rose and stepped toward her, amazed at the transformation that'd taken place, from black leather to lace, Gina suddenly so soft and delicate-looking, her hair and eyes radiant, her cheeks blushing red as she gave him a hesitant smile. The corsage he'd sent her was around her wrist, and her hands were crossed in front of her, on the billowing folds

253

of her gown. Angelo and Nestor crowded in, checking her out.

"Looks alrigh', don't she, Ma?"

Mama Gabooch gestured again, as if she were about to sing an opera. "She's beau-tiful." Her hand went lightly along the edge of Gina's gown, tracing it in the air. She turned to Twiller. "We're very happy you're taking Gina. I know what a fine young man you are, Gina's told me all about you."

For a moment, Twiller wondered if he'd gotten into the wrong house, but Mama Gabooch put out her hands, taking his and Gina's. "Anthracite Academic is a very fine school. It produces true gentlemen." She raised his hand with somber formality, as if presenting him to the community. Her voice took on a deep tremor, like an afternoon soap opera, or a tight girdle maybe.

"Boys from Anthracite Academic have a future.' Mama Gabooch squeezed his hand warmly, then gestured tenderly toward Angelo and Nestor, the meanest, raunchiest cold-storage units ever to kick somebody under a car. "And mine have done ok too. Both with scholarships." She turned to Twiller. "Are you on to more school?"

"Yeah, I'm probably going to be studying at a small school . . ." He gave a vague nod of his head. ". . . up the line."

"Mom," said Gina, "I think we have to get going."

"Yes, yes, go on, both of you." The Mother of the Year put her hands lightly on their backs and escorted them to the stairs, her girdle squeezing a trembling farewell from her. "Have a won-derful evening, you look *so* nice . . ."

Twiller followed Gina down the stairs, feeling the incredible wonder of it all—gown, corsage, tuxedo, *an extra fee of $5.00 per day to be paid Sabowski & Sons for time exceeding said hours.*

They crossed the street to the big red Buick and he opened the door for her; she slid in past him, her hair alive with electricity, pointed spitcurls lying smoothly against her cheek.

She fiddled with her corsage. "I'm not gonna know anybody . . ."

He started up the car and pulled out into the street, looking at her, still amazed at the transformation she'd undergone. He realized he sort of expected her to come in engineer boots.

She looked at him, her eyes a little unsure. "The dance is at Masonic Hall, is it?"

"Yeah, ever been there?"

"No, you?"

"I was in a dance recital there once, in the auditorium part."

"What kind of dance was it?"

"Hazatska, stuff like that." He turned onto Main Avenue. "I tap-danced up a flight of steps."

"No kidding?"

"Yeah . . ." He shrugged modestly, and circled the big Buick toward town, along the streetcar tracks, the wheels biting and slipping on the grooves. Traffic grew heavier, town crowded with prom couples. He could feel the excitement in the air, for this night belonged to them, as did the future, at Bird Grooming School or the button mill, it was a hard decision to make.

He wheeled in alongside the Hall, the curb lined with MG's, Corvettes, custom jobs with flames painted on the fenders. His fenders were hand-painted too of course, with rust-preventive red, applied over the chicken wire of which they were constructed.

"No room here," he said, and turned into the alley, wheeling the big Buick through.

"There's a space."

"Too small." Having learned to park with only the use of second gear, he clung to this training habit now, searching for a space large enough for a two-ton truck.

"Here's a spot," he said, and prepared.

"Isn't that a loading zone?"

"I'll chance it." He deftly maneuvered the convertible back, scraping the whitewalls against the curb with a rubbery screech. "In snug," he said, turning off the key. He opened both doors and Gina stepped out, her gown rustling over the curb. He gave her his arm. Her dangling teardrop earrings swung back and forth, palely glittering in the twilight, and her heels tapped on the pavement. His gleaming patent leather pumps answered, steps echoing with hers.

"Don't introduce me to nobody," she said, "I'm feelin' kinda shy."

They turned onto the avenue and walked toward the Hall. The wide stairs were filled with couples, and he felt his stomach, and Gina's, drop.

She squeezed his arm nervously, and it suddenly seemed to him he'd been dating her for years; the single evening they'd spent together, when he'd fired a shot at her, was like a lifelong relationship. He was right in step with her, in mutual fear, because the class officers were on the marble stairs, looking like the Ivy League already.

Above their heads, strung across the doorway, was the banner bearing their class slogan.

RECTUM PROPTER SESE

He led Gina under the banner, through the open door into the ballroom. It was framed with tables, and he guided her to an empty one.

"It's nice," said Gina, looking at the streamered ceiling.

He glanced toward the bandstand, where Eddie Chanooga and His All-Stars were playing accordion, guitar, bass and drums—a big sound from the Dance Band Man himself.

He gestured toward the dance floor. "Want to?"

"OK."

She got up with him and slipped into his arms. He guided her with surprising ease. A seven-dollar tuxedo had done wonders; he felt loose and carefree, could hardly believe that the nightmare of high school was over, but it was, all the years spiraling into a single point, like the rainbow of streamers overhead.

"Eddie Chanooga played our last dance," said Gina. "He's really cool."

Eddie swayed with his accordion, and crooned into the mike; it had a tendency toward ear-splitting feedback that made Eddie's gleaming teeth seem like they were made out of metal—Mister Senior Prom himself, hitting the high notes, his toupee lifting an inch off his head.

Twiller glided with Gina toward the bandstand, her wrist hanging lightly on his shoulder, her fingers touching his collar. "What did you say you were going to be doing when you get out?"

"I've got a chance to work with birds."

"Really? Doin' what?"

"Well, it's a whole curriculum, you learn everything."

"It sounds unusual."

"Yeah, it's something a little different."

"That's the kind of guy you are, right?" Gina smiled, her dark eyes like a black shooter he used to have, with faint swirls of gray at the center. He looked at her, thinking about how it could be—him coming home at night, covered with feathers and birdshit, and Gina waiting for him, in a little apartment over on Drain Court maybe, with a view of the junkyard.

He turned her in his arms, past the far end of the bandstand. "I might look into something down at the button mill too."

"Oh Jesus, I worked there last summer. You don't wanna go there."

"Slave labor?"

"And the noise." Gina put a finger in her ear, above her dangling teardrop.

"My guidance counselor wanted me to take it."

"Well, it's nowhere." Her gown pressed against him, and

257

he seemed to spiral up the bright streamers, to the vanishing point again. He was free, he didn't have to do anything he didn't want to do. They could put Bird Grooming School up their Rectum Propter Sese, along with the button mill.

"You dance nice," she said.

"Yeah, well, I took some lessons."

"Yeah, right."

Her huge gown kept him far away from her; it was like dancing with an opened umbrella, but her shoulders were bare and felt warm and soft.

"It's a big dance," said Gina.

"The biggest."

Conversation was proceeding along in a sophisticated manner. He hadn't thought it would ever be possible with a girl. But it was easy. He was *on top* of things tonight. He pressed in closer against her gown, but it sprung him back out, to arm's length again. Mama Gabooch had probably wired the fucking thing.

But the night was long, there was no need to rush anything. He had hours and hours ahead of him. And after that the whole summer, riding around, hanging out, playing it cool. He was a member of the graduating class. He could now get a job pumping gas. He was on the way *up*.

He looked into Gina's coal-black eyes, and she lowered her lashes and turned her head a little. Her gown sprung him back out again.

"You really look sharp tonight," she said.

"Thanks," he said. "So do you."

Mature, intelligent, casual conversation. He realized he'd taken a tremendous step forward. From here on in, he'd be able to go to the dances at the Ukrainian Social Club and indulge in some banter.

Eddie Chanooga's band let out a drumroll, some teeth-shattering feedback, and the tune ended with the bass player kicking viciously at the tubes in his speaker.

258

Couples applauded around the dance floor, and Twiller led Gina off to the side.

"Lotta different types of corsages here tonight."

"I really like this one," she said, sniffing the little bunch of roses and then passing them under his nose. The scent of the flowers was all mixed up with Gina's perfume, and he swam in the warm smell for a moment, feeling how really close a prom date brought two people, like these flowers were their special secret nobody else could share.

"Somebody's comin' over," said Gina nervously, her arm dropping to her side.

Twiller saw George Huffnak, the class president, bearing down on them, hand outstretched, a pasted-on smile on his face. "Jack," said Huffnak, "I just wanted to say good luck."

"Thanks," said Twiller, taking Huffnak's hand. "Hey, whyn't you meet Gina . . ."

"Nice to meet you, Gina," said Huffnak, his gaze taking her in very slowly, lingering along her bare shoulders for a moment.

"I'm sure," said Gina, and Twiller saw her face going stony, even though Huffnak was looking at her like she was the Queen of the Prom.

"Hey," said Twiller, "we're gonna spin around the floor one more time . . ."

"Right," said Huffnak, "I'm just circulating."

They watched him move along toward another couple. "Next time," said Gina, "I'm duckin' into the ladies' room."

"It's just the class officers," said Twiller. "They've gotta do it. Y'know, come around."

"Are they friends of yours?"

"Hell, no." Twiller fluffed up the flower in his buttonhole.

"I think I'll go in now anyways," said Gina. She touched the back of his hand with her fingertips, and stepped away toward the ladies' room, leaving electricity shooting up through his arm and down into his rented underwear.

He stretched out a cuff, straightened the twisted silver link, and then let the sleeve of his tux slip back down into place, over his palm.

Hanging just a little long.

But if he kept his elbows bent, it was totally unnoticeable.

He gazed at his classmates as they danced by. After four long years, it was all coming to an end. The world was waiting for them, and for him. He'd march out of the last assembly with his diploma in hand and go straight to the Carvel stand and get a job peeling bananas. Nothing could stop him now.

The highway wind blew over them, the night sky rushing past their heads. Alongside the highway, the lights of the Colony Inn glowed, and he signaled left, turning into the gravel lot. The MG's and Thunderbirds were there, and he pulled the big red monster in alongside them, the engine coughing to a stop. "I don't wanna meet nobody," said Gina.

He climbed out and opened her door. She took his arm and they went along the sidewalk, into the inn. The lights were low and the tables crowded, a hum of voices filling the room. From the shadowy row of heads, Crutch and Floyd stood and waved.

He glanced at Gina.

"It's ok," she said. "I like your friends."

He escorted her to their table. Floyd stood, holding a chair for her. His tuxedo fit the way Twiller wished his own did.

"You're looking lovely tonight, Gina," said Floyd, sliding the chair in beneath her.

She half-looked at him shyly. "You guys don't have dates?"

Crutch bit into a cheeseburger. "I couldn't get my cocker spaniel to wear a dress."

Twiller felt the edge of Gina's gown touching his leg beneath the table. The secret was still theirs, the two of them enclosed together in an invisible bubble; they might seem to talk and be with classmates and friends, but they were sharing something else with each other. She shifted a little in her chair and her gown moved again; it was almost alive, and was maybe the thing that united them most—the big spreading umbrella that kept them constantly touching. And the corsage—he could smell the roses again, her wrist on the table near his as she turned to the waiter and ordered a cheeseburger, without onions.

That was significant.

No onions.

She was staying kissing-sweet, for a reason.

He ordered a cheeseburger and french fries and settled his elbows back on the table. His silver cuff links were catching the candlelight and he felt unbelievably Dubonnet.

The highway was empty, his big red clunker trailing far behind the sports-car set heading back toward town. He drove at his regular forty miles per, beyond which the red monster would emit wondrous steam clouds, its mighty insides bubbling at tremendously high temperatures.

"You don't have to be home or anything yet, do you?"

"No," said Gina. "Mom knows a prom date lasts all night."

He slowed, looking for a particular turn-off he knew, by the old reservoir. As he scanned the wooded roadside, he noticed his headlights suddenly growing dim. A second later he was driving in total darkness.

"Jesus Christ . . ." He brought the monster to a stop, on the shoulder of the road.

"What's wrong?"

"The lights."

"I saw."

"Like that . . ." He snapped his fingers, as if making a swiftly penetrating diagnosis of the situation.

He opened the glove compartment and took out his flashlight. "Let me just check this." He stepped onto the roadway, and walked around to the front of the car. Had he been graduating from Manual Trades High tonight he would know exactly what to do; instead he was opening the hood on the eternal mystery.

He flashed the light around, and spoke softly. "*What are you doing to me?*"

The big red monster remained silent and dark, eyes closed.

"*This is my big night, you fuck . . .*" He rapped on a wire with the end of his flashlight.

"*Screwed . . .*" He slammed the hood. The rusting teeth in the grillwork smiled crookedly at him. He walked back to the door and crawled in behind the wheel, onto his dashing leopard skin cushion.

"Did you fix it?"

"No." He handed her the flashlight. "Shine it on the highway." He gunned the big V-8 motor, seven cylinders of which were actually firing, sand filling the eighth one; he limped the big red monster back onto the road.

Driving in total darkness, he leaned out the window, trying to see the faintly winding white line. He followed it closely, the warm confident glow of the night of nights running down his rented pants leg.

He drove on past the reservoir, would never chance trying to handle the road in there now; the big red monster would sense water and head right into it, feeling like it was home again, down at Snake's Riverside Junkyard.

262

"Fifty bucks I paid for this car." He spoke into the wind, neck craned around the side mirror.

"Well," said Gina, "there's nobody but us on the road."

"Yeah, we should be able to make it back in about three hours." He crept along, tracking the line, lost it and hit the brakes. Gina flew against the dashboard, flashlight falling on the floor.

"Sorry."

" 'Sok." Gina picked up the flashlight.

He found the line again and hugged it, hands clenched on the wheel. If a truck came barreling out of nowhere from behind them, it would cut a new asshole in the red monster. Somehow he had to avoid it, with all the skills at his command; he'd been trained in a car that went only ten miles per, and now, traveling at that same speed, he felt a certain familiarity taking over his limbs again. He'd bring them through this, drawing on all his knowledge of extremely slow driving.

The solid white line turned to broken bars of white, his lane becoming a passing zone, through which he tracked from bar to bar.

Gina stood, pointing her flashlight over the windshield, and he saw them—two cars rounding the near bend and heading for the passing zone, one of them already pulling out, into his lane.

"He can't see us—" He edged to the right, toward the shoulder, totally disoriented, feeling an immense chasm must be there. Gina moved her light quickly, shining it onto the guardrail, and he tucked in on the narrow patch of gravel, as the cars sped by him.

Gina fell back down in her seat. "Christ, ain't this somethin'?"

"We'll make it." He inched slowly back out to the highway, all the old reflexes coming back, the important responses a driver had to have when he was competing at speeds like this—nine miles per hour or less.

"It's kinda nice drivin' with the lights out," said Gina. "You feel like you're hidin' or somethin'."

He glanced at the stars above the dark treetops, and it did seem like he and Gina were hiding. The moon slipped by and then fell out of sight as the highway dipped down and around the wooded hills.

"Shooooo-doooooo-mmmmmmmm . . . shoooooooo . . ."

Gina started singing softly. He was amazed, as always, at the way girls could get all the frills of a tough tune *down,* making all the little dips and rises just like the record. Himself, he liked to mouth the words, while the record was playing. He had some powerful renditions of "Heartbreak Hotel" where he slid across the bedroom floor on his knees, nothing coming out of his mouth but a big silent *". . . ho . . . tel . . ."*

Gina stood up again and shined the light over the windshield. The wind played with the top of her gown. "This is a real kick," she said, one hand braced on the windshield, the other holding the flashlight and working it slowly back and forth, the beam tracing the road ahead.

"Yeah," he said, but how incredible the night could have been if he'd had a decent car, instead of this blind red monster limping through the darkness.

"Yeah," she said, "I'm not nervous anymore."

He glanced over at her and she looked back. "Y'know, the prom made me kind of nervous. Could'ja tell?"

"I was nervous too," he said, feeling suddenly close to her again, like it had always been the two of them against the odds. She looked down and smiled, her face relaxed, all the tension from the dance gone now. The wind was blowing in her hair and she was singing to herself and beating time with her ring finger on the edge of the windshield.

He mouthed the words of the tune, checking his mouth out in the sideview mirror to see he had his lips shaped right.

Perfectly natural.

"Where'd you get this car anyway?" asked Gina.

"Snake's."

"It's a crazy set of wheels."

"When we get back to town, I'll switch over to my old man's car. It's a new Chev."

And then he would put the last piece of the night into place. The close feeling with Gina was developing into something so warm inside himself; he'd never felt anything quite like it, as if she were somehow already in his arms. The dark pocket of highway they moved in was part of their secret, the night hanging around them like a curtain. Her gown was the color of the moon, which shone behind her now, through the trees. It was like a movie almost, like something that might have happened to James Dean—a *situation*.

He held his foot lightly on the gas pedal, and the highway kept coming at him slowly, the broken white line going under the front wheel, stitch after stitch, up a long black pants leg.

◇ ◇ ◇

"We made it." He limped the big vehicle around the corner and swung it sightlessly through the intersection. His knuckles were white on the wheel and his neck was twisted like a flamingo down toward the dim street, but his house was just ahead, with his father's car setting in the driveway. He pulled in at the curbstone, tearing a last little bit of whitewall off his tires, and parked.

"I'll get the keys," he said. "It'll just take a second."

He dashed across the lawn, toward the sleeping house, and went through the front door. Upstairs, he heard his father's heavy breathing. He tiptoed along the hallway and took his father's car keys from the night table, as the old man's muffled voice echoed through the house, the usual nightly dream discussion about the Democrats in full sway.

He tiptoed back along the hallway, and out again, across the lawn.

265

"Come on," he said, holding the car door for Gina. "I've got a good set of wheels now."

"I was startin' to get used to these," said Gina, with a little laugh, and crawled out. Holding her gown up from the dewy grass, she walked with him, over to his father's car.

He opened the door, to the brand-new smell inside, and they climbed in, onto the smooth plastic seat covers. He adjusted the seat, having no need for a leopard skin cushion to place him securely behind the wheel.

"Aren't you going to turn the lights on?" asked Gina.

He switched them on, the street strangely bright in front of him. "We're cool now," he said, though the car felt odd, with no frightening noises coming from under the hood, no sand clogging the brake drums, no scented pine tree hanging from the rearview mirror. But it would get them to the nearest make-out land, to which he had to hurry, as the night was almost gone already, lost on the blacked-out highway back to town.

"I'm gonna drive up through the college, ok?"

"Sure."

"Just see what's up there . . ."

He turned on through the main gates and cut left, toward a little road he knew, at the very edge of the campus. He circled, approaching the make-out lane from behind, so he'd be facing downhill into the valley, an inspiring sight for the night of nights.

He coasted over the top of the hill, his headlights falling onto another car—a familiar rear end, constructed of body filler like his own.

Crutch's shadowy form came bolt upright in the car, shocked into fast action. His tailpipe blasted, Twiller's headlights still shining on him through the rear window, as he pulled away.

"He's alone," said Gina.

"Yeah." Twiller watched Crutch barrel off down the road. A wave of sadness hit him for having spoiled a prom-night

266

jack-off session. A magical, once-in-a-lifetime moment had been interrupted.

"I coulda fixed him up with somebody," said Gina. "Lotsa girls would wanna go to Anthracite's prom, they wutn't care who with."

He gave her a pained look of inquiry. Had she herself been one of them?

She looked back at him. "Y'know?"

"Right. Right, I know."

He drew a long breath and turned back, looking down into the valley. The dark hills were lit by streetlamps, like single beads on a stretched-out chain hung through the distant trees.

From the corner of his eye he could see Gina staring into the dark valley.

He put his nose in his boutonniere. "It was quite the dance, huh?"

"Really swell." Gina turned toward him for a moment, and then back, to the distant valley lights.

He breathed the expensive new fabric of the seats, missing the smell of his perfumed little pine tree, and the smooth synthetic fur of his leopard skin seat covers that made you break out in hives. The old man's car was so clean and unbroken-in. Beer and sneaky-pete wine hadn't been spilled on the floor. No one had passed out in it, or fallen out with a wild cry; the top wasn't dashingly open to the stars. It was another world.

He looked toward Gina again, trying for a little sophisticated conversation. "Eddie Chanooga really played his wig off, didn't he?"

"Yeah," said Gina. "Eddie's cool."

"Place was decorated up, wasn't it?"

"Really neat."

"Yeah . . ." He stared down into the valley. His arms seemed paralyzed; he wanted to slip them up and across the seat but they wouldn't go there.

Gina touched the dashboard. "Your father's car is really sharp."

He could feel the dawn, only a little ways away. The night of nights was on the edge of fading forever.

"So what are you gonna do for summer?"

"I'm workin' at Luna Pizza."

"A really good crust. Really crisp." He gestured, wanting to continue with his fingers along the bare slope of her shoulder, drawing her to him, but his hand dropped back down onto the new gleaming seat, where he traced the pattern of shining vinyl.

He stared back out the window, into the valley, and saw the blackness turning ever-so-slightly to gray, just the faintest tint disturbing the magic darkness, but it couldn't be stopped; he raced against it, trying to make *his move.*

"A really really good crust . . ."

"It's starting to get light," said Gina.

Her hands were folded, sunk in the sheen of her gown, the corsage blooming out of her lap. She shifted her hands, putting the corsage under, and then put it back on top again.

Wheels spun inside him, through the spreading gray, going nine miles an hour, nowhere.

The edges of the trees were coming into view all along the rim of the valley. On the slopes, rooftops were emerging here and there, as the curtain lifted. He leaned forward on the steering wheel, to get a better look, as if he were a specialist in checking out sunrises.

Do it, do it

He shifted his hands on the wheel, preparing for a Big Move, but there was no imitation leopard skin on the wheel to give him that sleazy feeling that was *himself.*

Gina opened her evening bag, looked into it, and closed it up again. Houses were coming into view in the valley, the gray light creeping in through everything. He steeled himself for a *maneuver.* He couldn't back down, he had to act.

268

He unscrewed the shifting knob, looked at it, and screwed it back on again.

"There go the streetlights," said Gina.

He looked, and they were gone, switched off like the headlights on his big red monster.

An hour more, and I wouldn't have needed headlights.

He put his foot on the brake pedal and pressed down. There was lots of new brake. On the good old monster you pressed down through the floorboards and prayed. He flashed on going back for it, but realized it was too late; he'd made the switch, derailing himself, and the night was over.

"That was something, huh, us driving all the way back in the dark?" He looked at her, trying to recapture the feeling of the two of them, together on the highway, struggling along.

"Yeah," she said, "it was a kick, wasn't it?"

He nodded, wanting to kick himself, as he saw—the big red monster had smiled and given them the gift of darkness, had wrapped them in a deep black curtain and locked their souls together, Gina holding the flashlight over the windshield, her gown blowing in the wind, and himself, hanging out the other side, staring at the creeping white line, functioning brilliantly at his best speeds—five, six, and eight miles per.

"Yeah," he said, pulling the visor down, "a real kick."

Attached to the other side of the visor, facing him, was his father's parking permit for the company lot—a big, glossy number, edged in black.

He put the visor back up and closed his eyes, seeing the white line of the highway again, running inside his eyelids like a thread through a labyrinth. He'd followed it without a mistake, but hadn't realized the big red monster was his ace, that his and Gina's shadows were still back there in it, coming closer and closer, leaning together for a kiss.

"There's a milk truck," said Gina.

He opened his eyes, feeling only half-there, some part of him missing, skinned off, his leopard skin gone.

He watched the milk truck go by, up the block and out of

269

sight. He raised his eyes toward the far hills, where the tree-tops were starting to glow. The climbing sun shimmered through the branches and then came up over the treetops, shooting its rays across the valley.

"Pretty, ain't it," said Gina.

The sunlight spread across the valley, and suddenly the chrome was glistening on the car; one of Gina's earrings glittered for a second as she turned her head toward him. "I'm glad we could see it. You know, to remember . . ."

"Yeah, to look back on, yeah, I know."

The campus was visible now, dormitory windows reflecting the sunrise. A door opened in one of the buildings and a maintenance man stepped out.

Twiller touched the ignition and looked at Gina. This was her last chance to attack him, maddened by his after-shave.

She looked down at the clock on the dashboard, where the second hand was sweeping the minutes around with a faint little tick. "Mom'll be expectin' me."

Through the window of the Texas Weiner, he could see tuxedoed forms hunching at the counter, having an early-morning heartburn special. He walked through the door, into the sound of the clanging pinball machine. Crutch waved from alongside the machine, while Floyd swayed at the front of it, working the ball on down. Twiller joined the gathering.

"So," said Crutch, "did you score?"

"Hey, did I score . . ." He played it as nonchalantly as possible. "On a prom date? Hey, come on . . ."

It had been an Unforgettable Moment—sitting alone on the old mine road, the sunlight shining, the birds twittering, his right hand tenderly stroking into a Kleenex.

Spider looked out from behind the pinball machine,

toward the counter, where the owner was serving the other tuxedos. A long wire dangled from Spider's sleeve. He pulled it out and nodded to Floyd.

"Just keep playin'."

Floyd released another ball and Spider slipped behind the machine again.

Twiller moved to the far side of it, where Spider was inserting the wire through a hole he'd made in the scoreboard.

Ten games racked up on the little counter in the upper left corner.

Spider wiggled the wire again and ten more racked up.

"We're in five bucks," said Crutch.

"Hit it again, Spider," Floyd faked some fancy body English and Spider clicked twenty more games up. The owner looked across the counter, his expression growing still more weary as he saw he was going to have to pay off first thing in the morning.

Spider slipped out behind Crutch, wire up his tuxedo sleeve once more. Floyd walked over to the counter and pointed to the game score. The owner nodded unhappily and hit his cash register.

Twiller turned toward the window. The miniature golf course sparkled, empty greens covered with dew. Beside it, Hamburg Heaven was doing business, tuxedoed figures sitting around the counter.

It was something to remember.

"Alright, so what are we gonna do . . ."

"Whyn't we take a ride?"

"Yeah, somethin' might be shakin' somewhere."

They moved toward the door together, and on through, into the sunlight. Twiller adjusted his bow tie, and looked down the stretch of road. The other breakfast joints were opening their doors, and store lights were coming on.

"Take my car?" Crutch pointed to his Plymouth, sagging over broken shocks.

"You got gas?"

"We've got ten bucks—"

They climbed in, the car settling with a clunk. "Let's just *circle* . . ."

"Yeah, right."

They pulled away in a cloud of burning oil. The perfumed lady on the rearview mirror swung back and forth, winking at them.